A DC KENDRA MARCH CRIME THRILLER

ROAD TRIP

Book 3 of the 'Summary Justice' series

Theo Harris

Road Trip
Book 3 of the 'Summary Justice' series

Copyright © 2022 by Theo Harris
All rights reserved.

Paperback ISBN: 979-8-359553-38-4

Second Edition, © 2024

No part of this book may be reproduced in any form or by any electronic or mechanical means, including information storage and retrieval systems, without written permission from the author, except for the use of brief quotations in a book review.

This is a work of fiction. Names, characters, places, and incidents are either the product of the author's imagination or are used fictitiously, and any resemblance to actual persons, living or dead, business establishments, places of learning, events or locales is entirely coincidental.

PRAISE FOR THEO HARRIS

'Couldn't put the book down. Loved it.'

'The pacing of the book was impeccable, with each chapter leaving me hungry for more.'

'WOW! I was not expecting much but totally surprised.'

'One of my favourite reads of the year, waiting for the rest of the series!'

'Really gripping storytelling that is clearly well researched and engaging.'

Cool gritty romp... Excellent lead character and plot - really enjoyed the story.'

**Before AN EYE FROM AN EYE...
There was**

TRIAL RUN

An exclusive Prequel to the **'Summary Justice'** series, free to anyone who subscribes to the Theo Harris monthly newsletter.

Find out what brought the team together and the reasons behind what they do... and why.

Go to **theoharris.co.uk**
or join at:
https://dl.bookfunnel.com/7oh5ceuxyw

Also by Theo Harris

DC Kendra March - 'Summary Justice' series

Book 1 - An Eye for an Eye

Book 2 - Fagin's Folly

Book 3 - Road Trip

Book 4 - London's Burning

Book 5 - Nothing to Lose

Book 6 - Justice

Book 7 - Born to Kill

Boxset 1 - Books 1 to 3

Boxset 2 - Books 4 to 6

Think you've gotten away with it? Think again!

CONTENTS

Prologue	1
1. Face off	5
2. Allegations	14
3. Suspicions	27
4. The Rejects	44
5. Dark web	55
6. London	64
7. Interview	73
8. Corruption	84
9. Meet with the boss	98
10. Sabotage	109
11. Kidnap	119
12. The Cemetery	132
13. Meet with the Devil	143
14. Delivery	153
15. Infiltration	162
16. Stinger	173
17. Drugs	188
18. Mischief	202
19. Auction	215
20. Beeston Bump	225
21. Arrests	234
22. Soggy Bottom	246
23. Funeral	253
Epilogue	259
Book 4 Preview	264
Acknowledgments	275
About the Author	277

PROLOGUE

They stood in silence, unmoving, two ranks, like sentinels, waiting for their leader to address them. Dressed in all-black, all-weather motorcycle gear with blacked-out visors, they looked like extras in a sci-fi movie, playing the bad guys. It was the part they were born to play. You had to look closely to see the black shield-shaped patch on their right arms, each bearing a capital R in dark grey. The large empty warehouse in which they stood had been provided to them for their forthcoming mission, which their leader was about to explain.

His footsteps broke the silence as he approached from a side office, flanked by a pair of his most trusted and feared men. One sported a Māori warrior tattoo that covered half his face and neck. The other had several piercings in his nose, lips, ears, and between his eyes. Both were bald, both were fierce, and both were evil in appearance. It was exactly what their leader wanted from them, to instil fear into everyone they encountered, including colleagues. The leader himself was neither pierced nor tattooed but wore sunglasses indoors, in what was a poorly lit warehouse. He was dressed exactly as the others in all-black but wore a blood-red bandana around his neck. He stopped in front of those gathered before him and spoke.

'Listen up, people, it's finally happening!'

There were hoots and hollers from the small crowd in appreciation; it was the news they had been waiting for.

'Our benefactor has given us the go-ahead to start our operation,' he continued, 'so as of tomorrow, we shall cause as much mayhem as we possibly can.'

More cheers and the stomping of feet.

'Our benefactor has been generous. Not only has he provided us with this base of operations, but he has also given us the list of places he wants us to target. But best of all, he has filled our bank account with lots of lovely money, so we can buy all the drugs and guns we need to make this operation the most spectacular yet. Oh, and there'll be a ton of money left for us all personally if we do the job within a couple of months.'

This time there were whistles and shouts of 'beer' and 'drugs', amongst other things. Motorcycle helmets were raised in the air in approval and salute.

'You'll have whatever you want when we're done. Remember what I told you, people, when I picked you for this special team? You were unwanted pariahs, known as troublemakers, and to be avoided. Nobody wanted to work with you, nobody trusted you, nobody had faith in you – except for me! You are all perfect for this, and you are perfect for us. You are perfect for the Rejects, and we shall show them all exactly what we are worth!'

He raised his arms in the air as his minions cheered raucously, his two lieutenants urging them on and raising their fists in the air.

'Rejects! Rejects! Rejects!'

1

FACE OFF

The campfire crackled, its sparks floating upwards, brilliantly bright against the night sky as they weaved magical shapes and raced upwards before spluttering and disappearing. The family sitting around the fire laughed and joked as their annual gathering gained momentum. They ate and drank well into the night, celebrating the seventieth birthday of Manfri, their much-loved *Rom Baro*, or Big Man, the tribal leader of the Romany family that had been gracing this campsite once a year for the past fifty-three years. It was a well-attended ritual and celebration; although their family had diverged so much over the decades, they could gather annually to reflect upon and cement their long, proud heritage.

Manfri stood, raising his glass. 'May you all live long and happy lives, dear ones.'

'Hear, hear,' came the shouts from many, before they went silent in respect for their elder.

'Some of you have travelled far to be here with us once again. Some of you have chosen a different path to that of your Romany traditions, which we all respect,' he added, to some boos and laughter.

'Not all of us!' shouted someone from the darkness..

'Yes, yes, we hear you back there, Patrick, always wanting to get a word in,' Manfri continued, 'but in all seriousness, the world has changed a great deal in my lifetime, and I see nothing wrong with that which some of our families have chosen. I respect their decisions – and let's face it, they aren't doing too badly, are they?'

'Yuppies, Rom Baro, that's what they be, yuppies!' Patrick shouted once more, to a round of laughter.

'Come round to mine in Surrey and I'll let you drive my BMW, Patrick,' shouted another, 'and I'll let you wash in my swimming pool too, before you come into our lovely house,' he added, to continued hilarity.

The banter between those who still travelled the roads of England and those who had forsaken their caravans for brick-built homes and plant their roots anew had been going on for years. It had become part of the annual ritual, and everyone looked forward to it as it kept them grounded.

'As I was saying,' continued Manfri, 'you have come from far and wide to this place every year, at the same time, the same place, and it has become an important part of our family's custom, where we all look forward to seeing you again. Long may it continue!' He raised his glass again.

'Cheers and good health,' shouted many, for the umpteenth time that night.

'Finally, let us not forget our honoured guest, the man who has made us feel so welcome each year. You have been a friend to us all for many years now and are as part of this family as anyone else here. In these times of hatred and mistrust in the world, you are our shining beacon of hope.

Knowing there are good people like you still around sustains us all. Please, all, raise your glasses to Mr. Rufus Donald.'

'Hear, hear,' shouted the entire family; there were almost fifty people gathered around the fire: men, women and children.

'My friends,' said the elderly landowner, standing to address them all, 'I have looked forward to your coming here every year for a long time now, much as my father did before me. It is you that gives me hope, not the other way round. I see the love and respect you have for each other, the way you look after each other and make sure that at least once a year you connect.'

Several family members hugged as his words hit home.

'I only wish that I could see my children as often,' Rufus continued, sadly, 'but the ways of this modern world have taken priority for many people now, especially the younger generation who feel compelled to match—or better—each other's achievements in the material world. The life you have chosen is far better, in my humble opinion, and I wish you all the very best for the future. You will always be welcome here. You have my solemn word on this. Cheers!'

Rufus Donald raised his glass high as he toasted his much-loved guests.

There were rapturous cheers as the old man sat down, a smile hiding the sadness that he had just reminded himself of. Manfri, who had sat next to him, lay a hand on his shoulder.

'Thank you, my friend,' he said simply.

'There is nothing to thank me for, Manfri. You have been one of only a handful of what I can call genuine friends over the years, so you have my thanks and I will always make this place available to you. I have made it official that when I pass, my children will save the place for you each year.'

'I hope that won't be for a very long time, Rufus,' Manfri replied, raising his glass once more. Their glasses clinked loudly, and their drinks were downed in one, eliciting more cheers from the family.

A stockily-built man approached and sat next to them. 'You're slipping, Pa.'

'I'll still drink you under the table, young whelp,' Manfri replied.

'Rufus, you remember my eldest, Jacob? He stayed here many years ago because the life on the road became too much for him, remember?'

Rufus and Manfri both laughed as Jacob shook his head.

'Pa, you know I see Rufus regularly, right? You do this every year, as if it's going to embarrass me, and it never does.'

'Yes, but it makes us both laugh,' Manfri replied, clinking his glass against Rufus's again.

'Sorry, Jacob, I have to humour your Pa. He's one of my oldest and dearest friends and we have to look after each other in our old age, right?'

'Don't you worry, Rufus, it's this old man next to you who thinks he's a joker, you're fine. I take it from your toast that you have seen little of Peter and Emily?'

'Sadly, yes. Peter is a partner in the accountancy firm now, so he's working long unsociable hours, and doesn't even call much anymore. Emily started her own publishing company and also works stupid hours. She hired a nanny, so she doesn't even get to see her kids much, let alone her parents.'

'Don't be too harsh on them, Rufus,' Jacob said, resting a hand on the landlord's arm. 'The world has changed a lot recently, and it's tougher than ever. They're just trying to make a good life for themselves and their kids, you know?'

Rufus smiled and patted Jacob's arm.

'You reared a good one here, Manfri,' Rufus said, 'strong and sensible. Tell me, Jacob, how is the boxing club coming along?'

'It's going great, thanks,' Jacob said. 'We're up on last year's numbers and training some good youngsters with potential. I reckon in a couple of years we'll have a champion from Norfolk. It's long overdue.'

'Hear, hear,' Manfri said, raising his glass.

'Now you know where he gets all his strength from,' added Jacob, pointing to his father. 'The number of times he raises that glass, it's no wonder he can still beat the living daylights out of us all.'

'Hear, hear,' Manfri repeated, raising his glass yet again.

Jacob and Rufus exchanged a knowing look and then both burst out laughing, spraying their drinks in the process.

'It's gonna be a long night,' Jacob said. 'Cheers!'

Before he could down the drink, Jacob paused.

'Do you hear that?'

'Hear what?' Manfri asked. 'Oh, that rumble? What *is* that?'

They listened for a few more seconds before the rumble became a roar and two dozen motorcycles entered the site. The chatter around the fire stopped dead as the family looked on in astonishment at the growing number of bikers. Once they had stopped in a long line facing them, the central rider raised his fist, and they switched all engines and lights off, leaving an eerie sight made visible only by the light of the fire.

'Who the hell are they?' asked Manfri, standing.

'Leave it to me, Pa, I'll go and see what they want,' Jacob said.

As he walked towards the riders, who remained silent and passive, the lead rider removed his helmet and strode out to meet him, with two of his riders in tow. As they walked, they too removed their helmets. They stopped ten feet from Jacob and stared at him. Jacob could see the leader's face. There was a piercing pair of eyes like nothing he had ever seen. Completely black. No whites.. As the firelight flickered across his face, it gave him a fiendish look as he tilted his head for effect. Jacob realised they were waiting for him to react first.

'Oh, I'm sorry,' he said sarcastically, 'are you waiting for me? Who are you and what do you want?'

The leader smiled and raised his arms, spreading them in the associated gesture of peace.

'We came to pay our respects,' he said, eliciting a laugh from his companions.

Jacob was not expecting that as a response, and he certainly didn't believe it.

'You've lost me, stranger. We don't know you and so there's no reason for you to pay any respects.'

'Ah, but there is,' said the leader, 'we came to tell you we'd heard good things about this site and wanted to find out for ourselves. We want to join your little party here and have some fun, we hear gypsies like yourselves are very welcoming. Isn't that right, lads?' He turned to his fellow riders and nodded, stirring them into replying with muffled 'yea's' and raised fists.

'Well, you heard correctly, we Romany are usually a fun-loving and welcoming lot, but there is no room for you here tonight, stranger. There are many other sites around here for you to stay on, and we wish you luck finding one.'

The leader stepped forward, closing the gap between he and Jacob to just three feet.

'That's not very welcoming, is it, friend?'

His two friends joined him at his side, all three staring at Jacob.

'Oh, I see. My apologies. Now that you're staring me out with your scary-ass faces, I should bow down to you and let you join us, right? You don't scare me, stranger, you don't scare any of us. We've lived for centuries putting up with scarier people than you clowns, so why don't you turn round and piss off back where you came from before you get the beating of your lives.'

The leader's companions made to move towards Jacob, who stood his ground and stared back.

'Everything alright there, Jacob?' asked Patrick, who had stepped from the crowd along with fifteen other men, all holding weapons.

The leader saw the women had also armed themselves and even some of the older children had, too. His riders could lose this fight; they'd certainly take a beating, and he'd lose a lot of the team finding out. It was too early to take that chance. He reached out his arms to stop his lieutenants and smiled a sinister smile.

'Nah, we're all good here, Patrick, thanks for asking,' Jacob shouted back, without taking his eyes off the interlopers. 'These nice people were just leaving, weren't you?'

The leader laughed, nodding in acceptance.

'We're leaving—for now.'

He and his men turned and walked back towards the rest of their team. The leader paused and turned to face Jacob once more.

'I'll see you soon, stranger.'.

'Not if I can help it,' Jacob replied, waving sarcastically. 'Goodbye, now.'

The men went back to their bikes, putting their helmets on. The leader raised his fist to signal the starting of their engines. The roar from two dozen motorbikes was mighty, and they sat there and revved them for several moments before they rode slowly out of the site and away.

'That wasn't much fun, Pa. We'll need to keep our wits about us with that lot.'

'Yes, son, we will,' Manfri replied, his thoughts troubled by the unexpected malevolence. He had seen many things in his long life, but nothing so evil.

'I've never seen them before, or even heard of a gang like that in these parts,' said Rufus. 'I'll spread the word and warn everyone. They could cause a lot of problems around here.'

'Hopefully, it's nothing,' Jacob said, knowing full well that he would be sure to see the riders again. 'Maybe they just don't like travellers and wanted a scrap. Who knows?'

'Whoever they are, you be very careful, you hear? I'm off to bed. I've had enough excitement for one night,' Rufus added, standing. He shook their hands and those of many others as he left.

'A good man, that,' Manfri said. 'It'll be a sad day for us all when he's no longer with us.'

'You heard him, Pa, he's left instructions with his kids to allow us entry here.'

'Yes, he did. As long as they own the land, but what if they decide that city life is for them, and they don't want to live here?'

'I hadn't thought of that, but let's not dwell on a problem that could be many years away, eh? Now, pass me that bottle before you finish it all by yourself, you greedy old man.'

THE RIDERS DIDN'T TAKE LONG to get back to the warehouse. As the leader took his helmet off, he called over his two lieutenants.

'Bring that bastard to me,' he told them. 'He needs to be taught a lesson.'

As it turned out, teaching was what they were best at.

2

ALLEGATIONS

Kendra logged out of her computer and stretched. It had been a long day in the office, most of it spent at the computer completing mandatory training exercises and reports. It was tedious but necessary work, which—fortunately — only came round once or twice a year.

'Well, that's me done,' she said wearily.

'Sarge wants a word before you go,' Jillian said, as she walked past her desk. 'He seems pissed off.'

'Uh oh. Did I forget to put sugar in his coffee again?'

'Have fun, whatever it is.'

Kendra grabbed her coat and bag and left her desk, one they had temporarily assigned her to assist with the missing Qupi gang investigation. Since that had been closed down, Detective Sergeant Rick Watts had suggested she keep hold of it if she was to continue being the Intel Unit liaison, so she flitted between this and the Intel Unit office on the floor below. It was the ideal set-up for Kendra. It allowed her to maintain regular contact with her old team and also to keep up to speed with ongoing issues that had been ignored or bypassed.

'Ah, there you are, Kendra.' Said Rick Watts. 'Have a seat. How was the training, as exciting as ever?'

'All good, Sarge, thanks. Jillian told me you wanted to see me?'

'Yes, I did. There's not a lot to tell you since the missing gangster investigation was called off, but I have some worrying news.'

'What's that?'

'Our mutual friend, Eddie Duckmore from the NCA, has been suspended for conduct unbecoming a police officer, and bullying, which comes as no surprise. The tosser has not gone down without a fight, though, and has made a bunch of allegations against a few of us here in the Met.'

'Uh-oh, I'm guessing that I'm involved in this?'

'You and me both, K. He's alleged overbearing conduct against me, also alleging that I threatened him with violence, and he has his sidekick Critchley as his witness. He's alleged a couple of things against you, too, namely that you also threatened him, that you neglected your duty, and that you did not comply with legitimate orders.'

'Wow, I guess the douchebag is throwing all kinds of shit against the wall hoping something will stick, eh?'

'Yep, so he can save his own shitty skin. He's a real keeper, that one. Anyway, the allegations have been made and they have to be investigated, so at some point in the near future we're gonna get a visit from the DPS, so brace yourself for the death stare,' Watts said, smiling at the reference. The *Directorate of Professional Standards* was known to use the long stare to terrify their interviewees. It only ever worked with young inexperienced officers being questioned for the first time, as many of those with long service and experience typically tried their best not to laugh and antagonise the interviewer.

'Okay, thanks for the heads-up,' said Kendra. 'It may open a can of worms that will make things worse for him.'

'Agreed, I plan on being honest when it comes to what I think about him. He's not going to like what he hears.'

'I couldn't care less about that dick anymore; I try to think about pleasant things instead. Anyway, I'm off, Sarge, I'll see you in a couple of days.' Kendra stood to leave.

'Come and see me when you're back. We should have a catch-up on some recent cases that I want to look at. Hopefully, you can do some of your magical research for me.'

'Will do. See you then,' she said, waving as she walked out of his office and headed for the stairs. It had been several weeks since they had dealt with the robbers in Hackney, and everyone was now recovered and refreshed, raring to go on to the next case. She was looking forward to meeting up with Andy that night, in what was becoming a regular get-together. They would catch up and discuss recent events and the future of their ongoing venture, and it was her turn to cook. They had turned it into something that included a little fun, and preparing an enjoyable meal seemed to work best.

The plan was to meet at his house, where they would take turns in cooking something new. Tonight, she was to attempt a moussaka, a delicious Greek dish she'd wanted to try making for years. The ingredients were in a carrier bag in the car, bought during her lunch break, along with a bottle of Châteauneuf-du-Pape, a wine they both enjoyed.

The drive was uneventful, and she was excited about the evening ahead as she arrived at Andy's terraced house. As she rang the bell, she could hear the funky sound of *September* by Earth Wind and Fire playing in the house, bringing a smile to her face. It was a song that brought back happy childhood memories.

'There you are,' Andy said, answering the door, a relieved look on his face. 'It's about time, Detective,' he added. He was dressed in jeans and a salmon-coloured polo neck. His eyepatch completed a dashing figure that Kendra approved very much of. Glancing down, she could see he had his prosthetic foot on and not the blade, allowing him to wear his beloved vintage Nike trainers that were almost twenty years old. He only ever wore them indoors, which was the only reason they had lasted so well.

'What's up with you?' she asked, stepping into the hallway. 'I'm only ten minutes late, that's pretty good for me.'

'Yeah, well, that's ten extra minutes that I had to–'

'There you are, love,' Trevor said, suddenly appearing from the lounge. 'I didn't think you were going to turn up!'

'Dad, what are you doing here?' Kendra asked, startled.

'Well, that's not the welcome I was hoping for, that's for sure! I thought I'd pop over to catch you both up on what's been going on. We're in this together, remember? Or am I spoiling some sort of date night?'

'Dad! That's not what this is,' Kendra said quickly, blushing. 'I told you we were just debriefing and seeing what else was new, that's all. It's how we figure out what to do next.'

'Well, then, you won't mind at all if I stay, will you? After all, it's what I'm here for too, isn't it?' Trevor crossed his arms defiantly.

'Well, now that's sorted out, can we get out of the hall and into the other room?' Andy said.

'Yes, let's,' Kendra said, 'but let me put this away in the kitchen first. We need to thrash this out before it gets even more uncomfortable.'

'I don't know what you mean,' Trevor said innocently, ambling into the lounge and sitting in Andy's favourite armchair. Andy's glare was clear until he saw Trevor's expressionless stare, almost challenging him to respond. He chose instead to accept the challenge and stood there, motionless, trying not to blink.

Kendra returned a few seconds later and saw her two favourite men glaring at each other, like a pair of schoolboys having a staring contest.

'Will you just look at yourselves?' she said, putting her hands on her hips and making her anger clear.

Andy saw where this was going and quickly sat down, looking at her instead. Trevor did the same.

'Honestly,' she continued, 'I feel that this dislike of each other is getting worse, or am I wrong? I thought it was a little fun and banter, but this is not that, is it?'

'I don't dislike him,' Trevor said, looking back at Andy. 'I just don't like him sometimes. And I don't like his intentions towards you. It makes me uncomfortable.'

'What? You're the one that keeps threatening to kill me, Trevor. One minute you're patting me on the back and the next you're wanting to put a knife in my gut. It's not healthy, you know,' Andy added, hoping for the sympathy vote from Kendra. 'And for the record, my intentions towards Kendra are strictly honourable.'

She looked back and forth at both men before speaking.

'Listen to me, because this is getting out of control. If we're going to do this, then we have to do it together with nothing like this threatening to put us in any danger, okay? I need to know I can trust you, and that we can all trust each other, because what we're doing is a big deal. Please, put this shit behind you so we can move forward.' She needed a resolution soon before it jeopardised their operation. There was too much at stake.

There was silence as they looked at each other.

'He makes a good point, Dad. One minute you're fine and the next you're pissed off. It's hard to keep up.'

Trevor paused, considering his reply.

'I know, and I'm sorry,' he said, speaking to Andy. 'I just have a hard time watching you flirt with each other and keep secrets from me the way you have done. K, I don't want to be left out of your life again, that's all. Well, that, and some hairy-arsed copper leering at you the way he does.'

'I do not leer. I just process things a little differently, okay? And again—for the record, I'm not a copper anymore, so enough of the hairy arse comments, please.'

'And here we go again,' Kendra said, shaking her head, 'I'm going to go and cook the meal. You two sort your shit out by the time I'm done, otherwise I will kick both your arses, hairy or not.'

She stormed out of the lounge and headed for the kitchen, where the men could hear lots of therapeutic banging and crashing of utensils.

'Now look what you've done,' Trevor said, hissing.

'What? Come on, Pops, what the hell did I do? You're the one who just admitted being wrong,' Andy leaned in to emphasise his point.

'I didn't admit to anything, you arse. I was trying to compromise, so that Kendra doesn't blame me. And also for the record, I am not in any way happy that you have your nasty little mitts all over her every chance you get. And if you call me *Pops* again, I'll kick the shit out of you.'

'Well, you don't need to worry too much about my nasty little mitts, sir, because we decided we should cool things and make sure our focus is on what we're doing and not on each other.'

'Well, that's just—wait, what? When did this happen?'

'Weeks ago, during the whole new Hitler thing. Between you and me, as much as I'd love to have my mitts all over her —steady on, let me finish—the thought of her getting hurt or putting her in any danger made us realise that we'd lose focus. The tiniest loss of focus would be catastrophic and could end up with people getting hurt, or worse, so we've backed off and just have each other's backs now.'

'You decided together? Or it was Kendra's idea?'

'If that makes you feel better, then yes, it was Kendra's idea, and I agreed. It doesn't matter what I think or want, Trevor, it's all about Kendra and working together to change things, and that's good enough for me. I know she cares for me too, by the way. This way, at least I get to help and look out for her. And you, of course.' He smiled at the last, almost an olive branch.

'You know, I can't make you out, Andy. Half the time you're this weird genius nerd guy who can do anything, the other half you're a joker who gets up people's noses. Who the hell are you, really?'

'I'd like to think I'm somewhere in the middle, useful but annoyingly funny. I guess that's all I can be at the moment.'

'Yeah, well, you're very useful, but you're not funny,' Trevor conceded.

'I suppose I'll take that. So now that we've made up, shall we help your gorgeous daughter with the meal?'

'See what I mean? Not funny,' Trevor slapped Andy's arm.

Kendra heard him yelp and rolled her eyes.

'Idiots.'

'WELL DONE, BOYS AND GIRLS,' Jacob told his exhausted trainees. 'That was a good session. Remember to continue your good work at home. The more exercising you do, the better your fitness, the longer you can last. You know the drill.'

He was renowned for his training skills but more so for his strict regimen that separated the wheat from the chaff. But most of all, they knew him for turning wayward kids' lives around, with spectacular effect. Parents loved him for it, and many of his older trainees, who were now adults, always came back to pay their respects and thanks, some supporting the club for future generations.

'Woo hoo!' came the shouts from the relieved boxers. It had been a tough one, but they were all smiling, and felt good for the workout.

'Yeah, yeah, I hear you. Now get out of here,' Jacob said, with a wink.

'Thanks, coach Jacob,' one boy said as they walked past.

'You're welcome, son. Remember to keep your guard up when you're punching the bag. Get used to doing it and you'll be fine, okay?'

'Yes, coach Jacob, I will,' replied the teenager.

The small club was based on the outskirts of Sheringham, a small, picturesque town on the North Norfolk coast. Industrial units, the town football club, and a fancy new swimming pool that was attracting people from nearby towns surrounded it. Some parents were now taking in a swim after dropping their kids off at Jacob's club, so it was generating more visits to both club and pool. It was based in a converted garage, so although old-fashioned and grimy in places, it was spacious and well-equipped, thanks to the donations from those involved.

Jacob ran the club in the evenings, after working regular hours running his small security business from the office upstairs with his wife, Maureen. They would typically go home for their dinner, just a few minutes away, before Jacob would return to run the training sessions. He had help, but was involved in everything, such was his passion for helping the youngsters. He cleared away the equipment and made sure everything was in order and ready for the next day, before turning out the lights and locking up.

It was late at night and dark outside, so with everyone gone, it was eerily quiet in the car park around the back where he'd parked his white van. He whistled as he got his keys ready, looking forward to a good night's sleep.

He realised something was wrong when he saw the two brutes leaning against his van, arms crossed, waiting for him. He recognised them straight away, the two bald giants that had been with the leader when they'd had their confrontation.

'Seriously, lads? You trying to put the frighteners on me? I told you we don't scare easily, right?'

'Who said anything about scaring you?' said Snake, his Māori tattoo barely visible in the poorly lit car park. 'We just want a friendly chat, is all,' he continued, nudging his colleague Razor in the ribs.

'Well, let's get on with it,' Jacob said, putting his keys back in his pocket and clenching his fists in readiness. He knew he was in a dangerous situation, but was confident in his fighting prowess and would not be going down without a fight.

The two riders split and approached him from either

side, their leering grins suggesting they were looking forward to the fight. What they were not aware of was that not only had Jacob been a regional boxing champion for many years before hanging up his gloves, but he had also continued to train.

Razor moved first, coming in with a roundhouse punch that would have knocked anyone out had it connected. Jacob ducked and immediately struck him with a vicious uppercut to the body, connecting hard with the rider's ribs. The biker winced and hurried away, protecting his side, which was now throbbing with pain.

Snake immediately followed, coming in close and throwing two fast jabs that Jacob deflected with his forearms. He then went for an uppercut to the body, which glanced at Jacob's side enough for him to feel the searing pain. These guys knew how to fight. The tattooed rider followed up quickly with several more jabs and another attempt at an uppercut, this time to the head. An untrained man would have been on the floor by now, but Jacob's experience was kicking in and his muscle memory did not let him down. He moved in quickly to close the distance with Snake, before hitting him with a pair of body blows to the left side and a right hook to the chin. Snake went down to one knee, blood trickling from one side of his mouth.

Razor came back with several mis-timed roundhouse punches, hoping one of them would hit. All he managed to do was hit his opponent with a couple of glancing blows that did no harm as Jacob's feet moved him out of the way. It was then that he felt the searing pain in his side, worse than anything he'd ever felt. His hands immediately went to the side where the pain radiated, just as Snake was removing his six-inch stiletto knife. It was enough to distract Jacob, who knew now that he was in deep trouble, so he never saw the favoured roundhouse punch from Razor that connected perfectly with the side of his head. He was unconscious before he hit the ground, a pool of blood forming quickly by his side.

'I bet you're scared now, arsehole, aren't you?' Snake shouted at the prone body as he wiped the blood from his chin.

He pulled out his mobile phone and called Hawk.

'We have him, boss,' Snake said.

'Bring him to the Bump,' Hawk replied, ending the call abruptly.

'Shit,' Snake said, putting his phone away.

'What?' Razor asked.

'He wants us to take him to the Bump. We're going to have to carry the bastard up to the top of the bloody cliff,' Snake replied.

'Let's load him up in his van and go. The sooner we get out of here, the better,' Razor said, fishing the keys out of Jacob's pocket.

They bundled the unconscious Jacob into the back of his van and made the short five-minute drive to Beeston Bump, where they parked on the gravel leading to the path that snaked up the hill to the top of the sandy cliff. Beeston Bump, although only a couple of hundred feet high, was one of the highest points in Norfolk. The cliffs had been deeply eroded from the sea and inland water, causing several collapses over the years. It was a favourite for walkers from all over the country and renowned for the coastal views.

Late at night, though, there were no walkers or anyone in sight. It was easy to take Jacob out from the back with no one watching, but as Snake had mentioned, it was difficult to manhandle him up the winding path and the steps to the top. There were several places where the earth had been gouged away by the elements, giving the appearance that a giant had taken huge bites out of the cliffs.

They met with Hawk near the top and one gouge that was left from a recent collapse, where he stared out to sea at the blinking red lights of the wind farms in the distance, giving the appearance of a magical city out at sea.

Jacob was stirring back into consciousness, but the wound to his side and the blood loss had affected him badly. He shook his head to try to rouse himself, but alertness eluded him. Snake and Razor held him up as he faced Hawk. There was just enough light to see Hawk's malevolent face and demonic eyes.

'Well, if it isn't our welcoming friend. You don't look so good, old man,' Hawk said. Jacob could see the evil smile on his adversary's face.

'Piss off,' Jacob said, still unsteady on his feet.

'Let him go,' Hawk ordered.

His men released Jacob, who promptly fell to his knees, stopping himself from falling over by putting both hands down to keep him steady. He continued to shake his head, still groggy.

'What the hell do you want from me?' he asked weakly.

'I want nothing from you,' Hawk said, 'except for you to learn that acting the tough guy doesn't really work much anymore. It's a pretty harsh lesson.'

Jacob looked up, his vision clearing momentarily as Hawk reached down and pulled him up by his lapels.

Hawk slowly turned him around, so that Jacob had his back to the sea. He ambled towards the edge of the cliff as Jacob realised what was about to happen. As weak as he was, he thrashed about as much as his weak body could handle and tried to brush Hawk's arms away, to no avail, so he grabbed Hawk's leather jacket in both hands, holding on for dear life with what little strength that he had. As Hawk got to the edge, the leader realised what Jacob was trying to do and called out to his men.

'Break his fucking hands, will you? The bastard wants to drag me over with him.'

Snake approached and grabbed Jacob's hands, squeezing the fingers and knuckles together so that Jacob would release his grip. It worked, as Jacob gasped in pain, but he was able to make one last heroic attempt, scrabbling and scratching desperately at the leather jacket for one last firm hold. He almost succeeded, but wasn't quick enough, as Hawk finally pushed him off the edge of the cliff.

'Bye-bye,' Hawk waved, as Jacob fell.

He did not make a sound. His life ended instantaneously when he smashed onto the rocks below.

Hawk turned to his men. 'Good job, boys, now make sure you don't leave any trace of yourselves anywhere, okay? We have a lot more work to do.' He then walked off into the gloom in the opposite direction that his men had come from.

'Let's get rid of that van and head back,' said Razor.

Twenty minutes later it was back in the car park behind the boxing club. Any traces of blood and fingerprints had been wiped clean.

3

SUSPICIONS

Trevor, Andy, and Kendra were in the small canteen at the factory the following afternoon, discussing potential upgrades to the place when Trevor received a call.

'Maureen, how are you, darling? How's that horrible husband of yours?'

His smile disappeared instantly as he listened.

'Oh dear God, I'm so sorry, darling. Can you tell me what happened?'

As Trevor listened, Kendra saw an immediate change in his body language, suggesting that something was wrong. She watched as Trevor was visibly moved by the call.

'Dear God. What did the police say?' he asked. 'Mm-hmm,' he uttered in response to the reply.

'Maureen, listen to me. Do you need anything at all? All you have to do is ask, okay? Is Manfri and the rest of the family with you? Uh-huh... yes, please carry on. Okay, I want you to listen to me and pass a message on to Manfri. I'm coming over to see you tomorrow. Tell him to stay in the area until I get to speak to him, if you can. I know they're leaving Overstrand, but tell him to stay close by until we speak, okay?'

The conversation came to an end.

'Alright, love, I'll see you tomorrow.'

He put the phone down and slumped in his chair.

'Oh, dear God,' he said, holding his head in his hands, 'I can't believe it.'

'Dad? What is it?' Kendra asked, putting a hand on his shoulder.

'Poor Maureen,' Trevor said, his voice cracking. 'Jacob is dead. They found him at the bottom of a cliff.'

'What the hell? I'm so sorry, Dad. Do they know how it happened?'

'The police told his wife they thought it might be suicide, but she is adamant it was not. He had a run-in with a biker gang the night before and she thinks they had something to do with it.'

'Sorry for your loss, Trev. Was he a relative?' Andy asked.

'No, he was one of my closest friends from years ago. We started training kids together, along with Frazer. We all had the same vision, to keep kids safe and out of trouble, you know? And now he's dead.'

'Is there anything we can do, Dad? Do they need money or anything like that?'

Trevor wiped away a tear and stood, taking a deep breath, his face the picture of determination.

'We can do more than that, love. We're going to find out what the hell happened, because it stinks. I want to know who killed him and why. Then I'll destroy the bastard who did it. Andy, get Marge ready. We're going to the coast.'

ANDY WENT HOME to pack for the trip, whilst Kendra stuck close to Trevor to make sure he was coping with his loss. They went to their respective flats and packed before heading back to the factory the following morning. Kendra had called ahead and asked Rick Watts for the day off, which he granted.

As they arrived at the factory to meet with Andy, Trevor received another call.

'Frazer, have you heard, mate? Yeah, I can't believe it either. I'm gutted, mate. Did Maureen tell you about the biker gang? Yeah, I'm heading over to the coast now, just meeting up with some of the team and we're leaving straight away.'

Trevor listened to his friend from Walsall, who had helped so much with the robber gang in Hackney, and who was just as distraught as he was.

'Mate, that's excellent, thank you. Tell Darren to call when he's in the area, okay? Thanks again mate, I'll call you when I know more.'

'Is Frazer sending the boys to help?' Kendra asked.

'He is, and they'll be needed, from the sounds of it. Get your things ready. I'm going to speak with the twins.'

He found Mo and Amir in the gym, doing their usual morning exercise before training some of the younger trainees. They had taken on more responsibilities in recent weeks and were loving every moment.

'What's happening, boss?' Amir asked when he saw Trevor walk in. He dropped his weights and dried his face with a towel.

'Trevor, you okay? You look like you've seen a ghost,' Mo said.

'Sorry to intrude, guys. I'm going on a trip for a few days and wanted to check in with you before I leave.'

'Where are you going?' Mo asked.

'I'm taking the camper van with Andy and Kendra to Norfolk. A friend of mine died last night and I think it was foul play involving a biker gang, so I want to find out. Will you guys be okay running things while I'm away?'

'We can come with you, boss,' Amir pleaded. 'Charlie can look after things here. There's not a lot to do.'

'There isn't much room in the van, guys, but I'll tell you what: I'll call you if I think we need help, okay? Darren and his team are also meeting us there, in case there's any trouble with the biker gang.'

'All the more reason we should go with you, Trev. We can follow in one of the cars.'

Trevor thought for a few seconds before he replied.

'Alright, tell you what: come tomorrow. Ask Stav to get you one of the four-by-fours that he has there, the more rugged the better. Bring some equipment with you, like tools and anything else we might need to deal with a biker gang. I'll send you the address when we get there, okay?'

'Grand!' Amir replied, excited to be getting involved in another operation.

'Okay, I'll see you tomorrow then,' Trevor said, before leaving them at the gym.

Thirty minutes later, Andy, Trevor and Kendra were all aboard as they left in Marge for the North Norfolk coast.

'KEEP THEM MOVING, Patrick, let's get everyone out of here quickly and safely,' Manfri said, wiping his brow. He looked up at the dark clouds and shook his head. The past day or two had left him and his entire family bereft at the loss of their beloved Jacob, his eldest son, a loving husband and a father-of-two, a man who would always be there to help when you needed it. In the eyes of all that knew him, he was a significant loss to the world. Manfri had grieved privately in his own way, recognising the need to keep strong for his family, so it was an easy decision to leave this place now to ensure that nobody else would suffer the same fate as Jacob. He just couldn't take that chance.

The police had already concluded that Jacob had committed suicide, which made matters worse for them all. Everybody knew there was no chance in hell that Jacob would have taken his own life. No, someone had killed his son, he was sure of it, and the ache in his chest would take a long time to go away.

Jacob's wife Maureen had informed him of her conversation with Trevor, who had been a close friend. After speaking with his family and Rufus, who understood his plight, he decided to move from the camp in Overstrand and go to one further inland, away from the danger. He still did not understand why it had happened, what the bike gang actually wanted, and whether they were targeting his family in particular. Had Jacob been involved in something he shouldn't have been? Had anyone else from the family? Was Rufus the target? He went over the questions in his mind over and over, with no obvious conclusion.

The convoy moved out from the camp and turned away from the sea and towards another site in Felbrigg which Rufus had spoken to him about, and which had a similar layout, with pods for the non-travellers of the family. Rufus had called ahead and spoken to the owner, his brother-in-law, who agreed to take them all in for as long as they needed.

'Thomas will look after you, Manfri. He has taken no guests yet, so he can keep prying eyes away from you all until things blow over.'

'Thank you, my friend,' Manfri replied, clasping his friend's hand firmly. 'We won't forget what you have done, what you continue to do for us all, but please be careful yourself, there's a reason those bastards were there that night, and we may have just been in the way.'

'Don't worry about me, Manfri. I will be careful. I'm also speaking to the other landowners tomorrow to warn them all, so we'll be sticking together and looking out for each other.'

The site in Felbrigg was only a few miles away and their new host was waiting for them at the gates, which he closed behind them once they had all driven through.

'Thank you, Thomas, for helping us out here,' Manfri said, after they had parked up and met by the gate.

'Don't you fret, Mister Manfri, we'll look after you here. If there's anything you need, just give me a holler. I'm only the next field up, in the farmhouse.'

'Let's hope our stay here will be trouble-free. That's all I'm after for now,' Manfri said, looking around at his forlorn family. He had a tough job ahead, to cheer them up and rid them of the fear that had gripped them. They had all stayed, hoping they'd find out what exactly had happened. They wanted justice for Jacob.

'Aye, I'm sorry about your son, Mister Manfri. I hear he was a good man.'

'Thank you, Thomas, that he was.'

He turned and walked back to his family, who had settled into place on the site, but the difference in the atmosphere from the familiar jolly one they were used to, just a few nights earlier, was nowhere to be seen, and as *Rom Baro,* it fell to him to put things right.

THE JOURNEY to the North Norfolk coast was an uneventful one in the camper van. The mood was sullen and Kendra could see that Trevor was struggling with his emotions, so the conversation was kept light. After leaving the M11, they turned off onto the A11 and entered Norfolk, one of the few counties in England that didn't have a motorway running through it. The roads were pleasant; in some places they drove through long tree-lined roads that gave the appearance of a tunnel. It was a pleasing, stress-free drive as a result, especially as they got closer to the coast.

Trevor had been in touch with Maureen, who had messaged to say that Manfri and the rest of the family had moved to another site, giving the address and number for him to call. As they approached, he made the call.

'Mister Manfri, this is Trevor, sir. I just want you to know that it will be easier to come and see you first before we go to Maureen's, and we're only about ten minutes away. Is it okay to come now?'

'Hello, son, of course you can come straight here. I'll be waiting by the gate to let you in,' Manfri replied.

Trevor ended the call and shuffled up close to the driver's seat to speak to Andy.

'Stay on the A140 and then turn left at Roughton onto Chapel Road,' he said. 'The site is about a mile away on Cromer Road, and Manfri will be waiting to let us in.'

'All received and understood,' Andy replied. He glanced

over to Kendra to see that she was now holding her dad's hand and nodding in support.

'I'll be alright, love, just give me a little time. I'll feel a lot better when I know exactly what the hell happened and who this biker gang is.'

'We'll find out, Dad. Don't you worry,'

A few minutes later, they saw Manfri waiting for them by the open gate, which he closed after Andy had taken Marge through. He parked up close to the caravans, and they got out to speak with the head of the family. Manfri and Trevor shook hands warmly, holding on for longer than usual.

'Mister Manfri, this is my daughter Kendra and our associate Andy. We're so sorry for your loss, sir. It came as a shock to me, so heaven knows how you must all be feeling,' Trevor said.

'Thank you, son. It hasn't been easy, for sure. Jacob spoke fondly of you and Frazer often, so I know how much he meant to you. What are you hoping to find out here?'

'Answers, sir. That's all I want for now, answers. When I find them, I'll decide what to do, but for now I just want to know what happened. I'll keep you in the loop when I know more, I promise.'

'Thank you, Trevor. That means a great deal to me. There's nothing worse than not knowing, so anything you find may bring some peace and comfort to the family. As you can see,' he said, gesturing towards the sullen faces that were looking on, 'they are not in a good place at the moment.'

'You have my word, sir. What can you tell me about this biker gang?'

'Not a lot, really. They came here a few nights ago, about twenty of them, all dressed in black. They spoke with Jacob and asked if they could join us, which Jacob declined. He saw something was off and asked them to leave. It seemed they wanted trouble, but they didn't take the rest of us into account. We know how to look after ourselves, and they saw that and left.'

'Were they Hell's Angels? They rarely wear all black,' said Trevor.

'No, they were something different. Except for the three that spoke with Jacob, the rest kept their helmets on. They all had modern bikes, big expensive ones, but no chopper types or any of those fancy vintage ones that the Angels ride. Oh, and they had a patch on their arms, the letter R in grey, Jacob told me.'

'Okay, I've not heard of that before, but we'll check it out. Can you tell me more about the three men he spoke to? Did he describe them to you?'

'Yes. He told me the leader had evil black eyes, with no white showing at all. He kept mentioning it so it must have spooked him. The other two were big bald men, one had tattoos on the lower part of his face, and the other one had piercings all over his face. They sounded like a right bunch, if you ask me.'

'Okay, that's helpful to know. Thank you. Like I said, we're going to speak with Maureen now and I'll be in touch when I know more, okay? In the meantime, please stay safe. Don't let anyone out unless they are leaving the area completely. If you need anything, let me know and we'll bring it,' Trevor said, holding out his hand.

'Thank you, my friend. We are truly grateful. I'll let you out,' Manfri said, and the two shook hands again.

The trio walked back to the camper van. Kendra looked around at the family and saw fear and sadness on all their faces. At that moment, she made a vow to herself that she would help them any way she could.

'Those bikers sound ominous, don't they?' Andy said as they took their seats.

'I don't care how scary they are, we're going to sort this out, and if we find one jot of evidence that they're responsible–' Trevor's anger showed no sign of abating, and he didn't need to finish the sentence for them to know what he was thinking.

'Don't worry, Dad, if it's there, we'll find it.'

'Okay, here we go,' Andy said as he pulled away from the site and into the street, waving to Manfri as they left.

'He did well, that man,' Andy said. 'To lose his son and keep the family together takes some courage, that's for sure.'

'They're an amazing family, Andy,' Trevor said. 'They were always there for me when things weren't so good, you know? If it wasn't for them and Jacob, *especially* Jacob, I'd have been in prison. They showed me there were other ways of dealing with bad people, and I'll always be grateful for that.'

'We all are, Dad, and we will sort this out, I promise,' Kendra said.

'Right then, tell me how to get to Maureen's house, because I don't have a clue,' Andy said.

'You need to get on the A148, and you then follow the signs to Cromer and Sheringham, it's dead easy,' Trevor said. 'When you turn right into Holway Road towards Sheringham then I'll let you know where to go for Maureen's.'

They drove in silence for another ten minutes before they arrived in Sheringham. As they drove down the hill towards the coast, Trevor pointed ahead.

'Just over the rise is Snaefell Park, turn right into there

and then immediately take a left into the cul-de-sac. That's Jacob's house.'

Andy followed the instructions and took the tight turning, where he found parking at the end, close to the house. They got out and knocked on the door.

A petite, dark-haired woman wearing black trousers and a black jumper answered it, her face red from crying. She became tearful as soon as she saw Trevor and ran into his arms, bawling. He held her tightly and rocked gently from side to side for several minutes, giving her all the time that she needed.

'I'm so, so sorry for your loss, Maureen. He was one of the best, and I'm devastated for you and your family.'

'I've sent the kids to my mother for a few days. I have to be strong for them and I need a little time for that,' she replied. 'Please come on in.'

'This is my daughter Kendra, and our associate, Andy. We're going to do everything we can to find out what happened.'

'Please, come in,' said Maureen, taking Kendra and Andy by the hand. 'I'm so sorry for that spectacle. Jacob would laugh at me now if he were here.'

'Don't you worry, Maureen, you take all the time you need,' Kendra replied.

'He's told me so much about you, Kendra,' Maureen said, cupping Kendra's cheek. 'I'm so glad to meet you, finally.'

'I wish it were under different circumstances, but any friend of Dad's is family, as far as I'm concerned.'

They followed her into the lounge, with a pair of comfortable sofas and a bedraggled old armchair.

'Please, sit,' said Maureen. 'I'll make some tea.'

'That was Jacob's seat,' Trevor said, indicating to the old

chair. 'Sometimes he'd sleep in it all night. It was his favourite place in the house.'

The room was spotlessly clean, and it was clear Maureen kept it that way religiously. She returned after a few minutes carrying a tray with four cups and a teapot, along with a plate of custard creams. After making a fuss of Andy and Kendra, she finally sat next to Trevor on the sofa.

'I'm so happy to see you, Trevor. Jacob loved you like a brother, you know that, right?' Her voice trembled as she fought off the tears.

Trevor took her hand and said, 'He *was* my brother, and I will do anything for him *and* for you. Never forget that.'

'I'm happy to hear that, because I am convinced that there is foul play at work here, and the police must be involved in it because they were adamant it was suicide. I can tell you now, I will bet mine and my children's lives on the fact he would never do that.'

'I know, which is why we will look into everything,' Trevor said.

'Maureen,' said Kendra, 'have they mentioned the post mortem at all? Did they tell you when it would take place?'

'I think it took place today, but they mentioned nothing more about it. Why do you ask?'

'I think it's important to see what the medical examiner says. They should have been in touch by now.'

'No, they haven't said a thing to me,' Maureen said.

Kendra knew that the medical examiner should contact the family as soon as they had reached their conclusion. For Maureen to say that nothing had been explained other than the police mentioning suicide meant that there was indeed foul play involved. At this stage, it was difficult to say whether it was by the police or the pathologist, or both. They would have to investigate to find out, if only to bring closure to the family.

'Who did you speak to? Was it just the police?' Kendra pressed.

'Someone else came with the police. I think it was a coroner who asked some questions about Jacob's state of mind. I told him there was nothing wrong with his mind. He took some notes, and that was pretty much it, really. He told me he wanted to find out more about Jacob, but it was very confusing.'

'Okay, well, that's a start. A forensic pathologist would become involved if there was any suspicion, so it's important we find out as much information as we can so that we can get some answers,' Kendra replied.

'Thank you so much for this, all of you,' Maureen said, placing her hands on Trevor's again.

'Maureen, did you get any contact information from the police officer or the coroner?' Andy asked.

'The police officer left a card. Let me go and get it,' she said, going back into the kitchen.

She returned seconds later with a Norfolk Police business card in the name of Police Constable Rodney Fellows, the local beat manager of the Sheringham Safer Neighbourhood Team, and handed it to Andy. Andy took a picture of the card with his phone.

'Thank you, we'll try to speak to PC Fellows if we can,' he said, knowing full well that they would do no such thing until they were sure it was safe to do so.

'Where will you all stay while you're here?' Maureen asked. 'You're welcome to stay with me.'

'We don't want to be a burden to anyone, Maureen,' said Trevor. 'We've got a camper van, so we'll huddle down in that once we find a suitable site nearby.'

'Why don't you park behind the gym? We have a car park that isn't being used while we shut the gym and our office. You can stay in the gym, if you like, all you need is some sleeping bags and you're good to go. There's everything you need there: shower facilities, a small kitchen, everything.'

Trevor looked at Kendra and Andy, who both nodded. They had sleeping bags ready for their stint in Marge, but it would be more comfortable in the gym, for sure.

'Thanks, Maureen, that would help a lot,' Trevor said.

'Here's the address,' she said, writing it down on a piece of paper, 'and here's the key. I've written the alarm code on there, too.'

'Thank you. I have some more friends coming up tomorrow, so the gym will be perfect for us all.'

'Please be careful, all of you. Losing Jacob was bad enough, I'd hate to lose anyone else.'

Trevor gave her a hug and said, 'I'll call you with any updates. In the meantime, you stay safe and call me if you need anything at all, okay?'

Kendra hugged her too, before they left the house.

'Right, let's get some food and supplies and we'll find the gym and settle down for the night,' Trevor said. 'I'll call Darren and find out when they're due to arrive.'

Andy reversed out of the cul-de-sac and made for the town centre. The drive to the gym car park took less than a minute and they pulled around the back and parked out of sight of the road.

'I take it that's Jacob's van?' said Andy, pointing to the vehicle.

'Yeah,' Trevor said, 'but Maureen doesn't know where the keys are, and they weren't on Jacob's body. Nobody actually knows how he could have got to the cliff without driving there. I mean, it isn't a horrendous walk, but it's unlikely.'

'That's strange,' said Kendra. 'We'll have a look around the gym and see if we can find them. If we can get access to the police report, that would help tremendously, but I don't know how I'm going to do it from here.'

'Listen, I'm good,' said Andy, 'but there are certain systems I can't get into, and the police's is one of them, because it's a secure system with no external access except for police laptops that have the bespoke protected programmes installed.'

'Yeah, I get that. I'm just trying to figure out whether I can call in a favour from someone at work, while giving nothing away,' Kendra mused out loud.

'Be careful there, love. It could cause huge issues for us,' Trevor warned.

Kendra nodded. 'If I have to go back to London to do it then I will, so let's find out what we can for now and go from there.'

Trevor used the key Maureen had given him to gain entry into the gym. He tapped the four-digit code into the alarm system by the door and switched the lights on. The gym was roomy and well equipped, with a full-sized ring at the far end and several punch bags, ceiling balls and other equipment placed along each wall. There were mats stacked in the two corners closest to the door, and toilets and changing rooms on the left-hand side, giving the gym a stocky L-shape. The smell of stale sweat prevailed, along with the sharper smell of gym oils like eucalyptus and lemongrass that never seemed to go away.

'Well, that's a smell that takes some getting used to,' Andy said, covering his nose.

'That's the smell of hard work and success, man, and don't you forget it,' Trevor said. 'In an hour or two, you won't notice it anymore.'

'He's right, Andy, that smell doesn't bother me anymore, and these gyms are friggin' amazing,' Kendra added.

'He always kept a good gym, did Jacob,' Trevor said, looking around fondly at his old friend's pride and joy. 'He did some great work here and will be badly missed.'

'Well, I'm gonna pick a good spot. There's plenty of space in here for us all to camp out in,' Andy said, 'even when the Walsall boys turn up.'

'I spoke with Darren and they're driving up tomorrow in a couple of cars, so we should be ready to leave then. Amir is also coming tomorrow, so there will be plenty of us here if we have to deal with any problems,' Trevor said.

'Manfri said there were twenty-plus riders, Trev, which is ten more than we'll have,' Andy pointed out.

'Yeah, but they don't know we're here, and they don't know what we can do, so we'll keep it that way until we have a solid plan. If it turns out we need more bodies, then we can get them within a few hours. Those bastards will pay heavily if it turns out they killed my friend.'

'I'm going to see what the ladies' changing room is like, because I'd rather poke my eyes out than sleep in a gym with nine blokes. No disrespect intended,' Kendra said, heading off to investigate.

'I don't blame you, K, your dad is not shy about farting at every opportunity, so good call,' Andy replied, heading off to pick a corner to hunker down in.

'Don't you forget it, little man,' Trevor said. 'Now get some kip so that we're fresh tomorrow. I want you to start by seeing if you can access the coroner's office computer for his initial report. Kendra and I will try to find out more about the biker gang. My guess is that they are close by, or even maybe at the campsite where Manfri and his family were staying. It'll be a busy day.'

Andy waved in acknowledgement and dropped his rucksack on a mat next to the ring.

'No worries, Trev, no worries.'

4

THE REJECTS

They started bright and early the following day, having had a reasonably comfortable sleep in the gym. After a shower and a simple breakfast of tea and toast, they set to work on their allocated tasks. Andy took his mug of tea and set up in the back of Marge with the powerful computers, where he engaged both the Hades programme to search the dark web and the Cyclops system for access to the local CCTV servers. Within minutes he was immersed online, his tea forgotten, his fingers dancing over the keyboard, and the rest of the world forgotten.

Instead of hanging around for the rest of the team to arrive, Kendra and Trevor walked to the scene of the crime, the famous Beeston Bump, a distance of a mile-and-a-half. It took them more than half an hour to reach the top of the two-hundred-foot cliff from the gym, via the sandy, winding path that started at the top of Cliff Road by the putting green. They didn't know exactly where Jacob's body had been found, just the rough area. They walked back and forth, from the top to mid-way, trying to see if there were any clues. The views from the cliff were incredible, the sea calm and the cloudy sky epic. It was easy to understand why it was such a popular spot for hikers and tourists alike.

'If I were looking to throw someone off a cliff, I'd do it in one of those gouged-out areas, where there have been recent collapses and where it is easier to access,' Trevor said.

'It's also a lot steeper, so anyone falling wouldn't stand a chance,' Kendra added.

They leaned over one such gouge in the sandy, gravelly cliff and looked down to the ground below. It seemed rocky and treacherous at the base of the cliff, unlike the long, wide, sandy beach beyond.

'We should go down there and see if there are any traces left behind by the police,' Kendra said. 'You never know.'

They retraced their steps back towards the putting green and down the slope towards the beach. At the base of the slope, they turned right along the promenade and headed towards the area where they estimated that Jacob had been found, past the array of multi-coloured beach huts. Looking up towards the top of the cliff, they could see there were three potential spots for someone to be thrown from, so they examined the area at the base of each. The sandy gravel from the collapses had long been taken by the sea, so the area below was relatively compact, but rocky.

At the second spot, they noticed something.

The blue and white *POLICE LINE DO NOT CROSS* tape had apparently been tied to a heavy boulder, as a six-inch piece of it had snagged in a small crevice when it had been removed.

'What are the chances that the police have been here more than once?' Kendra said. 'This must be the place.'

They couldn't see anything obvious in the area and

widened their search, hoping to find the van keys. There were no clues, all having been taken by the police or the sea.

'Well, I'm still glad we came,' Trevor said, standing solemnly by the rocks. 'I can pay my respects.'

Kendra stood by his side, their arms entwined, as he stood silently for several minutes, head bowed, thinking of his friend and praying that his death would not be in vain.

'Let's go, love,' he said, 'we have work to do.'

They walked back via the slope and were back at the gym just before lunch, having taken a different route via the town centre. They wanted to see more of Sheringham, where Jacob had been extremely happy since moving here with Maureen.

'He always spoke fondly of this place,' Trevor said as they walked along the busy Station Road. There were various outlets, including a traditional butcher's shop, a fishmonger, a lovely red lobster-themed boutique gallery that sold paintings and arty goods, old-style sweet shops, even a model train shop, along with the other traditional outlets you'd expect to find in a seaside town, such as ice cream sellers, fish-and-chip shops, and more.

'It looks fab,' Kendra said. 'I can see why he'd enjoy living here.'

'I visited a few times. Jacob used to love showing me around. He was so proud of the place. He was a good man and deserved better, K.'

'He did. Remember,' she said, 'we're here to put things right and honour his memory. We won't let him or Maureen down.'

As they reached the gym, they saw that three more vehicles were now parked there alongside Marge. There was a grey Audi A5, a silver Ford Mondeo, and a Land Rover Defender in typical British racing green livery, complete with a snorkel and Terrafirma winch on the front bumper, ready for all terrains.

'He's a good lad, that Amir, that's exactly what we need,' Trevor said, patting the bonnet.

They went inside to find the Walsall contingent standing by the ring, teas and coffees in hand, talking with Amir and Andy.

'We thought you'd done a runner, guys,' Darren said. They shook hands and hugged, and thanked them for helping.

'Guys, I don't know what to say, but thank you–again, we just can't seem to get rid of you!'

The Walsall team laughed.

'Trev, we had such a good time last time that we couldn't resist it. Nothing like this ever happens in Walsall, so a bit of excitement is always welcome,' Darren said.

The rest of his team hollered in agreement.

'I wish I could say that it's something exciting, but it isn't, my friend, so be prepared for anything and everything. And Amir, you star,' Trevor continued, 'how on earth did you get a Land Rover Defender like that?'

Amir made a great show of rubbing his knuckles on his chest, happy to show off at every opportunity.

'You'll like this,' he said. 'It's actually one of Stav's personal motors, which he didn't think I would see. I had a good look around his site and that was the one that stood out. I also grabbed a bunch of tools from him, so we have everything we need to do some MacGyver shit.'

'Of that I'm sure,' Trevor said, clapping. Amir bowed.

'Always happy to be of service,' he said.

There was much laughter and good team bonding, and Kendra was proud to be involved in something that was looking to do good. Police officers' hands were tied so much nowadays that they didn't stand a chance, whereas this group of people had the freedom to do some good. Granted, it involved breaking the law, but the only people that would get hurt were the criminals–and she was more than happy about that, guilt-free and proud.

'Gents, it's great to see you all again. You know we've called on you because there are personal reasons this time. We believe that my dad's old friend was murdered, but the police say it was suicide. We think there is something going on in the background and we need to investigate. This biker gang we've been told about sounds like a nasty bunch, so we have our work cut out for us.'

'Like I said, we're happy to be here. What do you need from us?' Darren asked.

'Dad and I want to find this biker gang, see where they've pitched up. If we can't find them, we may need to play clever and draw them out. Can we grab one of your cars with a driver? Maybe you can take the other car and do the same. Have a look around?'

'Yeah, no problem at all. We can do that.'

'Thanks. Amir, you stay here with Andy and see if he needs any help, there's not a lot you can do until we find these people.'

'Sure thing, Kendra.'

'That's pretty much it for now. We can't do much else. Andy is trying to get some more information on the area and the police involved. We'll keep you updated if we find anything.'

Trevor gave Darren enough money to fuel both cars and to act as expenses for the next few days.

'Stock up on grub if you have time. We'll do the same so

that we have plenty to keep us going,' he said. 'Be careful, this gang is no ordinary bike gang from what we've been told. They all dress the same, in black. Their bikes are modern high-end bikes with plenty of horsepower, and their leaders are vicious. We're hoping they are staying somewhere that can be seen from the road, otherwise it'll be a struggle and we'll have to draw them out, like Kendra said.'

'Understood,' said Darren. 'I've told everyone to put GPS trackers in their vehicles and also on their person, just in case. I'm going to take a couple of spares with me if we come across any of the bikers.'

'Good idea. We'll all do the same. Best to be prepared, right?' Trevor said.

'What do you want us to do if we find them, Trev?'

'Nothing for now. Let's find them first and decide how we're going to deal with them after. Remember, there's more of them than us, and we have to play clever.'

'Got it.'

Darren took two of his team with him, leaving Jimmy and Izzy to stay with Trevor and Kendra. Rory stayed behind to take care of supplies and to help Andy and Amir if anything were to come up.

'Okay, let's go,' Trevor said. 'And remember to keep in regular contact.'

Jimmy drove the Audi A5 with Trevor in the passenger seat and Kendra and Izzy in the back. Izzy had been injured in the earlier operation against the robbers in Hackney, but had recovered well.

'I have the scar to prove it,' he said, about to lift his hoodie to show Kendra.

'No, you're good,' she said, laughing and stopping his hand from lifting the top.

'Izzy, stop showing off, man,' Jimmy said from the front. 'It's only a teeny scar, bro.'

'It's a proper war wound, Jimmy. I'll show it off every chance I get.'

'Okay,' said Trevor, 'let's worry about scars and showing off another time, folks. Keep your eyes out for the bad guys, remember?'

They drove along the coastal road, taking the scenic route to the seaside resort of Cromer. The road weaved through a number of quaint villages along the way, many of them lined with caravan parks and glamping sites for the multitudes that descended to the area from spring until late autumn each year.

'We'll check the regular sites along the way and then veer off and start looking at other potential sites if we have no luck,' Trevor said.

'I think we should check the site Jacob was at when the bikers first showed up,' Kendra said. 'They may have been there for a reason and have gone back.'

'Good idea. This is on the way, so we'll get there later.'

As they drove along, they were careful to check all the visible caravan sites along the route, some much larger than others, including those in the villages of East and West Runton.

'Blimey, there are a lot of these sites, aren't there?' Trevor said. 'And some of them are huge.'

'It's a lovely part of the world, Dad. I'm not surprised at all.'

'Problem is,' he said, 'we can't see all the sites when they're this big and crammed, just by driving along. If we don't have any luck spotting them from the car, we may have to go on foot to look closer.'

'If they're as menacing as we've heard, I'm sure we'll find them,' Jimmy added, as they left East Runton and continued towards Cromer.

'Where are Darren and the others checking?' Kendra asked.

'I told them to take the top road leading to Cromer. Holt Road, I think it's called. There are not as many sites as it's further from the sea, but there are still plenty of options.'

'I'll check in with Darren and see how they're getting on,' Izzy said, pulling out his phone.

'Good thinking,' said Trevor. 'We can meet up for something to eat if they're hungry. There's a nice pub just before Cromer that does some great grub.'

Izzy finished his call quickly.

'They've checked almost all the sites off the Holt Road with no sign at all,' he said.

'Okay, message him back and tell him to meet us at the Roman Camp pub on Holt Road in about half an hour. It's next to the petrol station, about a mile before the roundabout for Cromer.'

'Will do.'

'Jimmy, let's go to the site where Jacob was staying with his family. If they're staying at a site, then that may be the one now that Manfri has left. Drive through Cromer towards Overstrand and I'll show you where the entrance is.'

Jimmy continued into the busy Cromer town as instructed. As they left the town at the other end, Trevor showed him where to turn off for the caravan site. They drove down a narrow single-track road for about half a mile before coming to a small crossroads, where they turned left and then right down another single-track road. There was no traffic around, nor any people. It was eerily quiet.

'Okay, the entrance is just along here on the left. It's easy to miss, so drive slowly and I'll have a look at the site as we go past.'

Jimmy slowed the Audi as they approached the entrance to Rufus Donald's site with its traditional wooden gate. Trevor looked in and could see some activity, some smoke from a campfire perhaps, and some empty beer tins, but he couldn't see far enough around the hedge to see who was there.

'Damn it, there's someone there, but I couldn't see who, or any bikes.'

'Is there another way in, or a back gate or something?' Jimmy asked.

'I don't think so. Let's spin the car around and have another look,' Trevor said.

It was a while before they had the chance to turn around, but eventually they came across a farm entrance that allowed Jimmy to do so. A few minutes later, they were almost back at Rufus's.

'Okay, slow down a little, Jimmy. It's just up here on the right.'

As they approached the entrance, some hundred yards short of it, Jimmy had to brake to allow the six black bikes out, with their black-clothed riders. Fortunately, they turned right, away from the Audi, and sped off. As Jimmy drove past the entrance, Kendra saw another leather-clad rider closing the gate. He was a huge bald man with tattoos over half his face. They locked eyes briefly as the car drove past, before the man closing the gate vanished from sight.

'Dear God, did you see that man?' she asked.

'Yes, I did. Manfri said he was one of the leader's right-hand men. He's one nasty looking dude, that's for sure,' Trevor replied.

'What do you want me to do, Trev?' asked Jimmy.

'Let's see what those bikes are up to, shall we? Keep a loose follow on them. Hopefully, they won't be going too far.'

'Ooh, a surveillance follow,' Izzy said from the back. 'I've been wanting to do one of those for ages.'

As requested, Jimmy kept a suitable distance from the bikes. They turned left at the same crossroads but carried on, eventually ending up on the Norwich Road leading into Cromer. Thanks to the busy traffic, it was harder for the bikers to notice anything out of the ordinary, so they paid little attention to anything behind them. They eventually ended up in the car park of Morrisons supermarket, where they parked up at the far end and dismounted. Jimmy parked diagonally across from a space where they could watch without being spotted. One rider took his helmet off and laid it on his seat. He, too, was hefty and bald, but without tattoos. The other riders stayed by their bikes with their helmets on, ready to go at a moment's notice. The bald rider looked around and walked towards a white transit van nearby, stopping by the driver's side window. He looked around again as if to check the coast was clear, before reaching into the van and accepting a small package, which he put in his jacket pocket. He took something out of his other pocket and gave it to the driver, before giving a salute and walking back to his group. A minute later, the bikers were back on the move again.

'Well, if that wasn't a textbook drug deal, then I don't know what is,' Trevor said.

'Yep, it sure was. Quite brazen, too. They don't seem fazed by anything, do they?' Kendra added.

'Do you want me to follow?' Jimmy asked.

'No, I think we've achieved more than enough today,' Trevor said, 'let's meet the others at the pub.'

Jimmy waited for another minute before leaving the car park and heading back towards Sheringham and the pub. Kendra had a sinking feeling in the pit of her stomach, having seen the tattooed man at the site. *I hope I never have to deal with that piece of work.*

5

DARK WEB

'So now we know where they are. What are we going to do?' Darren asked.

They were now sitting in the beer garden of the Roman Camp pub in Aylsham, halfway between Cromer and Sheringham. It was a lovely traditional pub that was popular with the locals, not least thanks to its impressive menu. They sat around a large table under a parasol drinking soft drinks, much to the disappointment of the landlord, who'd perked up when they each ordered a main course.

'We need to think about it,' Trevor said, 'because this bunch are not your typical bikers, they don't have an honour code or anything like that. They're straightforward mercenary types who don't give a shit about anything or anyone else.'

'I think it's best just to keep an eye on them for now and see if Andy comes up with anything,' Kendra added, 'there's much more to this than initially meets the eye, so the more intel we have, the better we can deal with it.'

'I have no problem with that,' said Darren, 'but I can see we're going to have problems monitoring them, don't you think? I mean, that site is pretty remote.'

'Manfri told us that the site owner is a good friend, so maybe we should speak to him first and see if he can help.'

'That's a good point, K. I'll call Manfri and see if we can set something up to speak with him,' Trevor said.

It wasn't long before the food arrived. Many had chosen the fish and chips or the burger option, recommended for those that were hungrier than the others. Some were more restrained and went for the crab linguine. Nobody was disappointed.

Kendra was just finishing her pasta when she received a call. It was from her boss, Rick Watts.

'I have to take this, Dad, be right back.'

She walked down the steps into the ornamental garden, out of earshot of the rest of the team.

'What's up, Sarge?'

'Bad news, I'm afraid, K. The DPS has scheduled interviews for us both the day after tomorrow, in the morning. Just wanted to make sure you could make it; I know you're on leave.'

Kendra thought for a second before responding.

'No, I'll be there, not a problem. I can always rebook my leave. What time do you want me?'

'Can you pop in tomorrow afternoon so we can have a pre-interview catch up? I just want to make sure we're doing everything by the book, if you know what I mean.'

'Yeah, sure, I'll see you then,' she replied, ending the call.

She returned to the group and took a sip from her lemonade.

'Everything okay, love?' Trevor asked.

'Yeah, it's all fine, I need to go to London for a few days,' she said, 'but it's all good as it'll be an opportunity to check on some things we can't do from here.'

'Okay, we'll chat about it later, love. You can catch the train from Sheringham and get into Liverpool Street via Norwich. It's how I used to visit. There's one every hour so we can drop you after we finish up here.'

'I'll do that, thanks. I just need to pick my things up from the gym first.'

They finished up and left shortly afterwards, with Trevor paying the bill after thanking the landlord for the excellent food.

BACK AT THE GYM, Trevor and Kendra popped in to see Andy as he continued his searches.

'We found them,' said Trevor, 'but it's gonna be tough to keep an eye out so I want to speak with the owner to see if he can help. He's a friend of Manfri and Jacob's.'

'He can't be that much of a friend if he's letting those bastards stay on his site after they killed his friend.'

'We don't know what or why yet, Andy. That's why we're going to call Manfri and set up a meeting. Hopefully, we'll find out all we need,' Kendra added.

'Cool. I haven't made as much progress as I'd like. There's very little on this Rodney Fellows chap anywhere, except on the local police website where he's listed as one of the officers looking after the area.'

'That's a shame. Did you find anything useful at all?' Trevor asked.

'I found out a little on the dark web about the biker gang,' Andy said, 'which is a little disturbing.'

'Why's that?' asked Kendra.

'Well, for one, the *R* on their sleeves stands for *Rejects*. I found out that the gang comprises bikers who have been kicked out of their previous chapters for something out of order, misconduct that broke their internal rules, or they were dishonourable. They're basically biker outlaws that their new leader, a chap they call Hawk, has brought together.'

'When you say something out of order, what exactly did they do?' asked Trevor.

'Many of them got kicked out for assaulting their club leaders, mainly to challenge for the leadership, but doing so in a way that broke the rules. They arrested some for selling drugs to schoolkids, they kicked others out for grievous bodily harm to elderly burglary victims. The list goes on. There's about twenty-five of them according to current intel and they're nasty as hell.'

'So let me get this straight,' said Kendra, 'we need to come up with a way for ten of us to deal with twenty-five very nasty individuals while trying to find out who is responsible for Jacob's murder—and most of all, why.'

'That pretty much sums it up, Detective,' said Andy.

'I do like playing the underdog, but just once it would be nice for the odds to be stacked in our favour.'

'Never going to happen. We'll always be the underdogs, which is why we will always have to play clever,' Trevor said.

'Anyway, I'm off back to London for an uncomfortable interview. I'll try to get some intel on our police friend while I'm there, but don't hold your breath. It's likely to get messy.'

'DPS?' Andy asked.

'Yep, our old friend DS Douchebag's allegations have to be investigated. Not their fault. They're just doing their job, but it's frustrating as hell.'

'Try not to laugh. They don't like that, remember?'

Trevor dropped Kendra off a short time later and within ten minutes, the train to Norwich had arrived and she was on board. The one-hour journey went quickly, and upon arriving, she had ten minutes until the two-hour connecting train to Liverpool Street left. The carriage was less than half full, so she had the row of seats to herself, with space and time to think of the upcoming events.

These next few days are going to get interesting; it could hurt those I care about, my career, and harm everything that we're doing.

She started considering all potential eventualities and how to deal with them. It made the journey go quickly, but by the time the train arrived in London, she had a plan, giving her a little more hope and optimism for the future.

'DARREN, I've made the call to Manfri, and he has arranged for us to see the site owner, a chap by the name of Rufus Donald. You okay to tag along?' Trevor asked.

'Sure, when do we leave?' came the reply.

'How about now?'

'Great, let's go,' Darren said enthusiastically. Trevor was warming to him and the Walsall team. They had proven themselves useful and loyal these past few weeks, and he enjoyed their company. They were also tough as nails, which is exactly what was required.

'We'll take one of your cars. We only have the camper van

and the Land Rover and I'd rather those bastards see neither, not yet anyway.'

'No problem, we'll take one of the Audis and I'll drive.'

They drove back towards Cromer. Manfri had described Rufus's farmhouse and how to get to it, warning of the proximity to the bikers at the landlord's nearby caravan site.

'Manfri told me that the bikers have basically taken over the site and nobody else is using it, so they're using it as if it's their base of operations for the area,' Trevor said.

'Where were they before that, though?' Darren asked.

'Good question. Hopefully, it's one of the things we'll eventually find out.'

Trevor guided him to Rufus's farmhouse, which meant driving along the same road as the caravan site but turning off several hundred yards before it. They drove along a narrow, well-kept gravel road alongside the hedgerow before veering away from the road and towards a wooden gate that had been left open. As they drove through the gate, the restored nineteenth-century brick-and-flint farmhouse with its pantile roof came into view. The lovely two-storey building was immaculately kept and far enough away from the other farm buildings to be almost idyllic. As they pulled up next to a maroon Range Rover, the door to the farmhouse was opened by an old man wearing blue jeans and a tweed jacket, along with a flat cap. He waved as they got out of the car.

'Mr Giddings, I presume,' he said, offering his hand to Trevor. 'I'm Rufus Donald. Manfri told me you were coming over.'

'Please, call me Trevor. This is my colleague, Darren. Thank you for taking the time to speak with us. I hope it isn't too much of a bother.'

'Not at all, please. Come on in,' Rufus said, opening the door wider.

They walked into a spacious open-plan lounge, with a kitchen-diner at the back. In the middle, an open fire had been lit, giving the room a comfortable glow. There was an armchair and a sofa in front of it, along with a coffee table between the two.

'Please, sit,' Rufus said. 'What can I get you to drink?'

'Just water for me,' Darren said.

'Tea, please, milk, no sugar,' Trevor said.

'Be right with you.'

Rufus returned a short time later with a tray of drinks and sat down with them.

'How can I be of service?' he asked, sipping from a steaming mug of black coffee.

'Rufus, we believe that Jacob was killed by the biker gang that is now set up in your field. I need to know whether you have any information about them that might be useful. For starters, how is it they're in your field?'

'Those bastards have a lot to answer for if what you're saying is true. According to the police, Jacob committed suicide, which I find very hard to believe.'

'So how have you let them use the site?' Trevor asked.

'They came to see me literally minutes after Manfri and his family left. Frightened the bloody life out of me, they did. Their leader has the strangest eyes I've ever seen, completely jet black. It was like looking at the devil himself.' He crossed himself. The experience had clearly shaken him.

'What did they say?'

'Not a lot. He told me they were taking over Manfri's booking and staying for a few weeks. He gave me a bundle of money, several thousand pounds, and told me to make sure that nobody else booked while they were staying. I didn't really have much of a choice. His two colleagues were just as scary, huge bastards they were.'

'Both bald, one with tattoos and the other with piercings?' Darren asked.

'That's them. They wouldn't stop staring at me throughout the exchange. Never said a word, just stared. As much as I wanted to tell them to shove off, I just froze and took their bloody money, hoping I'd have nothing further to do with them.'

'I understand, and I probably would have done the same. I've seen them. They're scary as hell,' Trevor said. 'Can you tell me anything more about them?'

'Not really. Within minutes of them leaving, I could hear the rest turn up. They closed the gate behind them, so they're clearly not wanting to be seen.'

'Is there any way we can monitor them safely that you know of?' Darren asked.

'Yes, there is. My farmhouse and land are directly next door to the site. I fenced it off, but it's only a small part of the estate and it makes me decent money each year. Anyway, the power supply and water all come from my land, so when I converted it to a caravan site, I had to install specific lighting and power for visitors to plug into. I also installed CCTV on a couple of trees to overlook the site. It was for health and safety reasons, but I wanted it for security as well. The only problem is, a local security company manages it, so I don't have access to it.'

'That's actually great news,' said Trevor. 'If you can tell us the name of the company, we can speak with them, with your permission, of course.'

'That won't be a problem at all,' Rufus replied. 'You see, the security company that managed this site was Jacob's company. I'm sure Maureen won't have any issues with you having a look.'

6

LONDON

Kendra was at the office early the following morning, as she had promised Rick. They sat in his office with a coffee to discuss the forthcoming interviews, the door firmly closed.

'First off, this chat did not happen, okay?' Rick said. 'The last thing we need is an accusation of collaborating to make up evidence and whatnot—which this isn't.'

'Of course, Sarge, I'm not a newbie,' she replied, somewhat offended.

'Yeah, I know, but it still needed saying. What are your thoughts on the interview tomorrow?'

'I'm pretty sure I'll be accused of threatening him, amongst other things, such as insubordination and neglect of duty, blah blah. He's a dick, but he's a dick with experience, so he would have alleged several things to cover all bases.'

'You don't seem worried at all. You know he'll be using his mate Critchley as a witness, don't you?'

'I do, but there's not a lot I can do about that, is there? That's the whole point of all this, to get us both in the shit and teach us a lesson. Honestly, I'm just gonna tell the truth and hope they believe it.'

'That's exactly what you should do too, K, because I have no doubt they'll be looking to trip us both up, which would probably happen if we started making shit up. No point in doing that because we have done bugger-all wrong.'

'So, you're not worried either?'

'Not at all. I just wanted to make sure we're on the same page. I did threaten him, though, when you left the other day. He had a pop at you, so I told him he'd have to deal with me if he kept that shit up. He didn't seem to take it well, hence the complaints.'

'You didn't need to do that, Sarge. I can deal with idiots like him with my eyes shut. Don't get yourself into this shit because of me. That isn't right.'

'You'd do the same for me and you know it,' Watts said.

'Fair enough. So basically, we just stick to the truth and let them decide whether we're evil or not.'

'Yes, as it should be. Remember, I know how they operate. They try to catch you out, but ultimately, they just want the truth and nothing to cloud it.'

'I guess the complaints about Duckmore will also be looked into. Let's hope he tries a different tactic, and it trips him up, eh?' she said.

'I'm confident that his arrogance *will* trip him up, yes. His witness will need to be careful too, because he could also end up in trouble if they mess their stories up.'

'I couldn't care less about his witness, to be honest. He may not have done much directly, but he's giving his douchebag mate support,' she added.

'Okay, now that we have that straight, what else is going on with you? Everything okay?' Watts asked.

'I have no complaints, Sarge. Being part-time suits me just fine. There's less pressure and I can focus on other things in life, you know? I'm happy to continue this way.'

'Well, it's a little confusing to me. We already lost Pike and I don't want to lose you too, so having you here for a few days a week is better than not having you at all. I just hope one day you'll come to your senses and come back full-time. You can still have a great career, Kendra.'

'Thanks, Sarge, I appreciate it. At the moment, I'm happy as things are. Hopefully, I can continue to contribute usefully to the team.'

'Good to know. We can use your help today on an armed robbery gone wrong, if you fancy sticking around the office?'

'Can I pop up in the afternoon instead? I have a few things I want to take care of in the Intel office, if that's okay with you?'

'Sure, I'll see you later.'

Kendra felt bad about lying to Rick, but if he knew what she'd be doing in the next couple of hours, he'd be throwing her out of the third-floor window himself.

Right, let's go and get some intel on the elusive Constable Fellows.

AFTER A GOOD HALF hour spent catching up with her Intel Unit colleagues, Kendra finally sat at her desk and started work. She went through her email inbox and sorted out some admin that needed doing, as she bided her time. When the rest of her team invited her to lunch, she declined.

'I'm running late and they need some help upstairs, so I'll catch up in a while,' she said.

As soon as they had left, she logged into the police database as Geraldine Marley, her colleague in the unit. She knew she'd have to be quick and so immediately typed in *Rodney Fellows Norfolk* and waited for the results. It didn't take long, and other than the reports that he had submitted, there weren't many entries of note. She found the report pertaining to Jacob's death and made a note of the circumstances and evidence that Fellows had put in the report. Little of it made sense to Kendra, knowing full well that Jacob had been murdered, so seeing a fellow police officer suggest it was a suicide was disturbing. There was no other evidence of note. He didn't question Jacob's van still in situ at the gym; didn't question where the van keys were; made no recommendations to further investigate it as a suspicious death and made it clear this was a common suicide. He even said that he expected the medical examiner to determine it as such.

Kendra noted the name of the coroner, Mr Andrew Kirkbride, hoping she could eventually track down the postmortem report when it was submitted.

Finally, she searched for the Rejects biker gang. There weren't many entries, suggesting that the gang had been formed recently, but she found one report of interest, filed by Essex Police, detailing an assault, actual bodily harm, on a pub landlord in Harlow. Two men and a woman had attacked him, all dressed in black biker leathers with a grey *R* patch on their sleeves, and the victim had identified them as Kevin Talbot, Fabian Melrose, and Janice Brown. The victim had then rapidly retracted his accusation, and the matter was subsequently dropped, the crime report marked as resolved with no further action. She checked the alleged attackers' information and photographs.

'Jackpot!' she exclaimed. Talbot had half his face

tattooed and Melrose was covered in piercings. Finding information on the leader's two principal men was a significant boon and seeing a woman involved with the gang was bonus intel.

She quickly took pictures with her phone of the three and noted down their information, before logging out of Geraldine's account.

It was a productive ten minutes. Finding out the coroner's details, and especially the identity of the two bikers, meant that they now had a great place to start.

Andy should be able to take over from here. Now, time for some lunch.

Trevor stepped into Marge to see Andy working feverishly away at a terminal.

'How are you getting on, Andy?'

'Not too bad, thanks. Kendra's intel has been useful. We're building a decent picture of those involved. We're still way short, though. Nobody has a clue about the leader of this biker gang, plus the post-mortem report hasn't been sent yet, so I'll need to find a way to get that.'

'We'll get there. Don't worry,' Trevor said.

'I found out something interesting, though, not sure how it's fitting into all this, but the van that showed up at the supermarket where you saw the drugs deal belongs to a known drug dealer in Cromer, Bradley Starkins. He's got previous for possession and supply and has spent time in prison for it, but seems to be happily continuing his trade.'

'So, you think he's being supplied by the bikers?'

'I do. Maybe that's what this is all about. They're moving

into the area and controlling the drug supply, and perhaps Jacob and his family got in the way.'

'I don't buy that, Andy. Why pick on that site? Why kill Jacob? None of it makes any sense.'

'All we can do is keep looking and something will come up to make things clearer, I'm sure.'

'I agree,' said Trevor. 'When do you think you'll be able to access the post-mortem report?'

'Well, it's been almost a week, so it should be ready any day. I'll poke around and see if I can get access to the coroner's system. If I have any luck, I'll let you know.'

'Thanks Andy, I'll catch you later. We're going back out to see Rufus Donald, the landowner. He called to say he has more information, so I'm going back there with Darren.'

'Great, see you later.'

'THANK you for coming back at such short notice,' Rufus said, shaking their hands and letting them into his farmhouse again.

'Not at all. It's we who are grateful that you are helping us,' Trevor replied.

As before, Rufus fetched the beverages, and they sat around the fire.

'Something strange is going on around here, and I thought you should know of it,' he said. 'I met up with a bunch of local landowners and business owners in the area to tell them to look out for this biker gang.'

'That was prudent of you. Did anyone else mention being threatened or approached at all?'

'No, they did not know what had happened. Except for

one landowner who said something strange, which made me suspicious. His name is Jeremy Falconer, and he's the wealthiest landowner in the area, with thousands of acres. Horrible man, he is.'

'What did he say?' asked Darren.

'After I told them what had happened and then asked if anyone had seen or heard anything, they all said no or shook their heads, including Falconer. But then he told the group that just because they were bikers with strange eyes and tattooed heads didn't mean they were going to cause anyone else trouble.'

'Why did that make you suspicious?' Trevor asked.

'Because at no time did I mention the leader's strange eyes or the henchman with the tattooed head.'

'That is suspicious, indeed.'

'I gave him the benefit of the doubt, but later on I spoke to him again and he mentioned that he wanted to speak with me about buying my farm. He said that the area is going downhill and now would be a good time to sell up if I was interested.'

'That's mighty generous of him.'

'I've made it extremely clear that I'm not interested in selling up. I spoke to a couple of close friends at the meeting afterwards and they told me the same thing, that Falconer had offered to buy them out. His offers were lower than the valuation by at least twenty percent. I think he is looking to buy up as much land as possible on the cheap.'

'Hmm,' said Trevor. 'In Falconer's eyes, having a nasty drug dealing biker gang in the area is ideal for him, isn't it? If the locals get twitchy, he could buy up lots of land and businesses and dominate the area.'

'The thing is,' Rufus continued, 'he tried to do something

similar about five years ago, trying to buy up land around Overstrand and in the village itself, because he wanted to redevelop the area and build luxury accommodation. He has a lot of the land already, both in and out of the town, but if he had it all, he could destroy the place and turn it into a gigantic building site.'

'Wow, these rich dudes just wanna get richer, don't they?' Darren said, shaking his head.

'The fact that he spoke to many of us at the meeting again, but on the quiet, makes me think he's trying to do a landgrab on the cheap, Trevor, and somehow poor Jacob was part of the plan to scare the living daylights out of us all, and into selling up cheaply.'

Trevor sensed Rufus was upset, but he also saw a steely determination in the man, to do whatever he could to stop it from happening.

'Where does this lovely gentleman live?'

'He has a vast estate close to here,' Rufus said, 'with a farm and a small industrial estate at the far end. He's closed that down, for some unknown reason. It's a handful of warehouses and workshops that are now empty. Maybe that's part of his plan to redevelop. Who knows?'

'Thanks, Rufus, we really appreciate your help with this and will try to keep you in the loop. I'm popping over to see Maureen later to ask about the CCTV at the campsite. Maybe that will show something up too.'

'I'll let you know if I hear anything else in the meantime,' Rufus said as he walked them to the door.

'Thanks again,' Trevor said as they shook hands and left.

'That is one tough old dude,' Darren said as they drove away from the farmhouse.

'Yes, he is,' Trevor said, 'and he's on our side.'

'What's next?'

'Like I said, I want to speak with Maureen to see if we can access the CCTV footage at the site. At some point we'll need to pop over and check this Falconer's estate out, which sounds like it's huge and may take some time.'

'Sounds like a plan,' Darren said. 'This is becoming one of those big, unexpected adventures again, isn't it?'

'Unexpected *dangerous* adventures, yes,' Trevor replied grimly, 'and let me tell you, Darren, we can't afford to mess this one up. My mate isn't dying for nothing. That, I promise.'

7

INTERVIEW

'Please take a seat,' the smartly dressed female detective said to Kendra as she entered the small, stark interview room. A male detective who sat opposite Kendra accompanied the interviewer.

Kendra sat down and looked at the two officers.

The man reached over and started typing into the screen of the recording device that was secured to the wall and desk, preparing it for the interview.

'Is it K-E-N-D-R-A?' he asked as he struggled to type with his chunky fingers.

'Yes, that's right.'

'Thanks.'

It took a couple of minutes for him to type all the relevant information into the recorder, but finally, they were ready to go.

'Okay, ready to record,' he said, and pressed the button on the device, 'the time is two minutes past eleven in the morning.'

'My name is Detective Inspector Hannah Woodruff.'

'And my name is Detective Sergeant Christopher Oakley,' her colleague stated.

'Please state your name and rank for the record,' Woodruff said.

'Detective Constable Kendra March,'

'Detective Constable March, you do not have to say anything, but it may harm your defence if you don't mention now, something which you later rely on in court. And anything you do say may be given in evidence. Do you understand?'

Kendra smiled and replied, 'Yes, I understand.'

'Something funny, Detective?' Woodruff asked.

'No, ma'am, it just sounds weird being on the receiving end of the caution that I have given myself hundreds of times.'

'Well, that's as may be, but you have to be treated the same as everybody else. I'm sure that you understand.'

'Yes, ma'am, I do,' she replied.

'I also want to remind you of your right to have a legal representative here. Did you not want a solicitor with you?'

'I don't believe that I will need one, ma'am. I have done nothing wrong.'

'Nevertheless, I will need a formal answer from you for the record. You have the right to a legal representative here to assist you and you have chosen not to have anyone. Is that correct?'

'That is correct.'

'Okay, then we can get started. We're here today because police officers have made several allegations against you, allegations that we are currently investigating.'

'Officers?' You mean there's more than one?'

The DI ignored her and continued.

'The allegations made against you are as follows. Allegation one—on Wednesday 16th of February, without lawful excuse, you made to another a threat, intending that the other would fear it would be carried out, to assault that person, namely Detective Sergeant Edward Duckmore. Allegation two—on Wednesday 16th of February, without lawful excuse, you made to another a threat, intending that the other would fear it would be carried out, to assault that person, namely Detective Sergeant David Critchley. Allegation three—on Wednesday 16th of February, you did fail to obey a lawful order that was given to you by Detective Sergeant Edward Duckmore and therefore failed to abide by the provisions of Police Regulations. Allegation four—on Wednesday 16th of February, you did fail to obey a lawful order that was given to you by Detective Sergeant David Critchley and therefore failed to abide by the provisions of Police Regulations. Do you understand these allegations?'

'Yes, ma'am, I do,' Kendra replied.

'Do you wish to respond to the allegations?' the DI asked.

'Ma'am, I can categorically tell you that I did not threaten either of those officers and I can also tell you I have never refused any lawful order that anyone ever gave me, let alone those two.'

'Kendra, do you know what the lawful orders were?' asked DS Oakley. He seemed less officious than the DI and smiled at Kendra knowingly.

'No, Detective Sergeant, I do not. Can you please enlighten me?'

DS Oakley looked down at the report in front of him and then at the DI, who was watching him disapprovingly.

'Detective Sergeant Duckmore alleges that you refused to assist him when he requested your help to find a missing

Albanian gang, the Qupis. He alleges that you told him to—and I quote—"*Take your head for a shit.*" According to Detective Sergeant Critchley, he then stepped in and asked you for the same assistance, to which he alleges you replied—again I quote—"*You take his head for a shit too, you limp-dicked wanker.*" Does any of this sound familiar to you, Detective?' asked the DS, who continued to smile at Kendra.

It was all Kendra could do to stop laughing. She put her hand over her mouth, taking a few seconds to compose herself.

'My apologies. I needed a second to think. This is my formal response to those allegations. I would be proud to have thought up those responses, but sadly, I did not. Those two buffoons were an embarrassment to the police service and deserve nothing but disdain from me. However, I categorically deny that I ever said those things or refused to obey a lawful order.'

'Thank you, Detective,' he replied.

'Moving on,' the DI said, looking back and forth between the two of them reproachfully, 'do you have anything further to say about the allegations of threats to assault? They are serious allegations, Detective Constable March, so simply denying that it happened may not be enough in this instance.'

'Ma'am, other than their claim that I said so and corroborating each other's evidence, is there any other evidence to suggest that I did what they allege? Did they say where it happened? Was it inside, or even outside, where I'm sure CCTV would show anything untoward? Those two are thick as thieves, and I can assure you that they have no evidence. You should think about speaking to them again and give them a couple of trick questions each.

I promise you they'll slip up and put themselves in the shit.'

'Trick questions? What do you think this is, some sort of training school exercise?' the DI said. 'I suggest you take this interview seriously, Detective, because if the allegations are proven, there's a chance you'll lose your job, do you understand?'

'Yes, ma'am, I do understand. But I have nothing else to add. I simply did not do the things that they allege. They took a dislike to me from day one. Duckmore, in particular, is nothing more than a bully, a misogynist, and an arse-licker who is after promotion and will steamroller anyone who gets in his way. Let me tell you this, too. If you pose a question that puts his partner in the frame for letting him down, he will capitulate and throw him under the bus quicker than you can state your rank. They may be thick as thieves, but they are also rotten to the core and will screw each other over if it suits them. If you want the truth, then that's the angle you should go with, not try to threaten me with my job, Detective Inspector. On that note, I invoke my right to stop the interview and request legal representation.'

'Why now, Detective?' asked DS Oakley.

'Because I have nothing further to add and my job has been threatened. I was quite happy to assist because—as I've said many times—I have done nothing wrong. That gesture of goodwill went out of the window with the threat to my job. Please reschedule the interview and allow me to get a brief.'

'Very well,' he said, looking at the DI, who nodded. 'This interview is hereby concluded at 11.23am,' Oakley added, turning off the recorder.

The DI stood up and gathered her paperwork.

'You've clearly done something to piss them off, Detective,

I hope you understand that it's our job to investigate and make sure that we get to the truth of things,' she said, on her way out of the room.

'Don't worry about her, Detective, she's stern as hell, but she means well,' Oakley said.

'I suppose, but the second she made the threat, the gloves were off. I honestly didn't think it would get this far and that anyone would believe those two wankers. Honestly, where the hell is the job heading if twats like Duckmore can do and say what they want and get away with it?'

'Off the record, we don't believe them, and I'm sure we will catch them out when we speak with them again. I've seen the complaints against them, but we have to stay impartial when investigating you and DS Watts.'

'So, you know what they're like and yet you still have to go through this charade?'

'Pretty much, yes. We have to cross the t's and dot the i's so that nobody will accuse us of not investigating fully. I will tell you this, though, Kendra,' he added, 'if they can't provide any evidence, then this is going nowhere, but we will also look into malicious allegations by them both—and that will be their undoing.'

'That's good to know. I appreciate you telling me,' Kendra replied, surprised but elated.

'Just do me a favour and don't say anything, okay?' he said, opening the door to leave.

'Thanks, Sarge, I'm grateful.'

'You're welcome, Kendra. I doubt we'll be needing to speak with you again, so look after yourself.' With that, he waved and left the room.

'Well, that was different,' she said out loud.

An hour later, Kendra met up with Rick Watts in his office, behind closed doors.

'I have to say, Sarge, that was bizarre, to say the least.'

'Why do you say that, K? Mine was pretty straightforward. That DI is something else, isn't she? Tried to stare me out throughout the whole interview. I almost laughed, which would have caused some difficulties.'

'The DS basically told me they don't believe either of them, but that they had to investigate, regardless. Apparently, I said some hilarious things to that pair when I refused to obey a lawful order.'

'Yeah, sounds similar to me. I threatened to kick them both in the nuts, apparently. I would have loved to have done that, but I didn't say any such thing. According to them, I also hindered an investigation they were on. It's all bollocks. They're just trying to cause us problems, that's all.'

'Well, it's done now. Hopefully, they'll not be back,' Kendra said.

'Thanks for coming in at such short notice, Kendra. I'm glad we could get this out of the way quickly.'

'No problem, Sarge. I'd better be off; I have a trip to plan.'

'Okay, see you in a week or so, right?'

'Yes, see you then.'

Kendra left the station and was in her car within minutes. Before setting off, she dialled a number.

'How are you doing, Charmaine? Are you free for a catch up? Great, I'll see you at the factory in an hour.'

That gave her enough time to pop back to her flat and pick up some clean clothes. It also gave her time to make a couple more calls. She had plans to make.

A SHORT TIME after a quick stop off at her flat, Kendra called Andy to update him on the day's events.

'That DI sounded harsh and unfriendly.'

'She was okay, just doing her job. I would have done things differently, but she seems to have a permanent frown which won't sit well with experienced officers. I'm sure she'll improve as she finds this out.'

'So, what else is going on?' Andy asked.

'I'm heading to the factory to meet Charmaine and the twins so I can give them an update. I also want to pick up some equipment that we'll probably need in the next few days.'

'Oh, good. I've been thinking about how to deal with the bikers, too. Can you stop off at a hardware store and buy some steel chains, please? We'll need about thirty metres of it and a handful of connecting links too.'

'Why do you... never mind, I'm sure you have your reasons. Anything else?' she asked.

'Yeah, get me two cordless angle grinders, half a dozen cans of expanding foam, a dozen bottles of Gorilla Glue, four cans of fluorescent pink spray paint and a one kilo jar of jellybeans.'

'Honestly, I don't know whether you are joking. Do you seriously want me to get all that?'

'Yes, yes, I do, Detective. Do you have a problem with that?'

'I know I can't see you, but I also know you are grinning like a Cheshire cat, you horrible man. I'll get the hardware even though I have no idea what you want it for, but why the hell do you need the jellybeans?'

'The hardware is for dealing with the bikes and the jellybeans are for me to snack on while everyone is doing their thing. I'll save you some if you want?'

Kendra ended the call, shaking her head in the manner that only Andy could make her do.

'Jellybeans. Buffoon.'

AS SHE ARRIVED at the factory, Kendra could see several cars at the rear car park. She entered the building at the back and headed straight for the canteen, where she knew they would be waiting.

'We thought you'd called us in for a joke and weren't coming. It's bad form to be late, Kendra,' Mo joked as she walked in.

'You know what they say, Mo, the stars always make a dramatic entrance, and for that, you have to be a little late.'

Mo gave her a hug in response. 'Well, you are a star, I'll give you that.'

'Thanks for coming, Charmaine, I appreciate it,' Kendra said.

'No thanks needed. I'm intrigued to discover what this is about,' Charmaine replied, rubbing her hands together. She had enjoyed her adventures with the Russians recently and was keen to be more involved.

'As you all know, a friend of Dad's was found dead at the bottom of a cliff in Norfolk. They reported it as suicide, but we're now sure it was murder. We're looking into the people involved, including a vicious biker gang that we think may have been responsible for his death. I'm going back there tonight, but I want to go with some back-up for us to deal with these nasty bastards. I was hoping you'd be up for a trip for a few days to help us. What do you think?'

She looked at them each in turn, thinking the worst but hoping they'd volunteer.

'Why are you even asking, Kendra? You know we're up for it. Count us in,' Mo replied, quick to show unity.

'I was going to say the same thing,' said Charmaine. 'Of course I'll help, happy to.'

'Do you think you can drag any more people onboard? There are about twenty-five bikers and only ten of us at the moment, so even a couple more will help,' Kendra said.

'I know Zoe will be up for it, so I'll call her and tell her to get ready,' Charmaine said, walking away to make the call. Zoe was a capable boxer who had helped with the Russians and who was also keen to engage further with the team.

'You know what, I think it's about time young Gregory came out to play,' said Mo.

'Who's Gregory?' asked Kendra.

'You've seen him around but probably didn't notice him much, which is why he's perfect for this. You'll know him when you see him. He kinda blends into the background wherever he is, which will come in handy if we end up following the bikers.'

'Sounds great,' Kendra said.

'He's also a talented boxer, so he can take care of himself. He's only twenty-one, but he'll do well for us,' Mo added.

'Great, call him and see if he's up for a trip to the coast. In the meantime, we'll need a couple of cars to get there. I also need one of you to come with me to the hardware shop.'

'I can do that,' Charmaine volunteered.

'Come on then, let's go shopping.'

Mo waited for Gregory to answer the phone.

'What's up, Greg? You up for a trip to the seaside?'

THREE HOURS LATER, the two cars left the factory, heading for Norfolk. Kendra drove the silver Volvo estate with Charmaine as a passenger, while Mo drove the blue Vauxhall SUV, with Zoe and Greg keeping him company. Both cars were laden with the equipment and provisions that Andy had requested. Kendra had opened the large jar of jellybeans and was sharing them out in her car, having given Mo and Charmaine a good handful each. She had targeted at least half the contents by the time they got to Sheringham.

'That'll teach him,' she told her co-conspirators.

8

CORRUPTION

Trevor arrived at Maureen's house and parked in her otherwise empty driveway, with Jacob's van still parked behind the gym.

'It's lovely to see you again, Trevor,' Maureen said, giving him a hug.

'How have you been coping, love?' he asked once they were seated with their cups of tea.

'I won't lie. It's been pretty dreadful. I've had little sleep, and when I do manage to get some, I wake up in a cold sweat. I miss him so much, Trevor.' She dabbed her eyes with a handkerchief.

'We all miss him, love, but I can't imagine how much more difficult it is for you. Just remember, there are many people here for you if you need anything, okay? Absolutely anything.'

'That's very kind, thank you.'

'I'll get straight to it, if that's okay. Rufus told me that your company was hired to monitor the CCTV for his campsite, so I thought I'd pop over to see if you could help us.'

'Of course. What do you need?'

'The biker gang has set up there and they're not aware of any cameras overlooking the camp. Can you give us access to the CCTV so we can see what they're doing there?'

'If it's going to help find out who killed my Jacob, of course. I can give you the remote login so that you can monitor from your own computer, if that works?'

'That would be perfect. Is there anything else about the site that may help us? Even the smallest of details may make a difference.'

Maureen thought for a few seconds before replying. 'The only thing I can think about is the secret gate we installed at the back of the campsite that abuts to our farmland. We thought it would be useful to have another way in, just in case.'

'See? That is exactly what will help, tremendously. That's brilliant news, Maureen. Where is this secret gate?'

'It's in the top right corner of the campsite as you look at it from the road. There's a big tree in that corner, where we put one of the cameras. The gate is behind the tree, hidden by a holly bush. It may be a little uncomfortable getting in, but we thought it would deter anyone from snooping around.'

'Perfect. Can you write down the login info for the CCTV? I have someone who will put that to good use,' Trevor said.

'I'll get a pen and paper, please excuse me.' Maureen got up and walked towards the kitchen. Before she got to the door, she turned around.

'Did they kill my Jacob, Trevor? Is it them?'

Trevor paused before replying, trying to remain sensitive to the situation.

'Maureen, we have no evidence it was them, but we

suspect that it may have been. That's why we need to investigate further as we can't go pointing the finger until we know for sure. Your help will go a long way to finding the truth.'

'That's all I want to know, thank you,' she said, turning back towards the kitchen.

She returned a few minutes later with a piece of paper, which she handed to Trevor.

'That's the login address, username and password to the system. You'll find everything you need in the Rufus Donald account.'

Trevor took the paper and put it in his shirt pocket. He stood up and gave Maureen another hug.

'Thank you. We'll get them, I promise.'

'I know you will, Trevor. I know you will.'

Darren and Izzy arrived near the Falconer estate and aimed to park in a layby where many others had also parked before going cross-country with their dogs. The entrance to the estate was on a relatively busy road, unlike the campsite and where Rufus lived, which was a single-track carriageway. Entry was prevented by the huge wrought-iron gates that were controlled automatically from the security office in the manor house. Before parking up, Darren and Izzy had made a point of checking the entrance for future reference, just in case. They saw that there were two CCTV cameras mounted high on each of the two brick-built posts, pointing down towards approaching cars, along with another camera at the intercom that was mounted at driver level.

'So, we know he has on-site security,' Izzy said. Darren nodded in agreement.

'Yep, so this will be trickier than we thought,' he said. 'Let's take a walk around the perimeter to see if we can see the house.'

They had checked the area on Street View before heading out, so they had a good idea about the placement of the manor house and all the outbuildings, along with the adjoining land and boundaries. The estate was vast, but fortunately in a relatively busier area than Rufus's farm, so it wasn't unusual to see a couple of men walking in the vicinity. The small industrial estate was next to the grounds of the manor house at the far end. It was the last set of buildings before the road narrowed to a single-track carriageway again, suggesting that it was slightly more remote.

'Maybe we should get Andy to lend us a drone, or something,' Izzy said as they walked, 'because those hedges won't let us see much at all, will they?'

'Let's check it ourselves first. We'll be able to see things differently from the ground. As long as nobody eyeballs us, we'll be fine.'

As they approached the end of the hedgerow, they saw a wide wooden gate, with a cattle grid on either side to prevent them from leaving, if left open inadvertently.

'There's the house,' Darren said, nodding towards the end of the track. Fortunately, the track went in a straight line towards the manor house, which was several hundred metres from the gate.

'This must be their service gate for farm deliveries or collections,' Darren said. 'So this is how the rich live out here, eh?'

'Not for me, mate,' said Izzy. 'There's nothing around here for miles. No fried chicken takeaway, no burger joints, no bowling alley or arcade. What do they do around here for fun?'

'They probably have all those things in that house there,' Darren said, laughing.

'Yeah, well, if I had that sort of dosh, I'd be living in a penthouse in the centre of Birmingham with everything within minutes of my front door.'

Darren shook his head as they continued on.

'Listen up,' Izzy said, as they approached the small junction leading into the industrial estate, wary of the noise coming from the small warehouse closest to the road. They could see a faint light in one of the first-floor windows, but there was nothing else that showed any sign of life.

Except for the noise of a motorcycle engine being revved nearby.

It went on for a few seconds before the engine was switched off. There was clearly a problem with it, as it kept misfiring every few seconds. There was silence for about ten seconds before the revving started again. The misfiring was still there, but not as bad, and then the engine was switched off again.

'Let's go back,' Darren said, 'otherwise we'll stick out like a sore thumb if anyone comes out.'

'Didn't Trevor say that this industrial part has been empty for a while?' Izzy asked, 'because that sounded very much like a motorcycle engine being worked on.'

'Yes, he said that. Also, that was the sound of a Ducati Multistrada V4 engine, Izzy. I'd recognise it anywhere, and you should too.'

'Wait, is that the same bike that Frazer drives around, the one he's always boasting about?'

'Yep, that's the one, and I bet you a hundred quid that the one in that warehouse is black,' Darren added.

Izzy looked at him with incredulity.

'Seriously, how do you know that?' she asked.

'How many Ducatis have you seen around here, Izzy? Because the only ones I've seen were the ones being ridden by those bikers we saw the other day, the ones leaving the campsite. Two of them, in fact. I'm telling you they're using that warehouse, or they have some sort of access to it. Whatever it is, it puts this Falconer bloke in the frame as being involved with them.'

'This thing is getting weirder each day,' Izzy said.

'Yep, isn't it great?'

They both laughed as they made their way back to the car. They had much to report to Trevor and the team.

'I MANAGED to get hold of the post-mortem report,' Andy told Trevor as he stepped into the camper van. 'I've printed it out.'

'Dare I ask?'

'Not really, suffice to say that the coroner's server is just as badly protected as the local councils that we've dealt with in the past. Dreadful, really.'

'So, what did you find?' Trevor asked. 'Have they recommended an inquest?'

'No, they haven't, which in itself is suspicious as hell because even with the slightest amount of doubt, they should do so, and there is plenty.'

'Like what?' Trevor asked.

'Well, for one, there are still unanswered questions—why

was his van still at the gym, and where are his van keys? There was a deep wound to his side that they implied was caused by a sharp rock or a knife, and finally there is even a mention of some material found under his fingernails, which they have completely dismissed as unconnected.'

'What material?'

'According to the post-mortem report, there are minute traces of leather, and flakes of black dye under two fingernails on his right hand. They surmised it was unconnected to the fall and likely connected to his gym work. Absolute rubbish.'

'So, what does it all mean?' Trevor asked.

'It's basically as we feared, they have given the cause of death as a suspected suicide, because where he was found at the bottom of the cliff, there was no accidental way that he could have fallen.' Andy picked up the report and continued. 'Listen to this: "It is likely that Jacob veered deliberately off the path and walked directly to a place where he then jumped to his death"—hence suspected suicide. Honestly, I can't believe I'm reading this. Do you know what this means?'

'What?'

'It means,' said Andy, 'that we are dealing with a corrupt police officer, and potentially a corrupt pathologist and coroner. It means that someone powerful is pulling the strings here.'

'Shit, well, we were going to investigate anyway, so we may as well crack on and see what else we can find. Can you dig a little more into their backgrounds?'

'Who, the pathologist and coroner?'

'I think all three. I know we've looked into the police officer in the police databases, but there must be more to him than we have found so far, so dig a little further. We may as well see what links them all and whether they are connected to anyone else, that may shine some light on all this,' Trevor said. 'I'm sure it has something to do with that landowner, but we have to find some proof.'

Trevor's phone rang. 'It's Darren. One sec. How's it going, Darren? I've put you on speaker. Andy's with me.'

'We're just on our way back from the landowner's estate and we think we may have stumbled onto something interesting,' Darren said.

'What's that, mate?'

'We couldn't really see much into the estate itself, other than to see it's covered by pretty good security camera coverage. There is another entrance that we think is like a service gate or for deliveries at the side of the estate, where it is much quieter. What we found interesting was that the industrial estate next door has some occupants.'

'Really?' said Trevor. 'Rufus told us it had been closed for a while now. What did you see?'

'It's not what we saw, but what we heard. A motorbike was being worked on in the warehouse and it was one of those nice Ducatis that Frazer has, the same as a couple we saw the other day,' Darren replied.

'That is interesting. That's a pretty decent connection to the landowner if it is one of their bikes, isn't it?'

'Yeah, it would be nice to get some sort of confirmation, but we'll need some of Andy's secret squirrel kit, like those miniature cameras, and someone to install them.'

'I'll get Amir to pop over later tonight when it's all quiet. He loves that sort of thing,' Trevor added.

'Great. We'll be back there shortly.'

'Thanks, Darren.'

'Well, that is interesting,' said Andy. 'If the bikers are using that warehouse, then Falconer must have given him permission, right?'

'Logic would suggest that, yes, but I think we'll need more proof. If he's using these bikers to scare the hell out of everyone so he can buy up land on the cheap, then this guy means business. Jacob's death is on his head if he hired those thugs to kill him,' Trevor said.

'I guess I'd better start digging into everyone's background, then, to see if we can connect them and find that proof.'

'Thanks, Andy. Let me know what you find.' Trevor got up to leave.

'Trevor, just be careful how you move forward with all this,' said Andy. 'Don't let your emotions take over, because that's how we can screw up. We'll find what we need and then we'll find a suitable way of dealing with them all, like we always do.'

'Don't worry. I won't do anything to endanger what we do, that is foremost in my mind and trust me, I will find a suitable punishment for anyone involved.'

'I believe you,' Andy said after Trevor had left.

As Trevor left the camper van and walked towards the gym, he heard a car tooting its horn. When he turned, he saw two cars arriving in the car park and his daughter waving from one of them.

'Surprise!' she said, getting out and giving him a hug. 'I thought I'd bring a few friends to help out.'

'This is a nice surprise indeed. Hello, everyone. And who is this young man? I recognise you from somewhere.'

'Hi again, Mister Giddings. I'm Greg Petrucci, one of the interns at Sherwood Solutions. You've probably seen me around the factory a few times.'

'That's right, you've been learning about security consulting and products, haven't you? It's good to see you again. How have they roped you into coming here?'

'He wasn't *roped* into doing anything he didn't want, Trev,' said Mo. 'This boy is our best surveillance operative and can follow anyone. I thought he'd be useful up here, you know?'

'That's great. I'm sure we'll find something for you to do while you're here, Greg. Go and settle in with the others while I catch up with my daughter. Nice to see you too, Charmaine and Zoe. Welcome to the seaside.'

'Happy to be here, Trevor. We'll catch up later. I want to find out what the fuss is all about with this town. It looks lovely,' Charmaine replied.

'Get yourselves settled, I'm sure there will be plenty of time to sightsee later,' Trevor said.

Turning to Kendra, he asked the burning question, 'How did it go? Are you okay?'

'I'm fine, Dad. You don't have to worry. They know it's a sack of shit and are just going through the motions. I'll be fine.'

'Good. We're making some progress here, too. We just need to come up with a plan on how to deal with these bastards, but we can't do anything until we get some evidence, so there's still plenty to do.'

'Well, your finest investigator is back with you now, so leave it to me and your best mate Andy, and I'm sure we'll figure it all out. I'll just pop over there now to say hello.' Kendra giggled as she walked towards the camper van.

'Best mate, my arse,' Trevor said, waving a fist at her.

AMIR WAS DISPATCHED after dark and approached the estate as instructed. He quickly established something that Darren and Izzy hadn't spotted, that a CCTV camera also covered the side entrance. Fortunately, it was mounted on a post within the boundaries of the estate and pointed only at the gate, so nobody would be spotted walking on the opposite side of the road. He didn't want to take a chance that the camera had thermal capabilities, so he mounted the first miniature camera from across the road, affixed to a tree branch that faced the gate directly. That would give Andy a chance to identify vehicles and have a visual on the drivers and occupants.

He then approached the industrial estate with caution, anticipating that people would be there despite the late hour —and he was right to do so. From within the warehouse came voices, laughter, and the sounds of power tools being used. The warehouse entrance was on the opposite side, meaning that he could not approach from the roadway in case they had someone keeping an eye out.

Before making his move, Amir took a quick look around, and within seconds, had vanished into a small gap in the hedgerow and was quickly in the farmer's field adjoining the warehouse. Moving slowly in the shadows, he could get a view through the hedgerow at the front of the warehouse. It was well lit, making it difficult to approach directly. The loading bay shutters were down and the single doorway closed. A light was on in one of the upstairs windows, and another above the doorway, showing that there may be a mezzanine level.

Amir squirmed underneath the hedgerow, half expecting to encounter mice or other small mammals that had made it their home. He wanted to find a suitable point to attach a small camera, one that had clear sight of the shutters and the doorway. It wouldn't be perfect for identification, but it would give a heads-up that something was happening and there was some sort of movement. By snapping a couple of branches, he could find that line of sight, and quickly secured the camera with a pair of zip ties. Once he was happy that it was ready, he slowly made his way back towards the field.

Amir moved further along, towards another building that he had identified as unoccupied and in darkness. As he got closer, he saw it was a bin store for the estate, built with slatted pine so that it would hide the ugly industrial waste bins. Conscious of their regular use, Amir attached the camera to the side of the structure closest to the hedgerow, where it was unlikely there would be anyone to spot it. This time he was lucky, as there was a large gap underneath for him to crawl into and come out the other side next to the bin store. He quickly attached the camera using heavy-duty duct tape and a couple of small screws to be safe. The black tape helped to disguise the camera a little, which was fixed an inch from the edge and so was only visible if someone was really looking—which was unlikely.

Happy that it was pointing in the right direction, Amir made his way back towards the gap from which he had crawled. Back in the field, he slowly made his way back towards the road, stopping frequently to listen for anything hostile. He was about to exit through the gap to the road when he heard them. Several bikes, their engines growling, being revved as they turned into the industrial estate, confirming Darren's suspicion that the biker gang were using the warehouse. Amir went back towards the first camera that he had installed. If he could see anything useful, it would help them all later.

In position, he saw three black bikes stop by the shutters. Their riders all dismounted, and took their helmets off and placed them on their seats.

Amir gasped when he saw who the riders were. It was the two huge bald men, one with a tattooed face and the other with piercings glinting under the light that shone down on them. The third, smaller man had dreadful eyes that Amir glimpsed as the rider turned to walk towards the door.

'Well, Amir, you continue to live up to your reputation of being in the right place at the right time,' he whispered to himself as he took out his phone and took a few snaps. The three men all went into the building and the door closed behind them. Amir looked at the bikes and came up with several ideas about what he could have done to them in seconds. He decided not to take any risks and wait to see how long they'd be in there for.

Thirty minutes later, after shooing away half a dozen mice, Amir's patience was rewarded when the three men exited the warehouse. The man with the tattooed head was carrying a holdall that he hadn't taken into the building, which Amir assumed was contraband of some sort. More than likely, it was drugs for the local gangs that they were now supplying.

They were soon back on their bikes and heading away. Amir waited a couple of minutes before heading back towards the road, and before long he was in his car heading back to Sheringham. He was covered in twigs and insects and frequently shook himself to try to clear them—unsuccessfully—on the way back.

'Next time I am volunteering someone else,' he said out loud.

9

MEET WITH THE BOSS

'What the hell are you playing at? You weren't supposed to kill anyone, you fool, only to scare the shit out of them!' Falconer shouted, furious that Hawk had disobeyed his orders.

'I did what I thought was right. People are scared shitless now and questioning themselves more. You'll have many more willing to sell up on the cheap as a result, so stop worrying,' Hawk replied, taking his sunglasses off.

'Oh, for God's sake, put those back on. You know I can't stand looking at your eyes like that,' Falconer said, turning away.

'You may hate them, but they are very effective, eh guys?'

'They do work, boss. People back off when they're near Hawk,' said Snake.

'Yes, well, as true that may be, I don't like them, so please save those godforsaken devil eyes for someone else, okay?'

'You're the boss—boss,' Hawk replied, putting his sunglasses back on, grinning at his benefactor.

'So, where are you with the rest of it?' Falconer asked, ignoring the impudence that he had come to expect.

'We've taken over the entire wholesale supply in Cromer and Sheringham and everything in between, so we now fully control the flow to all drug dealers in the area, who love us. Demand is going up quickly because we are selling it on the cheap. We've set up a couple of crack houses in both towns. There's so many empty rentals it was easy. We made sure they were in prominent areas so people would notice them and spread the word. People are scared, and the fear is spreading quickly.'

'Okay, that's good. Keep that going, and remember: I'm keeping the police at bay by diverting reports to my source so that they are kept locally, which is helping. In the meantime, I may want you to ramp up your scare tactics to put pressure on a couple of stubborn old bastards who refuse to sell.'

'We're happy to pay them a visit, if you like?' Hawk said.

'Not now. Leave it for a bit. I want to find out what is going on with the bloke you killed. It cost me a bloody fortune to keep that under the radar. I want to check and see if anything has happened as a result.'

'We need more money to keep it going, though,' Hawk announced.

Falconer sighed, having half expected it. 'I'll add another fifty grand to the account, but do nothing else that will jeopardise the project, okay? I want the people of these towns to be frightened and desperate to leave, all of them. There will be hell to pay if you screw things up, I have big plans for the area.

'I hear you, boss,' Hawk said, still grinning.

Trevor gathered the team in the gym. He stood by the ring, with Kendra and Andy on one side and Mo and Darren on the other.

'Okay, folks, this is where we are at the moment,' he started. 'We have confirmation that the bikers are using a warehouse on the Falconer estate, suggesting that he is employing them to scare the hell out of locals into selling up on the cheap.'

'Evil bastard,' Charmaine said, to many accompanying nods.

'Yes, he is, and he will pay for what he's done and what he is doing, I promise you,' Kendra said.

'We have more pressing things to think about before we make those plans, though,' Trevor continued. 'For one, we now believe that the local cop who reported Jacob's death as an accident is crooked, along with the coroner and possibly the pathologist. That report isn't worth wiping our arses on, but it is an official document. It tells us that Falconer has friends in high places and is using many of them to carry out his plans, and there's bound to be more. We must find evidence to sort them all out, so please think about how we can do that.'

'What about the biker gang, Trev? How are we going to sort them out? There's a lot more of them than us and they are nasty as hell,' Izzy said.

'Yes, they are. I've mentioned before that we'll have to play clever with this one. As good as you lot are at fighting, this lot will not be easy to deal with. Young Andy here, has a few ideas. Over to you.'

Andy stepped forward. 'Thanks, Trevor. As our esteemed leader here has mentioned many times, we will be playing this clever. Brains over brawn and that sort of thing. So let me ask you, what is the most important thing to a biker like one of this lot?'

'Violence,' shouted one.

'Drugs,' shouted another.

'They hate everyone,' someone added.

'Yes to all those, but more so their bikes. If you've all noticed, they all have huge bikes that cost more than a few quid. That suggests they earn some good money from whatever it is they do. From what Amir has witnessed and what was seen at the local supermarket, they are supplying the local drug dealers.'

'I'm pretty sure they do it on a big scale, too,' said Amir. 'The holdall I saw last night seemed pretty heavy.'

'The plan is to hit them where it hurts the most. We'll damage or even destroy the bikes and we'll steal their drugs. They won't be expecting anything in this area, so their security won't be as vigilant as it should be.'

'Sounds good, Andy, but how are we going to do both those things?' Izzy asked.

'We have a secret way into the campsite, so when we are ready, we'll gain entry and damage the bikes. At the same time, we'll be breaking into their warehouse and stealing whatever we can carry out of there.'

'Sounds simple, doesn't it?' Trevor said, 'but as I keep saying, expect for it to be a lot tougher and also anticipate that something could go wrong. We need to keep our wits about us.'

'When are you looking to do this?' Charmaine asked.

'I'm thinking tonight or tomorrow. The earlier, the better,' said Trevor. 'I want to put a fire under their arses to let them know they have someone watching them. We'll leave clues that suggest a rival drug supplier who wants them out has attacked them. I want to see how they react to that and use it to our advantage later,'

'Isn't that going to make things difficult for us later with this Falcon bloke?' Charmaine asked.

'Falconer, Jeremy Falconer. The plan is to see how the bikers react first and also how—and if—that gets back to him. While all this is going on, we must find evidence, remember, so this should bring everyone out to play. We can then deal with those responsible for Jacob's death and all the other stuff that is going on.'

Those gathered nodded in approval, content with the plan, however loose it currently was.

'So, Andy, how are we going to sort their bikes out?' Amir asked, grinning in anticipation.

'Well, four or five of you will infiltrate the campsite, but you can't be one of them because you'll be breaking into the warehouse,' Andy said.

'Of course, 'cos nobody else can do that here, right?' he swaggered from side to side like a rapper on stage going through the motions.

'Okay, Amir, we acknowledge that you're the best burglar here, respect to you,' Kendra said, which led to much laughter from the rest of them and forced Amir to bring the curtain down on his performance.

'Moving on,' said Trevor, 'Andy has something to say about the campsite.'

'Yeah, so, we now have access to the CCTV covering the site, which, luckily, they do not know about. What I have seen is that the bikers park close to where they sleep, either the static caravans or the pods.'

'Are we looking to damage or destroy them?' asked Izzy.

'Neither, for now, and this part is important. Two of the

static caravans are being used by the two bald musclemen and the leader. The leader is sharing his with a young lady, who we believe is Janice Brown, while the other two are sharing another. These two caravans are slightly away from the others, and we don't want to damage their bikes,' Andy continued.

'Why's that, Andy? Rory asked.

'Because we are going to attach trackers to them and see where they go over the next few days. We want to see who they connect with, and that they hopefully lead us to that evidence that we need.'

'We'll split into two groups to sort out the details,' added Trevor. 'Kendra and Amir will take four others to the warehouse, so grab those you want to take and go and discuss the details.'

Amir picked Darren, Izzy and Jimmy to tag along while Kendra asked Charmaine.

'Okay,' said Trevor, 'so the campsite team will be Mo, Rory, Clive, Martin and Greg. That should be enough for what we want to do. Zoe and I will be in a car as back-up in case something goes wrong, or if we're required to follow behind a tracked bike if they go on the move.'

'I'll crack on and see if I can find out more about the cop, pathologist, and coroner,' Andy said before leaving.

Trevor rubbed his hands together as he saw the team that he and Kendra had assembled get busy with their tasks.

'And so it begins,' he said.

THEY WENT JUST AFTER MIDNIGHT.

Kendra, Amir, Darren, Charmaine, Izzy and Jimmy left in

two vehicles to get to the warehouse next to the Falconer estate. They took very little with them. Amir carried his toolkit for breaking in and the others each brought something to carry whatever they would be stealing. Between them, they had managed to grab a couple of holdalls, a pair of pillowcases, and a handful of plastic bags.

They parked the cars far enough away so that they wouldn't easily be picked out, but close enough for the walk to the warehouse to be a short one. Amir led the way and took them via the same hedgerow opening he had used the night before.

They moved in silence towards the camera that was covering the doorway and shutters. Andy was monitoring the cameras in both locations to give them all the heads-up, sending messages if required to the now-silent mobile phones that Kendra and Mo were carrying. He had reported no movement at the warehouse other than the four men that had locked up and left at around eight-thirty. The warehouse was empty.

Although it was the middle of the night, the light above the doors and shutters was still on and there were several streetlights illuminating the estate and the road leading into it.

'Okay, see that window up high on the side? That's my way in,' Amir whispered.

'Be careful, Amir,' said Kendra. 'It might be empty, but they may have cameras or other security in there.'

'Don't worry, K,' I have this. Just be ready to join me. I'll open the door for you.' Within seconds, he was climbing the drainpipe that ran about four feet from the window he was aiming for. He made the jump easily and was soon sliding his thin, flexible slim-jim type tool to release the catch. He then squeezed through the small window and disappeared from sight.

The others waited for his signal: the door opening. It was eerily quiet, and the wait seemed to go on for much longer than it should.

'Look, he's at the door. The coast must be clear. Let's go,' Darren whispered.

They took turns to slide under the hedgerow and then run across the short patch of concrete to the door where Amir waited. They were soon all inside and the door closed behind them.

'I've had a quick look around,' he told them, 'and there're no cameras or alarm or anything that should worry us. The warehouse is pretty bare, to be honest. They probably haven't been here long, so there's not a lot of gear here, a few bikes, some tools and bits and pieces.'

'We'll split up and look around,' Kendra said. 'Take anything of value and remember, we want to find the drugs more than anything else.'

They turned on their small torches and split up.

The ground floor was littered with black motorcycles in various states of repair, along with a couple of toolboxes. There were a couple of tables along one side where the bikers kept a coffee machine, a small fridge, and a biscuit tin. On the opposite side, there was a row of metal lockers, a kitchenette, a shower, and two toilets. There was a screened-off area that Kendra could see hid an office desk and several chairs.

'You guys crack on down here while I check upstairs with Darren,' she said.

They went up the stairs to the mezzanine, where they saw another desk and chair, a couple of double-sized metal lockers, and a deep shelf rack that had been used for storage back when it had been a functioning warehouse. Now it only stored some used parts from a motorcycle engine and a cardboard box full of tins of lubricant and grease.

Kendra searched the desk and found nothing much of interest other than a grubby laptop, along with an equally grubby tablet, both of which she took.

'Andy should be able to get some intel from these.'

'One of these lockers has got a bunch of nasty overalls and boots in it, but the other one is locked, so I'm guessing this is where they're hiding their good stuff,' Darren said.

Kendra called Amir, who was soon examining the lock.

'The lock on this is new, and pretty good, but it shouldn't be a problem,' he said.

He took out a couple of lock picks from his small bag and soon got to work.

'This is too simple for my skill set,' he said as he picked the lock in less than five seconds. 'Can you give me something a little more challenging next time, please?'

Kendra smiled and said, 'Yes, oh glorious one, thank you so much.'

'Bingo!' Darren said, pulling open the door.

Inside the locker were four more holdalls, similar to the ones Amir had seen the leader taking. They were stacked one on top of the other. There was also a locked cash box perched on top. Darren gave the cashbox to Kendra and took the top holdall and placed it on the floor.

'It's really heavy,' he said, unzipping it.

'Bloody hell,' Amir said as he peered inside. It was full to the brim with cellophane-wrapped white bricks.

'That's cocaine, isn't it?' Darren asked.

'Yep,' Kendra replied, 'a lot of it.' She placed the cashbox into the bag she'd used for the laptop and tablet.

'Guys, these are one-kilo bricks, worth around thirty grand each,' Amir said. Kendra hadn't seen him this one-eyed since they'd met.

'There must be twenty bricks in this bag alone,' she said, 'which makes this bag worth around six hundred grand. If the others are the same, then we're talking almost two-and-a-half million quid street value.'

'Shit,' was all Darren could say.

'Okay, we need to get this out of here, sharpish,' Kendra said. 'Amir, can you relock this, so it confuses them a little?'

Amir laughed. 'Yeah, sure. That will have them scratching their heads for sure.'

They went back downstairs to meet with the rest of the team. Between them, they had recovered another laptop, which had been used for calibrating engines; a small wall-mounted safe that Charmaine had easily pried off the wall and which she assumed held keys for motorbikes; and a bag filled with power tools.

'I thought we should take these to cause them more problems,' Jimmy said, taking out an angle grinder to show the team.

'Perfect, I think we've picked them clean, so let's get out of here. Amir, leave the door unlocked. Maybe that will confuse them too and they'll blame each other.'

Darren was first out, cautiously looking around before giving the all-clear.

They were soon on their stomachs again, crawling under the hedgerows, passing their loot through to the other side. The holdalls were heavy and difficult to carry but they got to the cars with no issues. Minutes later, they were on their way back to Sheringham and the gym, whooping and hollering the entire way.

10

SABOTAGE

Just a few miles away, the other team had made their way to the gate hidden behind the big tree. They stopped one last time before entering the site, for a last-minute briefing by Mo.

'Okay, guys, we'll only have one shot at this, so let's make sure we do it right. Remember, this lot are vicious bastards, so try not to make any noise, otherwise we're done for. Do you each have everything you need?'

Rory, Clive, Martin and Greg all nodded.

'Any questions?'

They all shook their heads. They were ready and raring to go.

'Okay, let's move,' Mo said, and headed towards the gate.

They had approached it from Rufus's land as he had directed, and quickly found it behind the bush that Rufus had described to Trevor.

The wooden gate was well hidden. Nobody would have found it unless they were looking for it. Mo quietly unlatched it and kept it open for the rest of them to come through, before closing it gently behind him. They quickly spread out to their allocated areas and began their silent sabotage.

Mo stayed behind and watched, trying not to laugh at what his colleagues were now doing. Rory was injecting industrial strength expanding foam into the sports exhausts of every bike he came across. It wouldn't permanently damage the bikes, but would certainly inconvenience the rider who had to clean it out to enable the bike to start again. Greg was spraying fluorescent pink paint on every tyre and petrol tank, including obscene messages and the occasional mention of *Nomads*, a notorious biker gang that had disbanded years earlier—intending to confuse the Rejects into thinking a rival gang was responsible. Martin was adding Gorilla Glue to the seats and handlebars. Mo came up from the rear and helped where he could so that none of the bikes were missed, except for those intentionally left out. The scene seemed quite unreal as the team worked in complete silence, causing the Rejects a great deal of damage.

While the team was cracking on with the sabotage, Mo took out the four small GPS tags he had brought, especially for the leader and his deputies. He walked around the back of the static caravans to the two that were slightly more remote. They wouldn't suspect they'd been spared, but consider themselves lucky to be hidden around the back. He prepped each tag and stuck them carefully on the underside of the seats, where they wouldn't be spotted. Happy with the result, he went around the front and gestured to his team that it was time to pull out.

A couple of minutes later, they were silently crossing over Rufus's land and to safety. They didn't dare make any noise until they were in the car and safely out of earshot. Once in and the doors were closed, they burst out laughing, real belly laughs, finally able to enjoy the exhilaration they had experienced at the campsite. They laughed for minutes, unable to contain their joy.

'Oh man, I'd pay real money to see their faces when they get up in the morning,' Rory said, wiping the tears away.

'Well, if we set the alarm, we can watch it. We have CCTV, remember?' added Mo.

'We should stop off and get some popcorn,' said Martin. 'This will be the best movie ever!'

The laughter started again, and it was a good thirty minutes before it was safe enough for them to drive back.

It was close to two in the morning when everyone was back at the gym. There was more laughter and back-slapping as they regaled Trevor and the team with the details of their mission.

'I honestly don't know what to say,' Trevor said, looking at the holdalls and the other bags of loot. 'Well done, all of you. If this doesn't put the cat amongst the pigeons, then nothing will.'

'I got some great video feed from the campsite too,' Andy said. 'It was hilarious to watch. Those bikers will be properly angry when they see what we have done to their pride and joy.'

'Okay, you all go get some sleep and I'll take care of this,' Trevor said, pointing to the drugs.

'What are you going to do with it, Trev?' asked Amir, trying to sound uninterested but failing miserably.

'Let me tell you one thing,' Trevor said. 'This shit will not be used by anyone.'

'So, you're going to dump millions of pounds' worth of gear?'

'Maybe, maybe not. I have a plan brewing, so we'll see how it goes.'

Amir walked away, muttering to his brother, 'There's so much money there, bro, I feel a bit sick.'

Mo laughed. 'Good,' he said, 'I'm glad. Anything to do with that shit will make you sick, so best you leave it to Trev; he knows what he's doing.'

'Yeah, I guess.'

He continued to shake his head as he made his way to his corner, while his brother continued to laugh.

'SO, WHAT NOW?' Andy asked Trevor as he and Kendra stayed behind to talk.

'Now we wait and see what the response is,' Kendra said. 'I'm guessing you're going to be busy tomorrow keeping tabs on the campsite, the warehouse, and the bikes that have been tagged. You should get some sleep while you have the chance.'

'Like she said, mate, there's nothing else you can do here at the moment, so get some rest and be ready for tomorrow because that's when we can get lucky.'

'Okay, you'll get no argument from me, Trevor,' Andy said, holding his hands up and walking off towards the exit.

'That camper van must be minging by now,' Kendra said as she watched Andy walk back to the mobile home.

'Surprisingly, not,' Trevor replied. 'When I went to speak to him today, he actually had Marigolds on and was polishing everything. It's his pride and joy so he'll keep it spick-and-span.'

'Huh, well, there you go. Every day is full of surprises.'

'Okay, help me with these holdalls, I want to keep them out of sight of that Amir. Let's not give him a chance to be tempted, eh?'

'So, have you decided what you're going to do with them, yet?' she asked.

'I have a rough idea, love. Keeping hold of them may help us a lot later, but until I have a proper plan, we need to keep them well hidden.'

'Okay, let's go then,' she said, picking up one of the heavy holdalls.

It took a few minutes, but the bags were soon safely sealed away in one locker that Trevor had emptied of kit, the key safely tucked in his pocket.

'We'll move them somewhere safer tomorrow,' he said as they walked back. 'Let's get some sleep now. It'll be daylight soon.'

Minutes later and the gym was silent, apart from the occasional snore, the recent events temporarily forgotten and the forthcoming adventures—and the dangers associated with them—already intruding in some dreams.

THERE WAS a buzz of excitement in the gym as morning came. Sleep had not come quickly to most of the team, the adrenaline taking its time to work through their bodies, but everyone seemed upbeat and excited to see the response to their early-morning raids. Trevor and Kendra had joined

Andy in the back of Marge to review the camera feeds for the biker responses.

It didn't take long.

First up: the mechanics, arriving bright and early at the warehouse. Kendra giggled as she saw the bemused reactions to the door being found unlocked. Just a few seconds later, one mechanic ran outside, looking around as if he were about to catch someone red-handed with their equipment. He pulled out a phone from his back pocket and made a call.

'Here we go,' Andy said as he turned to the other monitor.

The door to Hawk's caravan flew open as he ran out, barefoot and bare-chested with just a pair of jeans on, holding a phone to his ear and seeming to shout angrily. The leader ran around to the other caravans and started banging on doors. He did that to two before he noticed that the bikes had been spray-painted in fluorescent pink. He ended his calls and started banging on more doors as some of his riders emerged slowly from their slumber.

They soon woke up when they saw the condition of their bikes. Many had their hands on their heads as they approached, devastated at the damage to their babies. Some of them did a double-take when they saw expanding foam, now completely solid, coming out of their exhausts. Keys were quickly retrieved in an attempt to 'blow' the foam out by starting the engines, which failed miserably..

It was only then that further horror dawned upon them, when they couldn't remove their hands from the handlebars or their backsides from their saddles, thanks to the super strong Gorilla Glue that had been placed there for that exact purpose. The jerky movements from those firmly stuck in position made for hilarious viewing to those in the van, who rolled about with tears streaming down their faces.

Hawk ran back to his caravan, banging on his deputies' door again to get them up. He was very animated as they emerged, angrily pointing toward the bikes and holding out his phone to explain that there had been a break-in. It was then that his phone rang again, which resulted in the most animated result yet, throwing his arms into the air and roaring in anger and frustration, his deputies shrinking away and back into their temporary homes, presumably to dress.

Hawk ran into his home, brushing aside the semi-naked tattooed woman who had been watching from the doorway. The chaos continued as Trevor, Kendra and Andy rolled about in stitches; the result was far better than they'd have ever hoped.

A few minutes later, the four of them re-emerged, fully dressed, crash helmets in hands as they approached their bikes. They were clearly weary of any sabotage to their own as they closely inspected them. Finally, happy that they had been spared, the four riders rode towards the exit. Before doing so, they stopped and spoke to two of the un-stuck riders, gesticulating towards the damaged bikes, giving instructions. One of them opened the gate and let the four leave the violated campsite.

'I'm guessing they're heading for the warehouse. It's where I'd go first thing,' Kendra said.

'Are the GPS trackers all working, Andy?' asked Trevor.

'Yep, all four are working just fine. We will know exactly where they are now.'

'So, what now?' Kendra asked.

'They're likely to get desperate now, love, with no drugs and their bikes out of action. It'll be interesting to see what they do next because they no longer hold all the cards, do they?'

'I'm guessing the local suppliers will be screaming for gear soon and when they find out there isn't any—well, there may be a backlash. We can only hope.'

'I have a plan brewing, which may work. Let me have a think and I'll let you know. In the meantime, let's see where they go,' Trevor said, before leaving.

'You okay in here? Do you need anything?' Kendra asked as Andy continued to monitor the feeds.

'I'm good, thanks, I have everything I need. I've got a couple of laptops and a tablet. I need to check when I get the chance, so I'll be pretty busy back here all day.'

'Right then, I'll see you later,' she said, unsure why she was miffed at his indifference. She left the camper van and headed back to the gym for a coffee, trying to take her mind off him.

TREVOR EASILY PRISED open the cashbox that had been taken from the warehouse. Inside, he found three bundles of fifty-pound notes, each nicely wrapped and labelled £5,000.

'That's handy, we just found ourselves some extra funds for the kitty,' he said to Darren, Amir and Charmaine, who were watching keenly.

'That's good, Trev,' said Amir, 'because I ruined a perfectly good tracksuit in that damned hedgerow, so you can buy me a new one now.'

'What is this?' Trevor said, picking up a bank deposit book. 'Well, now, this is very interesting. This must be a new account because they've only made a couple of deposits, both for thirty grand.'

'Ooh, can we steal that, too?' asked Amir. 'Like we did with the Albanians?'

'It's not that easy. We'll need their phones for that to work because they'll have security measures in place. We'll certainly try it. Maybe we'll go back and get the phones, too. Who knows? Anyway, I'll give this to Andy, who may be able to work his magic.'

'That safe won't be as easy to break into, will it?' asked Darren.

'You'll be surprised how easy it is,' Trevor said, knowingly. 'Follow me and I'll show you.'

They took the small safe outside to the car park.

'Now watch and learn, children,' Trevor said as he lifted and then threw the safe up in the air. It landed with a thud on its side, but remained intact.

'The trick is to have it land on a corner, which may take a few goes,' he said when he saw their bemused expressions.

It took three more attempts before the safe landed on one corner. The door instantly flew open upon impact as it warped and released the lock, spilling its contents onto the ground. They weren't expecting anything other than motorbike keys, so it was surprising to see a blue security cash pouch amongst the contents.

'Well now, this day just gets better and better,' Trevor said, picking up the pouch. It was less than a foot square and only a couple of inches thick, but Trevor could tell that it held a fair amount of cash that was intended for deposit in the bank night safe. It was the ideal way for criminals to deposit cash in legitimate bank accounts, with no tellers to deal with, or CCTV to identify them.

As it was sealed, Trevor took out a knife and slashed it open within seconds, revealing six more bundles of five thousand pounds inside, along with a completed deposit slip, ready to be taken to the bank.

'It looks like we'll be able to afford two of those nasty tracksuits now, eh Amir?' he said, laughing.

'Those bastards are going to be extremely pissed when they find out what's been nicked, aren't they?' Charmaine said.

'Yes, they are, which is why we need to be vigilant and expect some sort of retaliation. Let everyone know what we've found, and warn them to be extra cautious while we plan the next steps. We've had it our way so far and this lot is gonna want to change that,' Trevor cautioned.

11

KIDNAP

'How the hell did you manage to leave the bloody door unlocked, you stupid bastard?' Hawk said as he continued to pummel one of the mechanics at the warehouse. The man was curled up on the floor in the foetal position as Hawk continued to rain down the kicks.

'Boss, I'm sure he locked it. We all left together. Pete was the last man out because he was locking up,' another man said in his defence.

Hawk stopped his assault and turned on the other man, who immediately backed away from the malevolent eyes, his hands raised.

'So, explain to me how they got in, then, smart-arse, where's the signs of a break-in? Or was it your fault? Maybe it should be you getting a kicking, eh?' Hawk spat.

'No, boss, you're right, my mistake,' the man said, holding up his arms in surrender.

'Tell me again, what have they taken?' Hawk asked, eyeballing the three men, one after the other.

'They took the wall safe, our laptops, the iPad, and some of our tools, boss,' the same man answered.

'Are you sure?'

'Yeah, the lockers haven't been smashed open or anything. They're still locked.'

'Who has the key?' Hawk asked, holding out his hand.

'That'll be Pete, boss.'

Hawk turned back to the man on the floor and was surprised to see one of his hands up in the air with the keys that he had swiftly retrieved from his pocket.

'H... h... here you go, b... boss,' the injured man said.

Hawk grabbed the keys and said, 'get up and lead the way.'

Pete slowly got up from the floor, wincing in pain as he did so. He limped towards the stairs and went up to the mezzanine where the lockers were. When he got there, he turned to Hawk, who threw the keys back at him.

'Open it,' the leader said.

Pete's hands were shaking as he unlocked the metal cabinet. As he opened the doors, he gasped in horror when he saw the holdalls were missing.

Hawk darted over manhandled him out of the way. He stared inside the empty locker as his anger built up.

'Shiiiiit!' he shouted, slamming the doors shut. He turned to Pete, who was still shaking, grabbed him by the collars, and dragged him over to the railings overlooking the warehouse below. Without pause, he threw the mechanic over, the poor man screaming as he fell to the concrete below—his scream ending immediately as the warehouse fell silent. Hawk looked at the other mechanics below, who were tending to their injured and unconscious colleague.

'That's what happens when you screw up! He's lucky I

didn't kill him. Make sure you tell him that when he eventually wakes up,' he shouted, making his way back down the stairs.

'Someone is going to pay heavily for this. Nobody fucks with the Rejects and gets away with it, you hear?'

The mechanics all nodded, fearful for their lives. They were an important part of the gang, responsible for the maintenance of the bikes and more, but still susceptible to reprisals by their leader if they screwed up. And it seemed to all and sundry that they had screwed up—royally.

Snake walked over to them and said, 'Get yourselves ready to sort out the rest of the bikes. The gang is bringing them over soon and we need them back on the road yesterday, understood?'

'How many of them, Snake?' asked one mechanic.

'All of them, except for ours.'

The mechanics looked at each other, trying to determine who would be the bravest and ask the question.

'What's wrong with them, Snake?' one of them eventually asked.

'They've had expanding foam sprayed up the exhausts, which has set hard. They'll also need glue removing from the seats and handlebars and spray paint removed. Just be ready. I want them back on the road as soon as possible, okay?'

'We'll do our best,' came the reply.

Hawk and his companion had left. He was too angry to do or say anything useful now. It had all been said and done, in his opinion.

'Let's get the hell out of here,' he called to his deputies, 'before I do something I'll regret.'

The four of them were soon on the road again. Hawk's mind was in overdrive.

Who has done this to us? Why have they done this? Where are my drugs? What now?

The questions went on and on, and he had no answers for any of them. His anger boiled inside him as he contemplated the things he would do to those responsible. None of them were pretty.

ANDY CONTINUED to monitor the feeds, occasionally switching to see if he could get anything useful from the laptops and the tablet. By the time the other two returned, he had trawled through the three devices and gleaned what he thought would be of interest.

'Not really a lot to tell you, guys, other than we now have access to some online accounts that we can certainly have some fun with later.'

'Like what?' Kendra asked.

'Well, for one, we have several suppliers that they regularly order bike parts from—some bike parts are really expensive. They've had accounts with them for years and so can buy now and pay later, which is very good for us. We can order a ton of shit and have it sent elsewhere without them knowing for a while. We can even arrange for them to deliver to the warehouse when they're not there, but when we *can* be.'

'Yep, we can have a ton of fun with that, for sure. What else?' asked Trevor.

'I had to have a giggle, but the gang is on the move with their bikes, pink paint 'n' all,' Andy added, leaning back and laughing.

'How is that possible?' asked Trevor. 'We stuffed their exhausts with—well, it may as well have been concrete!'

'I said they're on the move, not that they're riding them. They're pushing them along the road. We think towards the warehouse so they can be fixed. Honestly, you've never seen anything like it: they all poured out of there, dressed all in black like evil demons, pushing their mean black bikes, with glowing pink paint all over them.' He continued to laugh.

'Well, lucky for them they haven't got too far to go. What is it, a few miles?'

'Yeah, they should get there early afternoon, we think. It may be worth someone doing a drive-by to see where they are.'

'Good idea, fancy a drive, love?'

'Yeah, why not? I could do with another laugh,' Kendra said.

'Before we leave, hide this somewhere, will you?' Trevor handed Andy a carrier bag filled with the gang's money. 'It's probably safest in here with you.'

'Cool. Marge could do with a few more gadgets,' Andy said.

'Let's sort this lot out first, then we can decide what we're gonna do with that. I think Maureen probably needs some help. Maybe Manfri, we'll see.'

They left Andy to continue with his work and drove towards the industrial estate, taking the route that the bikers were likely to take, pushing their bikes. It didn't take long to catch up to them, maybe a mile or so from the warehouse, moving slowly, exhausted with their efforts so far. They were lucky to be in Norfolk, probably the flattest county in England.

'Look at that,' Kendra said, laughing. 'Have you ever seen anything like it?'

Trevor started overtaking the convoy. 'They look pathetic, don't they? 'He tooted the horn as he drove past, earning middle fingers from the riders that had the energy to flip them.

'Let's get back,' said Kendra. 'We should have a chat about what we're gonna do next.'

'Yeah, but we'll go via the scenic route. There's a lot of shit on this road,' Trevor said. They both laughed out loud.

'I still have this nagging feeling though, Dad, this is very different than what we've dealt with so far, you know? I feel like we're missing something.'

'I get that, love. That landowner bloke is set on destroying this area for profit and he has the police and some powerful friends helping him. We may have damaged a few bikes and stolen some of their drugs and money, but you can bet your bottom dollar they have tons more where that came from. They can still do a lot of harm. We've only inconvenienced them and pissed them off, that's all.'

'We need to do much more,' Kendra said.

'Damn right.'

'LISTEN UP, everyone. Just a quick update so you all know what's going on,' Trevor shouted, gaining the team's attention and commanding silence. 'Kendra?'

'You've done great so far, guys and girls, but we've just scratched the surface. We've angered them and are now waiting to see how they respond. It's what we need to see. We need to step things up and have come up with a plan–or three.'

'If it's as much fun as we had last night, then you can count me in, with bells on,' Izzy said.

'Yeah, that was all great, but never forget this lot are serious, guys,' Trevor added.

'The gang has now taken all the damaged bikes to the warehouse to get repaired and cleaned,' Kendra continued. 'And yes, it was fun to do that to them. Yes, it was fun to watch their reaction, and we had lots of laughs watching them wheel their babies to the warehouse. But guess what? We're going back to finish the job and to flush them out.'

'Won't they have secured the place better?' Jimmy asked.

'I'm sure they will have, but they won't have had time to install an alarm. At best, they'll have done something to the doors or possibly kept someone there during the night as a watchman. Either way, it won't matter because we're going in through the window again, right, Amir?'

'Yes, ma'am,' he replied coolly, saluting.

'If there is someone there, then we'll draw them out with a diversion so we can do our thing,' she added. 'What we're doing won't take long, either, as long as we are sure the place is clear for a few minutes.'

'Same team?' asked Charmaine.

'Yes, it may as well be, you know the lay of the land. We'll do it at the same sort of time, too. Andy can give us a heads-up in advance, which will let us know if anyone is staying behind. We're hoping they won't expect anyone back so soon.'

'Boy, are they in for a surprise,' Amir said.

'Okay, you may as well chill out and get some rest until then,' Trevor said.

'What about the rest of us, Kendra?' Mo asked.

'Your team has a slightly unfamiliar task, Mo. We need you to kidnap someone.'

It was early evening when Mo, Rory and Clive left in one car, with Martin and Greg in another. Their task was difficult, to locate Bradley Starkins, the local drug dealer in the Cromer area and supposedly one of Hawk's better suppliers. Their job was to trawl the streets of Cromer to confirm not only that Starkins was still actively supplying drugs, but also to see if he still frequented his favourite haunts.

'I know it isn't a huge town, but where are we supposed to look for this bloke?' Rory asked Mo as they drove along the coastal road.

'He can't be in too many places, mate. There's a few coffee shops that open 'til late, the drive-thru McDonald's, and a few fish-and-chip shops he may use. Between the two cars, I'm sure we'll find him.'

They kept in touch with the other car so that they could cover as much of the area as possible without overlapping. It took several hours, but they finally tracked him down.

'Isn't that the van that was involved in the drug deal?' Greg asked as they drove past the entrance to the drive-thru.

'Yep, that's the one. That's Starkins' van,' Martin replied. 'Good spot, Greg.'

'Give the others a call. I'll jump out on foot and keep an eye on it,' Greg said.

Martin pulled over and Greg was out in seconds. As he walked along Middlebrook Way, he could see a Co-op supermarket opposite the drive-thru. He walked towards it, knowing he'd have plenty of cover from which to keep an eye on the way out, as well as the van, which had parked in a quiet corner of the car park. He could see there was only one occupant, the driver, presumably Bradley Starkins. Greg messaged Martin to let him know, to keep the others updated. Five minutes later, his phone vibrated with a response.

'*Keep watching. We'll be parked nearby. Call when he's leaving and I'll pick you up.*'

Greg responded with a thumbs-up emoji.

He watched from his vantage point for almost thirty minutes, during which Starkins carried out half a dozen drug deals.

This guy is busy, he thought.

Eventually, he saw the headlights come on and the van slowly move out of its parking space. He called Martin.

'He's on the move. Stay on the line and I'll tell you which direction he takes when he turns onto the main road.'

The van meandered around the car park and eventually reached the junction at Holt Road.

'He's indicating right. Let the others know.' The van turned a few seconds later, disappearing out of his view. He walked down to the junction and crossed the road, his timing perfect, as Martin pulled over to pick him up.

'I've got Mo on speakerphone, the suspect's behind the van towards Sheringham,' Martin said. 'I have Greg, Mo, let me know if you need relieving.'

'Thanks, Martin. We're coming up to the roundabout, so can you take over there? Hopefully, he'll stop soon and we can grab him.'

'Will do,' Martin replied. He could see the roundabout in the distance and the van going straight over. Mo's car turned left, so he sped up to close the distance between his car and the van.

'Following cars is nothing like you see on the telly, Greg. It's bloody hard, and you usually need a team of five or six cars to do it properly. We'll struggle if he doesn't stop soon.'

About a mile further on, the van indicated and turned left by a large pub.

'Mo, he's turned left by the Roman Camp Inn. It's very quiet there and I can see brake lights, so I'll let young Greg out for another wander.'

'Alright, mate, we'll be back with you in a minute.'

Martin pulled over at a service station just before the pub and let Greg out, who walked towards the junction Starkins had taken. He turned left onto a dark single-track road and could see the entrance to the pub car park at the rear. As he got closer, he could see that it was very quiet there, only two or three other cars, parked with no occupants and likely to be staff cars. The van was parked in the top corner by itself as Starkins waited for his customers.

Greg called Martin, who had ended his call with Mo.

'He's alone in the car park, top corner. It's quiet, and he's waiting for customers. If we're going to do anything, it needs to be now.'

'Stay by the junction and keep an eye out. We're heading there now,' Martin said.

Seconds later, he saw the two cars turn onto the side road and head for the car park. He stayed in the shadows of an old tree in the smaller car park at the front, which again had very few cars parked there. He was now on the lookout for potential addicts looking for their regular fix.

He saw a car coming from the opposite direction indicating

for the side road and decided to head it off. As the car, an almost new BMW with a single occupant, turned into the road, it braked sharply to stop for the arm-waving lunatic that was in the way.

'What the hell...' the driver said as his window lowered. He was a man in his thirties with a well-groomed beard, dressed in a sharp suit with no tie, possibly a local estate agent or solicitor.

'Dude, you need to leave. The old bill is staking the car park out, and my dealer just drove in there. I think he's in the shit,' Greg said, his eyes darting about as if alarmed and distressed, missing his daily fix.

'Shit, thanks, mate. I'm out of here,' the BMW driver said, reversing back into the main road and driving away.

Greg smiled and went back to the welcoming shadow of the tree. The BMW driver looked well off, so had possibly been the only deal that Starkins was looking to do here tonight, but Greg wasn't taking any chances and remained vigilant, keeping his eye out for more visitors.

As Greg had told them where the van had parked, Mo and Martin could drive straight to the top corner and park in front of the van, blocking him in. Starkins looked nervous as he watched the men approach. He wound his window down a little to speak.

'What's going on, mate?' he said as Mo came over.

'How's it going, Bradley? We just want a quick word with you, that's all,' Mo replied.

'Nah, I'm good, mate, I don't know you from...'

The passenger door opened, distracting him from Mo.

'What the hell are you doing, man?' he shouted at Rory, who had climbed in to sit next to him, stony-faced.

Mo opened the driver's door and took the keys out of the ignition.

'Like I said, we just want a chat, okay?' he repeated, 'now please get out of the van and join me before things turn nasty for you.'

'Look, man, this is my turf,' Starkins replied, thinking that the four men were rival drug dealers. 'I'm not trying to take your business. I know my boundaries, okay?'

'Yeah, well, you'll have to explain them to my boss. He's waiting to speak to you, so you'll be coming with us.'

Mo grabbed his arm and guided him towards the car. His colleagues quickly searched him, taking his wad of cash and two mobile phones from his pockets. Mo then opened the back door and gestured for Starkins to sit in the back seat, where he was soon flanked by Rory and Clive.

Mo leaned into the car. 'Where are you hiding the gear?'

Starkins knew it was futile to argue. 'Under my seat,' he replied.

Mo went to the van and looked under the driver's seat, where he found a men's shoulder bag tucked towards the back. Inside, he saw a small, clear grip-sealed bag that contained several wraps. There was also another wad of cash in there, nicely bound by a thick rubber band. Mo took the shoulder bag and its contents and went back to his car. Martin had checked the rest of the van and had found nothing else worth taking, except for a hammer that Starkins had strategically placed in the side pocket. They left immediately.

'What about my van?' Starkins asked.

'Don't worry about your van, Bradley, it'll be there waiting for you when you come back,' Mo said as he dialled a number.

'We have our friend Mister Starkins with us. Where shall I bring him?'

He waited a second or two for a response.

'We'll be there in fifteen minutes,' he said, ending the call.

'So where are we going?' Starkins asked, getting more nervous by the minute.

'Like I said, I'm taking you to my boss so that he can have a quiet word in your ear. You are lucky, my friend. He sounds like he's in a good mood. Usually when we do this, he's very, very angry and chops fingers off.' Mo was trying very hard not to laugh.

'Wait, what? My fingers? Why... why would he do that? I have done nothing wrong here, mate. Can't you see it's probably a stupid misunderstanding?'

'Well, I'll be sure to tell him you said he is stupid. Maybe he'll change his mind,' Mo answered coldly.

Starkins shook his head and decided not to say anything else until he was in front of the man who was likely to chop his fingers off.

12

THE CEMETERY

Trevor had instructed Mo to meet him at West Beckham cemetery, which, as it was surrounded by farmland, was not overlooked by anyone.

Starkins' facial expressions worsened as they went deeper into the dark lanes. He was now deeply worried about his future—if he had one. It took close to the anticipated fifteen minutes for them to arrive, and Mo drove slowly into the cemetery where, as expected, another car was waiting.

'Bring him,' he told his colleagues in the back, relishing his role.

With straight faces, Rory and Clive did as they were told, and dragged the now whimpering Starkins over to Trevor's car. As he got out of the driver's seat, they pushed Starkins to his knees.

'Well, now. If it isn't the infamous Bradley Starkins, as I live and breathe,' Trevor said, in his most menacing voice.

'S... s... s ... sir, there must be some mistake,' Starkins snivelled. 'I've been working that patch for a year. Please believe me.'

'I don't give a shit about that, boy,' Trevor continued, 'but I do give a shit about your friends who have set themselves up nicely around here. It's very, very disrespectful, you know?'

'M... m... my friends? Who do you m... m... m ... mean, sir?'

'You know who I mean,' Trevor said, flicking Starkins on the forehead, 'don't test my patience, boy. Those bikers seem very friendly with you.'

'Oh... oh, you mean the Rejects? They're not my friends, sir, they're my suppliers. Well, apart from—'

'Apart from what?' Trevor pushed.

'N... nothing important, sir,' Starkins whimpered.

Trevor looked up at his men and said, 'He's a waste of my time. You know what to do.'

'I'll get the machete, boss,' Mo said, moving towards Trevor's car.

'W... wait! Please, w... wait!' shouted Starkins.

'What is it, Bradley?' Trevor asked. 'Last chance, or you lose fingers. Your call.'

'W... w... what I wanted to say is that they're not my friends, apart from George.'

'George? Who the hell is George?' he pressed.

'He... he... he's my... brother, sir,' Starkins replied. It wasn't what Trevor had been expecting and took him completely by surprise. It took only a second for him to compose himself and continue.

'Your brother is a member of the Rejects?'

'Y... y... yes, sir.'

'Well? Is that it? Or do I need to get the machete?'

'My... my... my brother George is Hawk, s... sir.'

It took a couple of extra seconds for that information to soak in.

'Your brother is the leader of the Rejects? The one with those stupid-ass eyes?'

'Y... yes, sir. W... w... well, he's my half-brother, but yes, the one with the scary eyes.'

'Well, you could knock me down with a feather, Mister Starkins. I did not see that one coming,' Trevor said, thinking fast. 'Did you guys see that coming?'

'Nope. No, sir,' came the replies.

'Anything else you want to tell me, while we're so friendly here? Remember, I have a machete and I'll use it,' Trevor continued. 'Why have the Rejects—your brother—why have they come to this part of the world, suddenly?'

Starkins looked horrified, thinking that he had offered enough information to be spared.

'I'm waiting, boy,' Trevor urged.

'S... s... sir, my dad called him, t... t... to cause trouble around here, s... s... sir.'

Trevor wasn't sure just how many surprises he could take. Again, taking a few seconds to compose himself, he pressed on.

'Who the hell is your daddy, Bradley?' he asked, leaning in close.

'S... s... sir, it's Jeremy Falconer, s... s... sir.'

'What? That rich dude is your dad? And Hawk's too?'

'Y... y... yes, sir. He was a bit of a playboy when he was young and basically shagged everyone he could. He paid my mum, though, as he did with George's, so we kinda kept in touch. To be honest, he's a bit of a wanker, but he's looking after us now, so it doesn't bother us much.'

'Well, now, this just gets more fascinating by the minute, right, boys?'

'Sure does, boss,' Mo replied.

'Let me think for a second, will you?' Trevor said, walking away slowly, pacing up and down between the graves.

Starkins watched as the madman with a machete walked alongside the headstones, the moonlight accentuating the scene. What little other light there was came from Mo's car. If he had been there alone, he would have been frightened witless, so to be here with a machete-wielding madman played tricks on his mind.

Trevor returned after a few minutes.

'This is what's going to happen, Mister Starkins. I want you to tell your brother that I have his drugs and his money and I will continue to cause him a ton of problems unless he agrees to meet with me. You got that?'

'Y... y... yes sir,' he replied quickly, jumping at the chance for freedom.

'In the meantime, I have one other message to show I mean business,' Trevor said, taking out his phone.

When the call was answered, he simply said, 'Do it now.'

Twenty minutes later, Mo dropped Starkins off at his van in the car park.

'Remember what the boss said, Bradley, or we'll find you again and do this all over. Only next time, there will be pain involved and maybe a few missing digits.'

'Trust me, mate, there won't be a next time. As soon as I've passed the message on, I'll be getting the hell out of this town. It's not good for my health to be here anymore. I haven't stammered like that since I was twelve.'

Mo drove out of the car park and was soon on the main road back towards Sheringham and the gym. Martin and

Greg, who had joined them at the pub, followed close behind.

'That's one of the funniest things I've ever seen, man,' Rory said, laughing out loud.

'I tell you, Trevor plays a mean gangster, doesn't he?' Mo said.

'I'm guessing Bradley will message to his brother right away. He has packing to do, right?'

KENDRA HAD TAKEN the call from her father and informed her team that they were moving early to their task. They took the two cars and left once more for the industrial estate. They were soon walking alongside the hedgerow in the dark, led by the competent Amir. He gave the signal for them to lie low as he looked through the gap in the hedge.

Andy had already informed them that all three remaining mechanics had left. Before leaving, they had used a heavy chain to secure the door and shutters, taking video of it as proof in case Hawk didn't believe them.

'Seriously, they still think we used the door?' Kendra said, trying to stifle a laugh.

Amir turned to them and said, 'It's all clear, so I'm gonna do my thing. You guys keep an eye out, not just at the front here, but also on the road, okay? I need plenty of notice if anyone is coming.'

He took a holdall with him he had brought especially and squirmed back through the gap, sprinting across the car park to the side of the warehouse where the window was. Putting the holdall carefully on his back, an arm through each handle, he climbed the drainpipe and reached the window in seconds. Like last time, he didn't take long to gain entry and had soon disappeared.

'Darren, can you go back and keep an eye on the junction, please?' Kendra asked.

'Sure thing,' Darren said, the two of them turning and going back.

'Izzy, Jimmy, can you go and get the cars ready? If you can get them closer but out of sight, we'll need to make a quick getaway this time,' she continued.

'Will do. See you in a bit,' Jimmy replied, as he and Izzy also left.

Kendra stayed behind to wait for Amir, hoping he wouldn't be in there for long.

AMIR HAD TAKEN a quick look around to see if anything else had changed other than the twenty-odd bikes that were now taking up almost all the floor space. He couldn't see anything, so he put the holdall down and got to work. Removing three plastic bottles that he had filled with petrol earlier, he carefully removed the lids and poured the petrol over the motorbikes, making sure that plenty of the flammable liquid was spread liberally over the warehouse floor. Moving upstairs, he took out a glass bottle from the holdall, also filled with petrol. He removed the lid and placed a wad of cloth into the neck of the bottle. He moved towards the window and had one last look around before lighting the cloth with a lighter. When he was happy with the flame, he nonchalantly threw the bottle over the side of the mezzanine to the floor below, where the bottle shattered and helped spread the flame from the wad to the floor and then to the bikes.

As the flames started licking at the bikes, Amir was climbing down the drainpipe and was quickly on the other side of the hedgerow, where he was met by Kendra. He gave a quick thumbs-up and they moved quickly towards the road. Darren and Charmaine met them and they made a call to Jimmy and Izzy, who they rendezvoused with in a side road, away from prying eyes.

By the time the first bike's fuel tank exploded, setting off the fire alarm, they were half a mile away. By the time they got back to the gym, the entire floor of the warehouse was on fire. By the time the fire brigade arrived, there was nothing left of the bikes but charred wrecks.

Andy showed Kendra and Trevor the aftermath on the camera feeds, showing two of the mechanics with their hands on their heads as the fire brigade put out the fire.

'Hawk is gonna take my message pretty seriously now, right?' Trevor said.

Bradley drove his van into the campsite; the gate had already been opened for him because of the call he had made to his half-brother. He was nervous about passing on the message, but also fearful of the all-out war he was expecting. He had no intention of letting Hawk know he was skipping town, no way.

'Well, if it isn't my little half-wit, half-brother Bradley,' Hawk said, walking down the steps to meet him.

'Hey, George,' Bradley replied as the two deputies arrived to join their leader.

'I told you not to call me that, you little shit. This isn't a good time, either. We're being attacked by some unknown gang that has something to do with the old Nomads that used to hang around here.'

'That's why I'm here,' Bradley said. 'It isn't the Nomads or anything to do with them. It's some evil bastard who chops people's hands off if they get in his way. He grabbed me off the street and asked me to pass a message on.'

Hawk grabbed his brother by the lapels. 'What the fuck are you talking about?'

'I just told you, George, this lot mean business, and he told me to pass on a message. He has your drugs and your money and wants to meet.'

Hawk lashed out and punched his brother in the face, instantly breaking his nose. Blood poured from his nostrils, but Bradley somehow steadied himself and stayed upright.

'I told you not to call me that!' Hawk shouted.

'S... s... s ... sorry, brother.'

'Ah, there he is, my little brother showing himself at last. T... t... t ... tell me again, little brother, tell me exactly what the b ... b ... b ... bastard said.'

'H... h... he said that you have to meet him if you ever want your gear back. He wants to know what you're after, 'cos it's messing with his business.'

'Shit! That idiot Rodney told me we wouldn't have any trouble here if we got rid of a handful of dealers, but now you're telling me we're treading on someone's toes? Shit!'

'What are we gonna do, boss?' asked the pierced deputy, Razor.

'Get that idiot on the phone,' said Hawk. 'I wanna know why he missed out this juicy bit of information.'

Razor walked away to make the call.

'Boss, you're not gonna like this,' Razor said on returning.

'What now?'

'I spoke to Rodney; he told me he was on his way to the fire.'

'What fire? What are you blabbering on about, man? Spit it out!'

'There's been a fire at the warehouse. All the bikes are gone, everything destroyed,' Razor said, stepping away in case of a backlash.

Hawk stood frozen to the spot, struggling to comprehend what he had just heard.

'What did you say?' he asked.

'Fire, boss, at the warehouse. Everything destroyed,' Razor said again.

'Sh... sh... sh ... shit, that's what he meant!' Bradley suddenly blurted.

Before Hawk could grab him, Bradley took a couple of paces back and said, 'The bloke also said he had another message for you, so you know he's serious. That must be the fire, right?'

Hawk spun around, hands on his head, struggling to believe the news. The plan, which had been going so well, was falling apart. If they were going to succeed, he knew he had no choice but to meet with these people. They clearly meant business.

'What did he say about the meeting?' he asked.

'To meet him tomorrow at midday, at the ruins of Beeston Regis Priory. He said to come alone, otherwise things will get a lot worse for everyone. He'll be there alone to meet you,' Bradley said, hoping that would be the end of his role in this debacle, enabling him to leave quickly and quietly.

'Did he now?' Hawk replied. 'Any of you know of this place?'

'No, boss,' said Snake.

'Never mind, I'll go and meet him. What choice do I have, eh?'

'What do you want us to do, boss?' asked Razor.

'Have a look online what the place is all about and we'll go from there. It sounds like somewhere deserted, probably in the middle of nowhere, easy to see all approaches in, that sort of thing. This guy has the advantage of knowing the area, so it'll be somewhere we can't react or double-cross them. Check anyway,' he said.

'That's it, Hawk. That was all he said. Can I go now? I need to get to the hospital. I think my nose is broken,' said Bradley.

Hawk looked at his younger brother in disgust, disappointed they were related.

'Get lost,' he said, turning his back on him.

Bradley was in his van and out of the campsite within a minute, relieved to have escaped with just a broken nose.

'Sod the hospital, I'm going home to pack,' he said out loud.

HAWK TURNED TO HIS DEPUTIES, his anger clear for all to see.

'Get everyone out there tomorrow and get them to cause as much aggro as they can in town and the surrounds. Just because they don't have any bikes doesn't mean we can't do what we're here for. I want to scare the shit out of everyone, you hear me?'

'Yes, boss, we hear you,' said Razor.

13

MEET WITH THE DEVIL

The following morning brought more surprises. Andy called Trevor and Kendra over to show them what was currently on his monitor.

The warehouse fire had been put out relatively quickly, so the building itself was still intact, the damage contained to the interior and the shutters, which had bulged outwards from the heat and the exploding fuel tanks.

'Look who we have here,' Andy said, pointing to the monitor.

'Well, well, well. It took a fire, but we finally got the man out of his cozy armchair,' Trevor said, recognising Jeremy Falconer. 'Smug bastard isn't having it all his own way, now, is he?'

'It looks like he's with his favourite son, too,' Kendra added. Hawk was gesturing to a police officer that made up the trio outside the front.

'That must be the elusive Constable Fellows,' Andy said, 'and we finally have our connection with the three. Now, if we can get some actual evidence, we can do more than set fires.

We can and should destroy them all for what they've done so far, let alone what they're planning.'

There was a lot of finger-pointing and gesticulating from all three, as they appeared to shout at each other.

'He seems very familiar for a cop, doesn't he?' Kendra said.

'Damn. I'd pay good money to hear what they were saying,' said Trevor.

'Sadly, not this time,' Andy replied. 'Sorry.'

'It's cool, Andy. We can't do everything, right? But can you help me with something else?'

'What's that?'

'I want to record my meeting later with that bastard,' Trevor said, pointing directly at Hawk.

THE TEAM GATHERED in the gym for another briefing. It was important that they were all kept up to speed, to avoid confusion.

'So far,' said Trevor, 'We've achieved everything we set out to do. We've given them a setback that they'll take time to recover from; but it isn't enough.'

'Yeah,' said Kendra. 'You've all been brilliant so far and we can't thank you enough, but we knew all along that the only way we could take on a nasty gang, a billionaire, and a bunch of bent cops was to use our brains and focus on what we're good at.

This is where we start the clever stuff, ladies and gents. We need proof of what they did. This job is very different from the others and it's important we all understand that,' she continued.

'So, what do we do next?' asked Charmaine.

'Next is Dad's meet with their leader, Hawk, at midday. It will give us some insight into their operations and maybe some evidence, too, we hope.'

'The rest of you will be divided up into smaller teams to look at the bent cop and the coroner. We don't have much info on them, but they're definitely involved,' Trevor said.

'Decide amongst yourselves and then find them both, wherever they are,' said Kendra. 'We need to find out where they work from, where they live, what they're driving, everything there is to know. If we can't get what we need, then we'll have to play dirty.'

'Who's going to go with you to the meet, Trev?' asked Darren.

'I'm going alone.'

'Seriously? Don't you think he'll try anything?'

'Only if he's stupid. We currently hold all the cards: we have his drugs, his money, and we've just destroyed his fleet of bikes. He's desperate to know what the hell is going on. He'll come alone but his mates will be somewhere nearby to be able to back him up in a hurry,' Trevor replied.

'I guess we should do the same, right?' said Darren.

'Fair enough, just a couple of you. Not too close: don't get spotted, otherwise it'll cause problems. Andy will be able to track the bikes, so will give you a heads-up where the maniac sidekicks are parked, but he can't help when they're on foot. Just be careful.'

'No problem, I'll take Jimmy with me,' Darren said, nodding to his colleague. 'We'll check the area where the bikes are parked and go from there.'

'Great, I will see you all later,' Trevor said.

Before leaving for the meeting with Hawk, Trevor dropped by to speak with Andy.

'I just want to make sure you can still track the bikes.'

'Yeah, all four are still at the site, but the meet isn't for another forty minutes, so it's still early.'

'Great. Did you have time to search for info on our mysterious Mister Hawk, aka George?'

'Why yes, I did, Mister Giddings. If you watch that monitor over there,' he said, pointing to the next one along, 'I'd like to introduce you to mister George Stellenberg, who, in his youth was a guest at His Majesty's Prison Cookham Wood, a prison for juvenile males. He spent eighteen months there for GBH when he stabbed and nearly killed a rival gang member.'

'No wonder he changed his name. George Stellenberg doesn't sound very menacing, does it? Is that German?'

'Actually, it's South African, which is where young George's mother came from. She was the landlady in a pub in Cromer, which Falconer frequented when he was young. Died about five years ago.'

'What else do we know about him?' asked Trevor.

'He's been living in London until recently, been cautioned twice for possession of cannabis. He was suspected of dealing drugs in London and a couple of operations were set up, but they failed to catch him—apparently, he was tipped off both times. One of the files is sealed, which tells me that the DPS were investigating, so maybe he had a London cop in his pocket, too.'

'Interesting. That's all good to know. I want to surprise him with my knowledge and see if I can bait him a little.'

'Just be careful, Trevor. He's as nasty as they come.'

'Don't you worry, young man, I know. He killed my friend, remember?'

Trevor walked out and went to his car, ready to go to the meeting. He was determined not to show any emotion there lest it ruin their plans.

'I'm coming for you, Hawk,' he said from behind gritted teeth.

THE MEETING WAS to take place at the ruins of the old Beeston Regis Priory. It was close to the Cromer Road but far enough away that it was pretty much out of sight. Surrounded by fields, and with public footpaths running close by, it was an unusual and unlikely place to meet. Trevor wasn't bothered by potential dog walkers; all he wanted to do was to have a chat with Hawk and try to glean more information from him.

He parked his car in a layby and walked along Cromer Road towards the Priory. He called Andy one last time to make sure everything was as it should be.

'Three bikes have parked up in Britons Lane, so he may be there waiting for you,' Andy said.

'Make sure Darren is aware,' said Trevor. 'I want to know where the other two are. Call me if there's any problems, okay? You may as well record from now.'

'Will do, to all that. You take care,' Andy said.

Trevor turned onto the track and strolled along it, watching carefully for places someone could step out from. Passing some cottages on the right, he turned off the track and onto the public path leading to the ruins. He saw nobody and relaxed slightly, passing the current functioning priory on the right before coming into sight of the ruins of the thirteenth-century church. As he walked towards it, he saw Hawk, leaning against the ruins nonchalantly, checking his fingernails, before looking up to see his adversary approaching.

'You're early,' Trevor said. He ignored the piercing, demonic eyes that Hawk used so effectively to frighten his rivals.

'Well, you know the old saying, early bird catches the worm, blah, blah, blah,' Hawk replied, still leaning against the ruins.

'Really? From where I'm standing, you don't seem to be catching anything, George,' Trevor said without missing a beat.

Hawk froze and stepped away from the wall.

'That arsehole told you my name, didn't he?'

'We didn't need anything from that idiot except to pass the message on to you, Mister Stellenberg.'

'Who the hell are you?' Hawk demanded.

'You don't need to know who I am. Just know that you're not welcome here. You're not the only one with the police in your pocket, George.'

He stared into the black eyes of a man who was getting angrier by the second.

'I don't give a shit about your connections. Just tell me why you've attacked us and what you're after,' Hawk continued.

'First off, you don't make any demands of me, boy. That's my job. You want to know what this is all about, then you shut up and listen, otherwise I walk away. Comprendez?' Trevor hissed.

Hawk smiled before replying, 'Go for it, uncle.'

Trevor paused and stared, showing that he wasn't biting at any insults or disrespect.

He walked up to Hawk and stood a couple of feet away, close enough to make it uncomfortable for the biker.

'You killed my friend, you piece of shit. I want to know why and I want to know *now*,' Trevor spat.

'What are you talking about?'

'Jacob was my brother and I want to know why you threw him off the cliff.'

'That was your brother? He looked nothing like you.'

'I won't ask again. You tell me or I walk away, and I carry on destroying everything you have. Your choice.'

Hawk's anger finally got the better of him. He stepped back a few paces and glared at Trevor.

'You're doing this because of that fucker? He's the one who started all this, insulting us and threatening us. All I did was nip it in the bud before he did anything to us,' he shouted. 'For what it's worth, it was quick. Like you said, I threw him off the cliff, but I could've done a lot worse. You want me to show you?'

He moved menacingly towards Trevor, who stood his ground and waited for the tell-tale signs of an attack.

Hawk reached out as if to grab Trevor's jacket, which wasn't what he was expecting. He immediately grabbed one hand and twisted it violently before pushing down and forcing Hawk to the ground.

Hawk screamed as the pain seared through his hand.

'You killed Jacob!' Trevor shouted in his face.

Hawk stopped screaming long enough to look into Trevor's eyes and sneered, pushing the pain aside.

'You'd better kill me now, mister. Because if you don't, I will come after you and everyone in this damned town with a fury you have never seen before. I'll go after them all, the old people, the women, the kids, all of them.'

Trevor could see that he was past caring what was happening to him. He was neither scared nor concerned about the future. He was cold, and evil as hell.

Trevor pulled his arm back and struck the biker on the left cheek with a powerful punch, knocking him down to the floor. The biker leaned on his elbows, shook his head, and laughed. A swelling formed on his cheek instantly.

'Let's call it quits, eh? I killed Jacob, you smashed my face in. Or I tell you what, you can kill my brother. How's that?' He laughed. 'Man, you're gonna pay for this.'

Trevor pretended to look around, as if he was expecting company.

'What, you got your boys hiding in the bushes waiting for me, eh? That's brave of you.'

'I don't need anyone to fight my battles, old man,' Hawk spat.

'I bet Snake and Razor do everything for you, don't they, like little puppies,' Trevor goaded.

'That's right, they do everything I say because they know I'm the boss. Without me, they're nothing, none of them.'

'That's just what I thought. You're just using them for your own gain, aren't you? You don't give a shit about anyone else.'

'You're clever, old man, but in this world you're the shepherd or the sheep—a leader or a follower. I'm the biggest, maddest shepherd you'll ever meet. Razor and Snake will do anything I say because they're the sheep, expendable. They all are. Once I'm done here, they'll all be inside or dead. I don't give a shit.'

'Wow, you're a lunatic, that's for sure,' Trevor said.

'That's right, grandad. Don't you forget it. You are all royally screwed.'

Trevor punched him again, this time knocking him out.

He searched the prone biker's pockets and took everything he could find: a mobile phone, cash, keys, and a piece of paper with a name and address on it.

'Shit,' he said.

He rushed back towards the main road and to his car. On the way, he called Kendra.

'They're going after Rufus, love. Get someone over there now before it's too late.'

BY THE TIME Martin and Greg arrived at Rufus's house, it was too late. There was a police car and ambulance parked on the road, so they carried on past.

Greg was dropped off further down the road and did a walk-by to see what he could find out. He saw the ambulance leave, an elderly woman with a handkerchief watching as it drove off. Next to her was a local police officer, none other than Rodney Fellows. Fellows said something to the woman, who nodded, and went back to his car and drove off.

'He's in an ambulance on the way to the hospital. I have no idea what state he's in or what happened,' Greg said when he called Trevor. 'And that bent copper was there, too. He's gone now.'

'I'll let Kendra know. If he's going back to the station, then we'll send someone over to keep an eye out. Thanks, Greg.'

Trevor called his daughter and arranged for a car to divert to the station and to expect Fellows to arrive shortly in a marked car.

'Will do, Dad. I'll call the hospital and see if there's any news about Mister Donald,' she said, hanging up.

'Damn them all,' Trevor said as he reached his car. He called Andy.

'Tell me you got that.'

'Yep, all received nice and clear,' Andy replied.

'Can you make copies and also do a little editing for me?' Trevor asked.

'Sure thing. What do you need?'

Trevor explained his plan.

'Nice. Devious, but nice,' Andy said.

14

DELIVERY

Back at the gym, Trevor met with Kendra and Andy to discuss the next steps.

'I spoke to the ward nurse at the hospital. Luckily, Rufus is out of danger. They attacked him when he answered the door, and broke a couple of ribs. He also has a couple of nasty black eyes and a broken wrist, so he won't be doing much on the farm for a while. They say he's out of danger but will be keeping him there for a few days.'

'That's good,' Trevor said, 'at least he's safe there.'

'They made his wife watch, Dad. She's scared shitless and wants to move away.'

'Which is exactly what Falconer wants,' said Andy.

'Bastard,' Trevor spat. 'We need to end this quick otherwise more people will be hurt.'

'Zoe and Clive are watching the police station and were there when Fellows turned up. They're staying there to see where he goes when he finishes his shift,' Kendra continued.

'Rory and Mo are at the coroner's office waiting for him to finish work. They sent a list of cars which they think belong to the staff there, from the car park at the back. I've checked them all and got an address for our friendly crooked coroner, Mister Andrew Kirkbride. I've told them to follow him loosely when he finishes to see if he goes home or not,' Andy said.

'Okay, that's good, having this info will help. Not sure how we'll deal with the coroner, any ideas?' Trevor asked.

'I'm sure we'll come up with something,' Kendra said.

'One bit of good news,' said Andy, 'is that I have a couple of numbers for none other than Jeremy Falconer, thanks to Hawk's and Starkins' phones.'

'That's good, those numbers may come in handy sooner rather than later,' Trevor said.

'So, what are we going to do about Falconer, Dad? I know Hawk and the bikers have done the damage, but he's the cause of it, the main man.'

'Yeah, there's a special place in hell waiting for him, love, we just have to figure out how we're gonna get him there.'

'Kendra, I have an idea how we can get some payback from Falconer,' Andy said, as they sat around the gym with a cup of coffee.

'What's that, then?'

'Well, it's pretty clear that the most important thing for this greedy bastard is the acquisition and development of prime real estate. He wants to redevelop the entire area and make it into a resort for rich people, filled with luxury homes that will be empty for eleven months of the year,' he said.

'Go on.'

'Well, a lot of this area is beautiful and still untouched by developers like the ones he wants to bring here. I looked into it and the people in North Norfolk are up in arms that so many people from big cities are buying up homes and keeping them empty most of the time. It's driven prices up and people out and they're not happy, they can't compete with city buyers.'

'Get to the point, Andy,' she said.

'If an area of outstanding natural beauty is under threat, then doesn't the National Trust step in and make compulsory purchases of that land or property?' he said.

'I have no idea. Where are you going with this?'

'I looked it up. Listen to what it says they can do:

"Land or property may be acquired to protect an existing property of inalienable standard. We may acquire land or buildings if their development could impact on nearby places of national importance."

'They can do a lot more but surely this covers an area such as this. I bet Falconer hasn't even considered it, that would surely scupper his plans, right?'

'Andy, that could be the stroke of luck we need to get him. Taking his dream away would be a great start. Can you look into it further?'

'Already started, I sent them an email today asking for clarity and what we need to do.'

'Fantastic. I'll let Dad know we're doing that. I'm sure he has something very different in mind for Falconer.'

'Good news, people. We now have addresses for the coroner and the bent cop. Great work, everyone.'

'What now, Trev?' asked Darren.

'Now we turn everyone against each other and watch them fight, while we record it all as evidence,' he said, smiling.

'I like the sound of that, where do we start?' Darren asked.

'First off, we're hearing that many people have made complaints or called the police. The bikers are basically trying to scare people away to make Falconer's job of buying everything up easier. We need to stop those shits from doing any more harm.'

'Are they still working out of the campsite?' Izzy asked.

'Yes, so we can stage another raid on the site and do some more damage. This time, let's slow them down a lot more, eh?'

'So, people,' said Kendra, 'how do we stop twenty-odd bikers from leaving the campsite?'

'Doesn't the water and electricity supply come in from Rufus Donald's property?' Charmaine said.

'Yes, why do you ask?'

'I know it'll only slow them down for a few days, but can't we dump a couple of bottles of laxative into their water supply and see what that does? I'm sure there's other stuff we can dump in there too to make them sick, so they won't leave.'

Everyone looked at Charmaine, stunned at her proposal. It was so simple, yet so effective that nobody would have even considered it.

'Charmaine, remind me never to get on your bad side,' Darren said, putting his arm around her.

'That will make for excellent viewing,' Andy said, laughing.

'Well, I guess that sorts *that* out. We can start with laxatives and look at alternatives after a day or two,' Kendra said.

'Okay, we'll buy some and go back tonight,' Trevor said.

'In the meantime, Rufus is going to need help with the farm now that he's in hospital, so I'm going to see someone who may be able to help him.'

'It's good to see you, Trevor,' Manfri said as they shook hands.

'Likewise, Manfri. How are you all doing here?'

'It's been tough, I won't lie. Some of the family went back home, but I felt we owed it to Jacob to try to carry on our tradition, you know?'

'I came over to let you know what's been going on. We know who killed Jacob for sure now, Manfri. His death was part of a big scheme to screw the local people out of their homes and land. We have plans to deal with them all, so please bear with us while we do our thing. In the meantime, I need your help with something.'

'Anything to help, my friend,' Manfri said.

'You probably don't know but they also attacked Rufus and put him in hospital. He's going to be laid up for a few days and won't be able to do much on the farm for weeks. Can you spare someone to help out?'

'Yes, of course,' said Manfri.'

'I'll let his wife know that you'll be sending someone over, she'll be very pleased.'

'We'll be here for another week or so and then most of the family will be leaving,' said Manfri. 'I'll be staying until I know that Jacob's death has been avenged, so anything else you need, you just come and ask.'

'Yes, of course. There is one other thing which may help

us later,' Trevor said, 'is there a holding tank for the water supply to the camp from Rufus's place?'

'There is, yes. I know because I helped install it when he replaced the old system a few years ago so that each caravan has its own supply. It's linked to the mains supply now and the tank is next to two of the older caravans, just behind them.'

'You mean the two bigger ones that are set slightly back from the rest?' Trevor asked.

'That's right, yes. They were the first two he put in before he expanded the site,' Manfri said.

'Excellent, thank you for that, it would've taken us ages to find them.'

They shook hands again before Trevor left, heading back to the gym. The plan he'd been working on in his head was coming together slowly, but it was getting there. He was used to adjusting plans for unknowns, so there was always a plan B or C. He'd lost count of the changes he'd made so far and so he knew it was time to turn the screws to maximum.

Tonight's midnight foray back to the campsite would be the start of what would be a very interesting couple of days.

'How are you getting on?' Trevor asked Andy.

'I've done some creative editing, like you asked. Here, this can't be traced and isn't much use as a phone. I've added the recording to the music app so you can play it back whenever you want.'

Trevor took the phone and unlocked the screen. The sound clip named *Hawk* was the only file on the music app. He pressed play and immediately heard Hawk speaking:

"That's right, they do everything I say because they know I'm the boss. Without me they're nothing, none of them."

He let the recording go on, which highlighted Hawk's disdain for pretty much everyone, especially his own team.

"Razor and Snake will do anything I say because they're the sheep, expendable. Once I'm done here, they'll all be inside or dead, I don't give a shit."

'Excellent, thanks, Andy," said Trevor. 'What about the rest of it?'

Andy handed him another phone. 'This one has Hawk confessing to Jacob's murder. It won't hold up in court, but it'll help the police focus. Once they re-open the case, they'll soon find the inconsistencies and deliberate misdirection by the coroner and that bent cop, Fellows.'

'Great, this will get both into a lot of shit. That's why this recording was important, just to get the police's attention and into conducting a proper investigation. Cheers!'

'Make sure you wipe it clean before you hand it over, okay?' Andy said.

'Will do!'

KENDRA HAD BEEN TASKED to write an anonymous letter to Norfolk Constabulary Serious crimes Unit, based at their headquarters in Wymondham, just south-west of Norwich. In the letter, she outlined the cover-up by PC Rodney Fellows and coroner Andrew Kirkbride, and suggested that the pathologist also be investigated.

Besides outlining the cover-up, Kendra included a list of the offences they had committed and a copy of the current coroner's report. She included salient points such as the location of the van, which had been cleaned and no fingerprints found, the missing keys for the van, the material found under Jacob's fingernails, and everything they had gleaned over the past week or so.

At the end of the letter, she clarified that PC Rodney Fellows was corrupt and connected to a large-scale plot involving Falconer and the Rejects and suggested they look into bank accounts and phone records to confirm the connections. She also included printouts of the meeting between the three outside the warehouse.

Finally, she also said that unless the matter was thoroughly investigated, then copies of everything would be sent to the press, to the Directorate of Professional Standards, and to the Police Ombudsman's Office—implying that there was large-scale corruption within the ranks of Norfolk Constabulary, particularly the senior ranks, who ignored solid evidence of bad practice and serious crimes.

Once she was happy with what she'd written, she showed it to Andy, who had been with her in the van checking the phones and laptops again and recording all the contact information separately.

'What do you think?' she asked, showing him the screen.

'That should put the cat amongst the pigeons,' he said, 'you're a pretty cool Detective, Detective.'

'That's very kind, Mister Pike.'

She printed out two copies, and, mindful of fingerprints, wore medical gloves before carefully placing them in envelopes and addressing one to the Chief Constable of Norfolk Police and the other to the Police and Crime Commissioner.

'I think I'll have someone drive to Cromer and post from

there,' she said, 'so it can't be traced to us here in Sheringham.'

'Good thinking. Want to know what I've been doing?' he asked mischievously.

'I dread to think.'

'I've just ordered two thousand pounds' worth of new tools from the biker's suppliers,' he said, grinning, 'and I paid a lot extra for overnight shipping.'

'Very devious, where are they sending them to?'

'That's the funny part. I told them we'd lost our other tools in a fire and it had damaged the workshop and they said they'd just knock and meet us outside. I'll send a couple of Darren's boys dressed in overalls and they can bring the tools back to us here. None of the mechanics are there, the place is deserted.'

'Excellent. You should have ordered more!'

'Well, I didn't want to take advantage of their generous nature. I did something else naughty, though,' he said.

'Uh oh, I daren't ask!'

'From another supplier, I've ordered a pallet of motorcycle oil, and a couple of hundred oil filters and brake discs. Nine thousand pounds' worth.'

'What are we going to do with all that?'

'Oh, that's not for us, that's for Jeremy Falconer, I've arranged for the delivery in a couple of days. I told them to use the side entrance.'

It took a few minutes for the laughter to die down, before Kendra finally had recovered enough to be able to leave.

15

INFILTRATION

'It starts tonight, folks,' said Trevor. 'Things are going to get pretty strange around here for the next few days, and it starts tonight. Tonight, we go back to the campsite to deliver a special gift to the guests there. The idea is to slow them down for a few days while the rest of our plan kicks in, to stop them from harassing the locals.'

'Same team as last time?' asked Mo.

'No, we don't need all of you. We just need one person to go in and one to keep an eye out. I'll leave that for you to decide, Mo.'

'No problem. I'll go with Rory.'

'It will be a little trickier this time around: the water tank is behind the two caravans that we left alone last time, where the leader and his evil sidekicks will be sleeping. You'll need to be very careful.'

'Don't worry, Trev, I'll give him some pointers,' Amir said, to much laughter.

'Moving on,' Trevor said, shaking his head, 'the rest of you chill out for the rest of the evening. For tomorrow will be a busy day for us all. The laxative won't kick in until they've left the campsite, so I'll need some of you to keep an eye on them. They'll start feeling it and return to the site pretty quickly, I imagine.

'Take lots of tissues,' Charmaine said. 'It's likely to get messy and stinky very quickly,' she added, to another round of laughter.

'You think she's joking,' Trevor said, laughing.

'Isn't it weird that we can stay upbeat when so much evil is going on?' Kendra said, 'but I guess that's exactly what we need to do to keep ourselves sane, right?'

'You'll get no argument from any of us,' Darren said, 'you lot have shown us a very different world to the one we know.'

'Well, let's try to make whatever small changes we can here,' Kendra replied, 'it's all we can do.'

'That's right, ladies and gents, it's serious—but remember, it's for the greater good. Continuing, we'll be sending some evidence tomorrow to implicate the bent police officer and coroner to the authorities. It'll buy us some time, but we will try to speak to the coroner ourselves before he is arrested, maybe he can give us more evidence against Falconer.'

'That plan is to approach him and also the police officer and let them know what we know. On top of that, we'll tell them that they've been sacrificed by their so-called friends. It should make them panic and give them up officially to the police – or so we hope. I know it's what I've seen happening all the time back in London, most of them are cowards,' Kendra added.

'Who's doing what, Trevor?' asked Charmaine.

'I'll be speaking to the cop and will take Darren with me,' said Trevor. 'Kendra will take Jimmy and speak to the coroner. I want teams of two to back us up in case they do something silly. I doubt they will, but you never know how people are going to react when they're panicked, right?'

'Clive and Izzy can cover us, Trev. Martin and Greg can cover Kendra's meet,' Darren added.

'Charmaine, can you and Zoe have a chat with Janice Brown? She's Hawk's mistress, for want of a better word, but she rarely hangs around with him during the day when he's off doing scary stuff. Andy will tell you where her bike is, and you two can have a friendly chat with her. We want to turn her against Hawk, too, so we'll give you a copy of the recording that Andy made – it will help,' Kendra said.

'No problem at all,' Charmaine replied.

'So, by my reckoning, that just leaves you, Amir. You okay working alone tonight? I have something special lined up for you. You keep asking for special, right?' Trevor asked.

'As long as it doesn't involve tissues and biker shit, then I'm your man. What do you need?'

'I want to see just how good Falconer's security is – think you can break into his house tonight?'

'That's the mansion with security cameras everywhere, right?'

'Yep, that's the one.'

'Do I look worried?' Amir said confidently. 'Count me in, this is more like the type of challenge I need.'

'Well, just be careful. I want to see how good the security is. If it's Amir-proof, then at least we'll know quickly. If it's second rate and you can get in and grab some intel, then we may upgrade our plans for Mister Falconer. Either way, it'll be good to know.'

'Like I said, not a problem. Mo can drop me off on the way to the campsite, right, bro?'

'Yeah, bro, we can do that. I'll give you some pointers on the way, refresh your memory a little.'

'I'll be wearing my headphones, so don't waste your breath,' Amir replied.

Trevor hushed the banter and said, 'Go safely, people. Don't take any unnecessary chances, okay?'

They dispersed, leaving Trevor, Andy and Kendra standing by the ring.

'Well? Can you think of anything else that needs doing?' Trevor asked.

'I think we've covered everything – for now,' Kendra said.

'I'll go and make another copy of the recording for Charmaine,' said Andy, walking off.

'Every day that passes reminds me how things should be at work, so we can do our jobs properly,' Kendra mused.

'At least we're doing something, love. Better than nothing, right?'

Mo, Rory and Amir left the gym at midnight. Earlier in the day, five of the team had visited different chemists, where they had acquired ten bottles of fast-acting liquid laxative that advertised relief in six to twelve hours. Trevor surmised the bikers would start feeling the effects after midday and begin their nervous journeys back a short time later.

They dropped Amir off a couple of hundred metres from the Falconer estate and turned back towards the campsite. Amir continued nonchalantly towards the estate, acting as though he belonged. He continued past the main entrance and again past the side entrance, knowing that there were cameras set up covering them. He walked towards the industrial estate and decided he'd go the long way around, via his familiar hedgerow, which he'd used to such great effect with the warehouse adventures.

He put on the night-vision goggles that Andy had supplied, and continued. This time, instead of stopping, he carried on way past the warehouse and the rest of the industrial units until he got to the end. He turned right and followed the boundary towards the Falconer estate, estimating that he'd be halfway along its flank and hoping there'd be no CCTV coverage there.

As he neared the Falconer boundary, he paused for a minute, listening for anything untoward or hostile – such as guard dogs. Content that he'd not heard anything, he found a small gap under the hedgerow that he then deepened by scooping out soil with his hands, making a gap large enough for his wiry frame to wriggle through. Once inside the estate grounds he paused again, hoping to hear nothing, but prepared for the worst. He was soon on his way, effectively doubling back on himself towards the main house. He could see a couple of faint lights on in the house, which was only to be expected, but there was no activity of any kind.

Andy had shown him a recent layout of the nineteenth-century house, which he had "acquired" from the local planning office. The house had seven bedrooms, over three floors. The ground floor had been extended in the past ten years to add a large single-storey L-shaped extension, adding a conservatory, a large office, and a garden-facing dining area to the side and the rear of the house. Andy had also shown him pictures of Falconer and his family, pointing out that he was recently divorced and had shared custody of the three children, aged nine, ten, and twelve.

One other addition was the security room that was based

in one of the outbuildings close to the house. It was a small bungalow with an office, a bathroom, and a bedroom for the night duty staff. According to the records and plans, it was intended to be manned twenty-four hours by one security guard, who checked arrivals and the CCTV monitors covering the entrances into the house. Amir had also seen several cameras covering the front and rear, but none on the side.

He was confident that despite twenty-four-hour security coverage, it wasn't comprehensive, and that he'd be able to check the house without being spotted.

It took a few minutes of keeping in the deep shadows and stopping to listen, but eventually he arrived within fifty feet of the house. It was still silent and his confidence grew that there were no guard dogs on the grounds – he hoped the same was true of the inside, too. He had targeted a gnarly old oak tree that grew close to the house and now moved swiftly towards it. The tree had been there for centuries and had been pruned many times due to its proximity to the house, where branches had grown close enough to cause damage.

Amir climbed, aiming for a thick, solid branch about halfway up. It was one of those branches that was likely to be lopped soon, so it was perfect for him to use. The branch grew toward the flat-roofed extension that would give him access to the drainpipes and the windows, allowing him the opportunity to further explore and test the security capabilities.

'Let's see how seriously you take your security, mister evil,' he thought as he made his way silently to one of several windows. The night-vision goggles were very effective, and he could see into a child's bedroom with an unmade bed. It confirmed that the children were not currently in the house,

which would make Amir's task simpler. He moved along to the next two windows and saw that they were also empty bedrooms. Moving around to the rear of the house, he double-checked to ensure that he had missed no cameras. The two he had seen were mounted up high at each end of the house, pointing towards the grounds, not the roof, so he could easily evade detection.

Moving along the back of the house, he saw where the faint light source was coming from: a hall light on the ground floor. It wasn't bright enough to affect his night vision, so he was able to continue. He'd noticed that the windows were all original sash windows with effective locks that screwed shut, making it impossible for him to use his trusted shimmy to gain entry. He checked all the windows on the first floor and decided that the only chance of getting in was likely from the second, where they were less likely to have secured the locks.

Looking up, he saw two windows, both in darkness. They were probably bedrooms, likely used for guests, or for storage. Either way, he was hoping they were an option for entry. One of them had a metal drainpipe close by, so he climbed it, slowly. Reaching over to the window, he got a good hold on the concrete sill and pulled himself over. He saw that the lock differed from those downstairs, as it was easy to slide to one side, which he did with the aid of his pocketknife. He dragged the lower window upwards enough to get inside.

He saw it had been a bedroom but now seemed cluttered, with lots of boxes stacked on top of each other. It had a musty smell to it, suggesting it wasn't used very often, or been aired at all. He slowly opened the door and listened carefully. It was still silent; he could see the faint light coming from the ground floor. He edged out and closed the door quietly behind him, tiptoeing along the hall towards the stairs.

Keeping to the side to avoid creaking stairs, he started for the first floor.

On the first-floor landing, Amir knew that there was likely to be someone sleeping in a bedroom – perhaps Falconer himself – so he avoided the floor completely and headed downstairs. He removed his goggles as the light from the hall was getting brighter, rendering them useless. One thing he noticed, as he continued, was the absence of artwork on the walls. There had clearly been pictures hanging but they had been removed, making the faint outlines of the dust visible.

As he got closer to the ground floor, a sound he wasn't expecting broke the silence: the sound of snoring. .

The snoring came from the office that he knew from the plans, towards the corner of the house. As he approached it, he saw the door was ajar, and the snoring was much louder. He peered inside and saw a luxuriously appointed office, more of a library, really, with one complete wall taken up by a floor-to-ceiling shelf crammed with books, and a vintage slide-along ladder to reach the top shelves. In front of the main window overlooking the grounds was an ornate oak desk, with a brass lamp that was switched on, illuminating two telephones and a pair of computer monitors and some clutter on the desk. Both computers had blinking lights, suggesting they were switched on. Amir again noticed the absence of any art on the walls, contrary to photographs Andy had shown him of prominent artwork on display in the house. This was the house that Falconer had once showcased to magazines, along with a valuable Vermeer that he had shown off in his office, where the wall was now bare.

Opposite the bookshelf was a brown chesterfield sofa, its leather aged and weathered. Sprawled on the sofa, with one arm hanging down towards the floor, was none other than Jeremy Falconer, in the deepest of drunken sleeps and snoring loudly. A half-empty bottle of Johnnie Walker Black Label whisky was propped against the sofa, and an empty crystal glass lay on its side next to it. A pile of documents was scattered across the rug in front of the sofa.

Amir tiptoed towards the sofa, careful to avoid stepping on any documents. Even in the gloom, he could see that many of them were legal documents, financial statements, and demand notices. This was valuable information that he needed to get to Andy as soon as possible.

He quietly gathered up the documents that seemed to be of high importance and took them out of the room and into the downstairs toilet. Grabbing a towel from the back of the door, he placed it on the floor to block any light before turning on the lights on. He lay the documents on the toilet seat and started taking photos with his mobile, one at a time. It took a couple of minutes to send them via email to Andy before he switched off the light, replaced the towel, and cracked the door to check if there had been any changes. He could still hear the snoring from the office, so he quietly returned and replaced the documents on the floor.

Before leaving, he grabbed a piece of paper and a pen from Falconer's desk. He made a note of the computer makes and models, their serial numbers, and whatever information he could glean from the labels on the back. He also made a note of the router information and password, to give Andy a better chance of hacking the system and potentially garnering more information about Falconer's businesses. When he was happy, he took one last look around before making his way out of the office and back towards the stairs.

He went quietly back to the second floor and into the room through which he had entered.

He climbed back out onto the windowsill, closing the window carefully behind him. Seconds later, he was climbing back down the drainpipe and onto the flat roof below. He made his way back towards the tree, but before he climbed back down, he removed a small camera from his pocket and placed it carefully against the end of some guttering at the front of the extension, which covered the front door and security hut, as well as the large garage and the other outbuildings. When he was happy, he taped it in place using black gaffer tape.

This should make Andy even happier, he thought.

It was trickier to get back onto the same branch: without his weight, it had now moved back to seven feet above the level of the rooftop, so he had to spring up to grab it. Holding on carefully, he climbed on and crawled the first few feet before it was stable enough for him to stand again. He reached the trunk and climbed back down easily. After one last look, he could creep back to the hedgerow and make good his escape.

It was only when he was clear of the estate that Amir took a deep breath and said out loud, 'Well, that was a bloody rush, wasn't it?'

JUST A FEW MILES AWAY, Mo was emptying the last bottle of laxative into the water tank that supplied the static caravans the rejects were using. He and Rory had used the hidden gate to access the site again and had skirted the boundary to avoid being spotted by the resident bikers. The only bikes left were those of Hawk, his deputies, and his girlfriend, so it was likely that they were well-guarded or stored somewhere safe.

Hawk had also been conscious of this, especially after the meeting with the unknown competitor that had knocked him out. He had turfed the occupants out of one pod and locked the four bikes in there for safety. They couldn't afford to lose them, too.

Mo had left Rory to keep an eye out between the two larger caravans and the remaining smaller ones, where the riders were all now fast asleep. He had moved silently behind one of them and found the water tank exactly where Manfri had said it would be. The large tank was made of heavy-duty black plastic, as you'd expect. Its lid was weighted down with a large rock to prevent any creatures from getting in. Mo had silently lifted the heavy stone and placed it on the ground before lifting the lid and sliding it along a few inches. He had then removed the bottles from his small backpack and emptied them all into the tank.

Once the last bottle was emptied, he replaced the lid and the rock before making his way back to Rory, where they then retraced their route back to the hidden gate. The entire operation had taken less than fifteen minutes.

'That was exactly how I like things to go,' Mo told Rory as they made their way back towards their car. 'Quick, easy, and without problems.'

'Let's hope they're all nice and thirsty tomorrow morning, eh?' Rory said.

16

STINGER

'How the hell did you manage that?' Andy had asked Amir, stunned by the information that the young twin had supplied. 'I thought you were just checking to see if it was good security or not.'

'Well. You know what they say, Andy. When in Rome... take every opportunity you can to break in and steal shit.'

'You just made that up, didn't you?' Andy replied.

'I'm sure I've heard it from somewhere,' Amir said, with a smile.

'Brilliant, Amir, just brilliant,' Kendra said, giving him a hug.

'Yeah, great work, young man,' Trevor added. 'It seemed the perfect challenge for you, right?'

'Yes, sir. I've had some sleep now, so I'm ready for more.'

'I'm sure something else will come up, Amir. Don't you worry,' Kendra added.

'Have you had a chance to look through the documents?' Trevor asked.

'Not thoroughly, but to be honest, I don't need to,' said

Andy. 'This guy is deep in the crap financially. He's mortgaged to the hilt on all his properties, including the main house. He's in big, big trouble and has gambled everything on the land grab and development to make good.'

'I thought he was super-rich,' Kendra said.

'His family may have been, but other than some holiday rentals, he doesn't have any income. The industrial estate gave him enough to get by, but when he closed everything down, gambling on the development going through, it all started going south for him.'

'Did I mention he has no paintings left in his house? The walls were bare and nothing like the pictures you showed me, Andy.'

'He must have sold them. They were worth millions, especially the Vermeer. I'll check online and see if I can find out what he did with them.'

'He must have raised millions by re-mortgaging his properties and selling off the family treasures, right? What the hell has he spent it on?' Kendra asked.

'I'm hoping he keeps accounts on his computer. Thanks to Amir, I have his router info and password, so I'll be able to hack into his computers and check later. At a guess, I'd say he's spent it on buying everyone else's properties and the plans for the development.'

'That's good news and bad news,' Trevor said. 'If he's in so much trouble, then he'll be desperate, which makes him much more dangerous than we thought. Until now, we thought he was just a rich arsehole wanting to become richer by screwing over the poor, the usual story.'

'What's the good news, Trevor?' Andy said.

'We know he is in trouble, but we can make it worse for him. A lot worse.'

Road Trip

LATER THAT DAY, the team were all ready and raring to go. Trevor and Darren were parked by the police station waiting for PC Rodney Fellows to show. They knew he was on the early shift, so he would be bound to come out soon.

Kendra and Jimmy had done much the same, parked near the coroner's office.

'Let's see what the day brings,' Kendra said to Jimmy as they waited. 'It's time to show these bastards they won't get away with it.'

FIRST OUT WAS FELLOWS. He stopped briefly and waved at a passer-by that he knew, before walking to the staff car park that was next to the station.

'There he is,' Trevor told Darren, who was driving, 'just look at the smug bastard, not a care in the world, and after all the shit he's done.'

Fellows got into his one-year-old Jaguar SUV, bought with the money that Falconer had regularly provided, and headed home. He hadn't tried to hide his good fortune. Along with the expensive car, he had also paid off his mortgage and upgraded his home. His luxury four-bedroom detached house was on a private estate where the residents raised eyebrows when the local bobby moved in. He told them it had been an inheritance and kept away from them all.

Darren drove out of his parking space and followed Fellows at a distance. There was no need to get any closer. Their plan hinged on Amir and his excellent timing. Trevor gave him a call.

'We're on the way, Amir. We'll be there in three minutes.'

After leaving town, Fellows turned onto a single-track road that led to the expensive development where he lived. There was a junction coming up before the entrance to the estate, not far from where Amir was waiting with a stinger. It was the only way they could realistically get Fellows to stop and talk to them.

Amir was hiding behind a tree fifty yards before the junction, within the braking zone of any approaching vehicles. He peeked around the tree and could see the SUV slowing down at the junction. Just before Fellows reached the tree, Amir flung the stinger part-way out onto the road just in front of the Jaguar. His timing was perfect, the stinger extending about a third of the way across the road, just enough for the nearside tyres to go.

Fellows couldn't stop in time and had no idea what had jumped out onto the road in front of him. By the time he'd braked, both tyres had gone over the stinger and were now almost completely flat.

Amir quickly retracted it and was soon skulking away into the trees where Fellows would be unable to detect him. His job was done, successfully–as ever.

Fellows got out of the car and looked around, wary of being carjacked. He held his extendable baton in his hand, but there was nobody to be found.

'Shit,' he exclaimed, kicking one of the tyres.

He looked back towards the road when he saw a car coming. He started getting anxious when the car stopped and two men got out.

'Constable Fellows, how's it going?' Trevor asked, his hands held out to show he was unarmed.

'Who are you? Stay back, I'm calling for backup.'

He reached into his coat and pulled out a mobile phone, which he quickly unlocked with his free hand.

'I wouldn't do that, if I were you,' Trevor said, 'we just want a chat, and if you call your colleagues, then we'll have to explain that you're as bent as a five-bob note and in the pay of Jeremy Falconer. You won't want that, now, will you?'

Fellows paused, unsure of his next move. When Trevor's words had sunk in, he returned his phone to his pocket.

'What do you want?'

'Like I said, we just want to chat, nothing more. You have been taking money from Falconer for years. You are in bed with a biker gang that is dealing drugs. We know about your plans to help frighten the locals into selling up on the cheap and moving away. We know it all, Rodney.'

'Who the fuck are you?' Fellows asked. He hadn't expected the adrenaline rush that came with the fear of being caught, and was very concerned for his immediate future.

'Who we are is of no concern, Rodney. What should be of concern is that we have sent evidence of your corrupt arse to your bosses. I'm sure they'll be paying you a visit soon. Your days of fancy cars and flash houses are over, mate.'

'What the hell have I done to you?' Fellows asked, knowing there was little point in denying anything.

'You helped an evil man, is what you did. You took money from him to fill your boots with nice things while people were dying and being screwed out of their land and their homes. You helped the scum of the earth when you were supposed to be protecting people from them, you piece of shit.' Trevor took a step forward and lowered his hands. He stared at Fellows, his face impassive and hard.

Fellows dropped his head in shame.

'You have no evidence of anything. You're lying,' he said, more in hope than expectation.

'You want to know what everyone is saying about you? Okay then,' Trevor replied.

He took out the phone containing Andy's recordings and pressed play.

There was no mistaking Hawk's voice.

"You're clever, old man, but in this world you're the shepherd or the sheep—a leader or a follower. I'm the biggest, maddest shepherd you'll ever meet. Razor and Snake will do anything I say because they're the sheep, expendable. They all are. Once I'm done here, they'll all be inside or dead. I don't give a shit."

'That's not all,' Trevor said. 'You should hear what your friend Andrew Kirkbride has told us about you.'

The mention of the coroner hurt Fellows badly, like a gut punch. He looked back at Trevor, who was now smiling.

'I haven't finished yet, shit head. By the time I've finished sending the evidence to your superiors, you'll be looking at a life sentence for so many offences you won't know what to do with yourself. They will shaft you for everything, make an example of you. You'll be in all future training manuals as the textbook example of a scumbag corrupt cop.'

Fellows hung his head, the baton dropping from his limp hand. He was done.

'Only one thing will help take some of that away, Fellows. Only one thing,' Trevor continued, now that he could see Fellows had completely dropped his guard.

The chance of some redemption and hope was all it took for Fellows to raise his head expectantly.

'What?' he asked meekly. 'What do you need?'

'I want to know everything. I want to know how much he gave you to bribe Kirkbride, and about all the other payments. I want to know everything else Falconer is trying to do and what the Rejects are planning. Everything. Times, dates, amounts of all past dealings–I know you'll have records, you're a cop. If you help with that then you'll only be nicked and charged with conspiracy to pervert the course of justice for the bribe and altering the coroner's report, perjury, maybe a couple of procedural offences, like fraud, but nothing as serious as aiding and abetting a murderer. You'll still have to do some time, don't get me wrong, but probably not for the rest of your life. Your choice.'

Knowing he was a beaten man, Fellows simply nodded.

'I'll tell you everything I know.'

Kendra and Jimmy had followed the coroner as he left work, waiting for him to stop at a junction or a set of lights. As they approached the junction with another road, Kendra nudged Jimmy, who was driving.

'Here's as good a place as any,' she said, looking around to see if there were any other cars around. There were none.

As Kirkbride pulled up to the junction, Jimmy drove their car into the back of his, just fast enough to cause a little damage to both cars. Kirkbride got out and came to look at the damage to the rear. Jimmy and Kendra joined him.

'Not being funny, mate,' Kirkbride said, 'but you need to pay more attention while you're driving.'

'Sorry, mate, she made me do it,' Jimmy replied, pointing to Kendra.

Kirkbride was bemused, looking back and forth between the two.

'You did it on purpose?'

'That's right, Mister Kirkbride. We wanted to have a chat and thought this was the perfect way to introduce ourselves,' Kendra folded her arms and glared at him.

'Well, I suppose we should call the police and let them sort it out, shall we?' Kirkbride pulled out a mobile phone and unlocked it.

'That's a great idea. That way, we can tell them all about you falsifying a report to conceal a murder. They love arresting people for crimes like that,' Kendra said, without missing a beat.

Kirkbride looked aghast at her suggestion.

'W... what?'

'You heard me. You concealed a murder by falsifying your report, showing it as a suspected suicide and recommending no further investigation. You took a lot of money from your pal, Constable Fellows. He told us all about it.'

'H... he what? He told you?' Kirkbride's voice became high-pitched as panic and realisation set in. 'The bastard grassed me up. After everything I did for him?'

'That's right, he told us everything. He told us about your friendship and how you've helped hide many other "*accidents*" over the past few years. You have taken a lot of money off him and Jeremy Falconer, haven't you?'

Kirkbride was stunned. He looked around, panicking, with no idea how to respond.

'So, here's the thing, Andrew,' Kendra continued. 'We have sent a nice long letter and lots of evidence to the local police, telling them all about you and how corrupt you have been these past few years. They are going to be paying you a visit soon, I can assure you. Your choice is very simple–you can help, or you can hinder.'

'What do you mean?' he asked, confused.

'You can help by telling us everything you know about Fellows and Falconer, which will lead to your being arrested and charged for less serious fraud and corruption offences. Or you can hinder us, whereby you'll be charged with helping a murderer commit the crime, plus all the other offences. Your choice.'

'THIS IS THE PLACE,' Charmaine told Zoe as they pulled up outside the Tea Room in West Runton. It was a popular spot for tourists and locals alike. They saw Janice Brown's motorcycle parked nearby and knew from Andy that she was here. As they walked through the front garden towards the shop, they saw her sitting outside at a table, alone, looking at her mobile phone.

They walked past her and into the shop, ordering a couple of coffees. The server said she'd bring them over, so they went outside and sat at the table next to Janice. They chatted while waiting for their drinks, Charmaine keeping one eye on what Janice was doing. Their coffees arrived, and they continued to chat about mundane subjects. Charmaine then nodded to Zoe, starting a new conversation.

'That bike is fab, isn't it?' Zoe said.

'What, the black Triumph?' Charmaine replied. 'Yeah, it's a good 'un, that. It's the Tiger 900 GT, lovely touring bike.'

Janice twitched when she heard them talking about her bike. Charmaine pressed on.

'I'd love to meet the man who rides that,' she told Zoe, winking. 'I bet he can show me a few moves.'

That was Janice's cue to turn around.

'Actually, ladies, sorry to burst your bubble, but it's my bike,' she said, laughing.

Charmaine pretended to be surprised.

'Well, I'm sure you know a few moves too,' she said, with a laugh.

'Sorry about that,' Zoe said. 'We're just impressed. Even more so now we know it's yours. You just passing through?'

Janice seemed to relax a little. 'I suppose. To be honest, I can't wait to leave. I'm here with my fella, but I haven't seen much of him recently. He's always in a foul mood. I just want to leave now.'

'Come and join us. We'll get some more coffees,' Charmaine said.

'Don't mind if I do, I've missed having company recently, so it's nice to chat, you know?'

'What do you fancy?' Zoe asked.

'Thanks, that's very kind of you. I'll have a cappuccino, please.'

Zoe went inside to place the order.

'So, where are you from, if you're not from around here?' Charmaine asked.

'I've been living in Kent for the past few years. I love it there. Things were pretty good down there until my fella got this new job. He keeps telling me it's only for a few weeks, but it's dragging on now,' Janice replied.

'He just leaves you on your own while he goes off to work? That doesn't sound like much fun.'

'It's not, really. Luckily, I have my bike, and he gives me plenty of money to spend on whatever I want. It helps. I think he does it to keep me quiet.' Janice laughed, unconvinced.

'Yeah, I guess it's okay, until the boredom sets in.'

'I suppose.' The server brought out their drinks, and Janice took a sip. 'Thank you,' she told Charmaine.

'You're welcome,' Charmaine replied. 'You know, it sounds like your bloke is using you. You should do something about that. I mean, it's not as if you can't ride off. Look at that beast parked out the front. It's a beauty.'

'Yeah, but he gave me that, so he'd take it back if I left him.'

Charmaine sensed that Janice wasn't entirely happy with her lot and wanted a better life. It was time to change tack.

'You know, Janice, Hawk isn't going to change. He'll always expect you to do his bidding, and all you'll get is the use of a nice bike and some money to buy trinkets with.'

'Yeah, I know, but he's not too... wait, how do you know my name? You know Hawk? Did he send you to check on me?'

'Calm down, we just want to tell you a few things and then we'll be on our way,' Zoe added.

'What? What the hell is going on?'

'Hawk is deep into some nasty shit, and you will pay the price for it. He's planning on grassing you all up. You, Snake, Razor, the whole team. When he gets what he wants, he'll shaft you all.' Charmaine took out the phone Andy had prepared for her.

"You're clever, old man, but in this world you're the shepherd or the sheep–a leader or a follower. I'm the biggest, maddest shepherd you'll ever meet. Razor and Snake will do anything I say because they're the sheep, expendable. They all are. Once I'm done here, they'll all be inside or dead. I don't give a shit."

Charmaine stopped the recording and put the phone away.

'Hawk is going to screw you over. There is more than just

that recording. You really need to watch your back, Janice,' she added.

'What the hell am I supposed to do?' Janice asked, panicking.

'Tell us what you know and then just leave. Leave tonight, ride out of here, and go somewhere safe. We have sent evidence that will lead to Hawk's arrest soon. Once he's away, you'll be safe from him. If you help us, we'll help you. If you don't want to help, then you should go back to him right now and tell him what we have said. We don't think it will be pleasant, do you?'

'I don't know much; he doesn't tell me anything. How can I help you?' Janice asked.

'Do you know what he's doing next? Where he's going? Where his bank accounts are? That sort of thing,' Charmaine said.

'His bank accounts. Why do you want those?'

'It'll help our case if we can prove certain people have paid him, it all helps.'

Janice looked back and forth between the two friends, unsure of what to do.

'Do you need more proof? Follow us and we'll meet another friend who can call Hawk on your phone. You can stand right there next to him, out of sight, so you can hear his response. It'll only take a few minutes. He's not far away,' Charmaine said.

Janice paused before deciding. 'Okay, that works for me. I'll follow you,' she said, standing.

Charmaine called Trevor, who had finished his dealings with Fellows.

'Can we meet you somewhere so you can make a call?' she asked him.

'Sure, meet me in the car park of The Reef and I'll walk round there from the gym.'

Janice followed them on her bike. The journey took just five minutes before they turned into the swimming pool car park. It was half empty, and they quickly spotted Trevor waiting in the corner.

'This is Janice, boss. She's Hawk's girlfriend. We're trying to prove to her he is bad news, so I thought you could phone him from her phone and pretend you have grabbed her off the street. I want Janice to hear his reaction so she can stand on one side and listen. Is that okay?' Charmaine asked.

'Damn, remind me never to get on your bad side!' he said, before turning to Janice. 'How are you doing, Janice? Don't be scared. We won't do anything to hurt you. We just want you to see that Hawk is not good for you. Can I use your phone to prove it to you?'

'I'm not sure this is a good idea, but if he does what you say he will, I suppose it'll make it easy for me to decide, won't it?' Janice unlocked her phone and handed it over.

Trevor dialled Hawk using FaceTime, ushering the women to one side and out of sight.

'Hey, bab... what the hell!' Hawk exclaimed when he saw Trevor's smiling face.

'How's it going, Hawk? How's your chin?' Trevor said, laughing at his adversary.

'What have you done with Janice?' Hawk sneered.

'I thought she'd be better off with us for a while. We'll keep her nice and warm for you when you're ready to get the hell out of Norfolk. How's that sound... George?'

Hawk stayed silent for a moment before answering.

'You think you're gonna scare me out of Norfolk, do you? I

ain't going anywhere, mate, not until I'm done here. You got that?'

'Well, that's a shame. Janice is so pretty. You know we'll have to do something about that, don't you? Then we'll come after the rest of your minions and do the same to them. By the time we're done,' Trevor said, 'you won't have anyone left.'

Hawk laughed, completely unperturbed.

'You didn't hear a word I said the other day, did you? I couldn't give a shit about any of them, not Janice or anyone. They're just tools that are useful for me now and again to get to where I want. Do what you damned well like, old man,' he snorted. 'I ain't going anywhere, anytime soon.'

'I should've finished you when I had the chance, Georgey boy,' Trevor pressed, 'but it looks like I'll be having a bit more fun with you all before we meet again, eh?'

'Go fu—' was as far as he got as Trevor cut off the call.

Janice had remained cool throughout.

'I was expecting you to be upset or angry, one of the two. You seem pretty calm about it,' Trevor said.

'I guess I needed to hear it for myself. I've been with him for years now. He's more trouble than he's worth, but I thought I loved him, you know? What he just said made me feel cold, nothing more, just... cold.'

'What are you going to do now?' Charmaine asked.

'That was my cue to get the hell out of Dodge. I need to find somewhere quiet and peaceful to live. I think I've outgrown this macho biker stuff.'

'As long as you're away from that creep, then life can only get better,' Zoe said.

'Listen, I appreciate it. This could've turned out really bad for me, but instead it's been a godsend, thank you.'

'Take care of yourself, Janice,' Trevor said, handing back her phone.

They watched her leave the car park and turn left and away from the town, away from the campsite and away from Hawk and the Rejects – for good.

17

DRUGS

'You need to come and see this!'

They joined Andy in Marge, where he pointed to a monitor.

'Watch that screen. It's from an hour ago.'

The feed was from the camera that Amir had installed covering the front of Falconer's house. Andy pressed a key, and the recording started.

A car arrived and parked next to the security hut. A few seconds later, Falconer appeared through the front door and approached the car as two men got out. The passenger shook Falconer's hand and the pair of them made their way to the hut. The driver stayed behind and opened the boot before joining them.

A couple of minutes later, they came out. The driver had a holdall in each hand, as did the passenger. Falconer carried one, for a total of five holdalls. After they were placed in the boot, the passenger and Falconer shook hands again and parted ways.

'Did you recognise the bags?' Andy asked.

'Wait... are they the same as the ones holding the drugs that we stole?' Kendra asked.

'Yes!' Trevor exclaimed. 'They are!'

'Now you know how desperate he is, Trev. He's turned into a drug dealer–a wholesaler, no less!'

'Wow, I did not see that coming,' said Kendra.

'Is there anything we can do?' Trevor asked.

'I hope you don't mind, but I made a call and circulated the reg number of that car, with a description of the men and the contents of the boot. They're from Ipswich, which helped. If they get stopped – and it's a big if, then they'll probably blame Falconer for it. They'll also want their money back, too, which will make his situation a lot worse.'

'We don't mind at all. Good work, Andy,' Kendra said, patting him on the arm.

'Damn, that man will stoop lower than a snake to get what he wants. He's going for glory, isn't he?' Trevor said.

'Let's hope it's a bust instead, shall we?' Kendra replied. 'Can you make a recording of that, please, Andy?'

'Sure, no problem.'

'I think I'll send another letter with more evidence,' she said mischievously.

'HERE THEY COME, a little later than we originally expected, but still–they're returning to the site,' Andy said, showing them the feed to the campsite.

The bikers had started appearing in the early afternoon. Within an hour and a half, they were all back except for a handful who had probably not drunk any water that morning. The feed had been amusing, showing them walking awkwardly to their caravan just in time, some running, and two had even removed their trousers and underwear completely, dumped somewhere. Their modesty had been protected by their shirts – just.

'That was a great idea, wasn't it? A non-violent way of putting them out of action,' Trevor said, laughing at the bikers' efforts to get to the toilet in time.

'You know, it's not going to stop them for long, maybe a couple of days,' Kendra said.

'Hopefully, that's all we'll need. If it looks like they're planning to go back out again, we can try something else.'

'Oh? What devious plan do you have in mind this time, Dad?'

'Originally, I was going to send Amir in to put some industrial glue on the toilets, because that would have been hilarious. For us, not for them: it would have been painful as hell. But then I thought it was too risky. There's a lot that could go wrong with that plan.'

'What did you replace it with? Come on, this is a great alternative to policing, this is!' Kendra laughed.

'I think we should double the dose and see what happens,' Trevor said. 'It worked a treat, didn't it? Okay, not all of them were affected, but look, most of them were. Imagine if we double it. They won't have a clue that we've spiked their water. They'll think it's something they've eaten.'

'You know what they say, Kendra,' Andy said. 'Keep it simple, stupid.'

'Well, we'd better go out and buy a lot more laxatives,' she said, still laughing.

Road Trip

WITHIN A COUPLE of hours they had returned from various trips to chemists in local villages, with two dozen bottles of the same laxative. Trevor gave them all to Mo, along with instructions to return that night.

'Man, I wouldn't want to be anywhere near that place for weeks,' Mo said. 'This lot will make it horrendous for them in there.'

'That's the plan, Mo. Keep them in the camp where they can't do any harm. There's something else I want you to do if you're up for it? It's the main reason I want you to go back.'

'What's that?'

'I want you to take some of the drugs we stole and plant them in the campsite, preferably in Hawk's caravan.'

'Damn, you really hate that man, don't you? Can I take Amir with me? Those bags were heavy.'

'Yes, I think you'll need to be a team of four tonight, so take whoever you need,' Trevor said. 'How do you figure on getting in the caravan?'

'I'll leave that to my baby brother. He's the sneaky one.'

'That, he certainly is. Go and sort out your team and I'll bring the bags to your car in a few minutes,' Trevor said.

TREVOR HAD THOUGHT LONG and hard about how to deal with Hawk. He had thought of ways to kill him, by himself, to avenge Jacob. None of them would bring his friend back—and Jacob would never have approved. When Andy had recorded the conversation with Hawk, another idea had formed that he was much happier to implement. The drugs would play a big part in that.

'I'm coming for you, Hawk,' Trevor said out loud, 'and you won't see me coming.'

Trevor retrieved two of the holdalls containing the drugs. It was all he needed to make his plan work, and he wanted to keep hold of the other two bags for later in case he needed a back-up plan.

'Here you go, mate,' he told Mo, placing them in the boot, 'remember, wherever you put them must be blamed on Hawk, okay?'

'Like I said, the youngster will sort that out, I'm sure,' Mo said, closing the boot.

As it was too early to go to the camp, they walked back to the gym. It was time for another update. Trevor could sense the excitement as they walked in. They were all talking enthusiastically and there were no signs of nerves or tension.

'Okay, you wonderful people, gather round so that I can tell you a bedtime story,' Trevor said, to much amusement.

'You're finally admitting that you're old then, Grandad,' Charmaine replied.

'Not at all. I feel like a young teacher about to tell off a classroom of toddlers, so less of the old, okay, or there will be no milk and biscuits for you later.'

He was enjoying their confidence and their current mood, so there was no harm in some good old-fashioned banter. If anything, it was a great way to integrate and bond as a team.

'Right then, to serious stuff,' he continued. 'I won't be patting you on the back anymore, it's clearly making some of your heads swell.'

'Dad, get on with it, please,' Kendra said. 'They got it the first time and you're no Kevin Hart.'

'Alright then, fine–hurtful, but fine. As you're aware, we've all been very busy these past couple of days. It's coming together nicely, but there's still much to do. Mo and his team have a tough job tonight. The rest of us will be planning tomorrow's activities.' 'Kendra will tell you what's needed, so listen up, as she'll be dividing you into small teams again.'

'Thanks, Dad. First off, Constable Fellows has promised us a nice parcel, so Darren, can you take one of your boys with you to meet with him? The plan is to meet in the community car park tomorrow morning at a quarter to eight, before he starts work. Does that work for you?'

'Yep, I'm okay with the early starts,' said Darren. 'I'll take Clive with me. He hates mornings, so will scare the bejesus out of the cop if he steps out of line.'

'Great, thanks. I'll be doing much the same with the coroner. I'll meet him before he starts work, to grab the records he's promised us. I'll take Jimmy with me for that. He knows us both.'

'Damn it, I was hoping for a lie-in!' Jimmy exclaimed.

'Well, you can get an early night then, young man,' Kendra replied instantly. His friends from the Midlands took turns in ribbing him.

Trevor let them have their fun before taking over.

'Izzy, Greg and I will go to the warehouse and wait for a delivery to turn up. Andy will let us know the time they're expected and has told them we'll be meeting them outside because of the fire. As a result, we'll have a couple of grand's worth of tools and equipment for the gyms back home, courtesy of Mister Falconer.'

'I'll be keeping a couple of those for Marge, thank you very much,' Andy said, claiming dibs before it was too late.

'Don't worry, Marge will be very well looked after,' Trevor said. 'Finally, Charmaine and Zoe will be our back-ups, floating in the car between us in case anyone needs help. Once Mo and his team are back up and running, we'll see about getting some help from them as well.'

'That's it, for now,' added Kendra. 'If you need anything, just let us know. In the meantime, get yourselves some rest.'

'Andy, did you grab the numbers for the bikers from any of the phones we took? I know Hawk got up and running again with a spare phone, so I'm hoping you have a number for his two deputies,' Trevor said.

'Yep, I have them all,' Andy confirmed.

'Okay, I'll need those for tomorrow.'

'No problem. You can use the phone with the recordings on, can't you?'

'Yes, can you add them to that?'

'Consider it done. You're gonna meet up with them, aren't you?' Andy asked.

'I sure am,' Trevor said, 'and I'll be taking a present for them.'

THE REST of the evening passed by quickly and it was soon time for Mo, Amir, Martin and Rory to go back to the campsite. Trevor and Kendra went with them to the car.

'Be careful, guys,' Kendra said. 'Some of them may struggle to sleep with the state their stomachs are in, so it will be tougher tonight.'

'Don't worry, we'll figure something out,' said Mo. 'My

chief concern is the weight of the bags slowing us down when we're inside, but I'm sure we'll manage.'

'It won't be a problem,' Amir added, 'we've got muscles coming with us, haven't we?' He indicated towards Martin and Rory.

'Always the funny man,' his brother said as they got into the car.

'Take it easy and come back safe,' Trevor said, waving them off.

'I have a funny feeling about this, Dad. Is it a good idea to go back there so soon?'

'Maybe, maybe not, but if you were that lot, would you think anyone would go back anytime soon?'

'I think I'd have someone acting as a lookout for sure,' Kendra said. 'I know they locked up the remaining bikes, but is it enough? I don't know.'

'Well, if there's a guard, then they'll be keeping an eye out on the bikes and not the caravans, I'm sure.'

'Well, it won't be long before we find out, will it?'

THE FOUR INTREPID invaders didn't take long to get to the hidden gate. The campsite was silent, but Mo was vigilant and expecting the worst. They took the long way around to avoid the front of the caravans by skirting the site boundary and keeping to the deepest shadows. They took their time, pausing several times to listen out. There were noises, restless sleepers, and the odd flushing toilet, but nobody had come outside yet.

They continued towards the far end of the site and the caravan behind the water tank, along with Hawk's neighbouring static caravan. After what seemed like an age, due mainly to their cautious approach, they arrived close to their destination. Mo indicated for Rory to give Amir the holdall he'd been carrying, with Martin carrying the other. He pointed to the caravan next to the water tank and gave the thumbs-up to them both. They responded in kind and walked towards it.

Mo and Rory went behind the caravan again and repeated the process from the other night. It took longer, as there was twice as much to be deposited, but he took his time while Rory kept an eye out. He couldn't see what his brother was up to and was a little nervous. He looked at Rory, who gave the nod that all was clear.

Amir and Martin had reached Hawk's caravan. Although it was silent, there was a light on inside, which meant there was a chance Hawk was still awake. That was confirmed almost immediately when they heard a string of profanities coming from inside. Much of his bitter diatribe was aimed at Janice and the rest at the *"Bastard who thinks he can stop me."*

Amir turned to Martin and put his finger to his mouth, to which Martin nodded. Amir then indicated for Martin to follow him, as he crouched low and headed for the opposite side of the caravan, the side closest to the boundary and hedgerow.

'We're not getting inside, mate,' said Amir. 'Even if he's drunk, it'll be a problem. You stay here while I see what the score is with the bikes. Maybe we can do something there, okay? I won't be long.'

He left his holdall with Martin and was soon out of sight. Mo had told him where the pod was that the bikes were locked in, and so he made for it, again keeping to the boundary and the darker shadows. The pod was one of four, so he had a fair amount of ground to cover. As before, he paused frequently to listen for potential danger, so it took longer than he'd have liked.

Reaching the pods, he immediately saw that he'd have problems. The pods had a small decking area in front for guests to sit and talk, or eat outdoors. Amir could see which one was playing host to the bikes because there were two very large Rejects sitting outside the furthest pod. One was fast asleep, his legs extended straight and his head leaning back at an awkward angle over the back of the chair. The other was clearly taking turns in watching the pod and looking at his phone, the light reflecting off his face as he watched a video.

'*Right, then. That's not gonna happen either,*' Amir thought. It took several minutes for him to get back to Martin, by which time he had decided what to do.

'We can't get inside and we can't do anything with his bike, so we'll have to improvise,' he said. 'I'm going to crawl underneath the caravan and hide the bags in the chassis. It's unlikely anyone has ever looked under there, so it's actually not a terrible place to hide stuff. The only issue might be hungry rats eating everything, but that's not our problem, right?'

'Sounds good to me,' Martin replied.

'When I'm under, pass the first one through,' Amir said, before he crawled backwards underneath and out of sight. Martin passed the first holdall to him, pushing it as far as he could before Amir grabbed it. He then did the same with the second. It took a few minutes before Amir reappeared, a big grin on his face.

'I nearly shit myself!' he said. 'There's a badger under there! Luckily, it's a youngster, and I was far enough away not to be a threat, so it just hissed and ran away towards the other caravan. They can be nasty, them things.'

'Man, those things frighten the hell out of me. I would have fainted!' Martin said.

'Well, it's done, so let's get the hell out of here,' Amir replied, happy with the close call and the subsequent result.

They slowly retraced their steps and were soon on the way back, having passed the other caravan and seeing that Mo and Rory had moved on. They were almost at the tree when it happened.

'Get out here, now, Snake!' Razor shouted as he exited the caravan, pulling on his boots. 'There's someone out here. I just heard something underneath.'

Fearing they'd been targeted, the riders were all in a heightened state and soon rushing out to investigate the disturbance. Several were completely naked as they ran over to Razor.

Snake ran out, half dressed, slightly confused but ready for action.

'What's going on?' he asked.

'I just got up to go to the bog–*again*—when I heard noises coming from under the caravan. I bet those bastards have come back,' Razor continued.

'You lot! Get over here and surround it,' Snake shouted to the other riders. They duly responded.

'What the hell is going on out here?' Hawk yelled as he came out to investigate. He was bare-chested and holding a half-empty bottle of vodka but seemed steady on his feet.

'We think they've come back, boss. We've got them trapped under the caravan,' Razor said.

'Well, what are you waiting for? Get under there and drag the bastard out!'

Razor and Snake looked at each other, each willing the other to volunteer. Snake frowned and said, 'You called it, so you go.'

Razor shrugged and took his jacket off.

'Sod this,' he said, crawling under the caravan. 'I can't see a bloody thing; anyone got a torch?'

'Here,' Snake shouted, leaning in and handing him his phone with the torch switched on.

Razor took it and turned the torch towards the dark recesses under their mobile home. He squirmed further in, waving it slowly from side to side. He almost did a double-take when he illuminated two piercing bright blue eyes and the snarling teeth of a juvenile badger, which hissed as soon as the torchlight semi-blinded it. Razor froze, but it was too late – the badger lashed out, hissing furiously. Razor had nowhere to go as the claws hit their mark on his hands, the badger getting more confident—and getting ever closer to his face.

'Aaaarghh! Get me out of here!' he screamed, trying to wriggle out backwards and failing to do so. His colleagues stood and looked at each other, momentarily confused and unsure of what was going on. Was he being attacked by the intruder? Their hesitation was momentary, and they eventually started to close in, making sure to leave no room for the supposed intruder to escape.

Snake reached in and grabbed Razor by the ankle, pulling hard to get his friend out. Another rider grabbed the other leg, and they quickly pulled him to safely.

Razor was shaking, his hands covered in scratches and his jacket slashed in several places.

'What the hell happened, dude?' asked Snake. 'And where's my bloody phone?'

'There's a friggin' dragon under there, man. I dropped the phone when you pulled me out. I think he ate it!'

'Useless idiot,' Hawk said. 'Are you just gonna leave them under there?' He didn't believe a word Razor had said.

'I'm telling you, boss, there's some vicious monster under there, all teeth and evil blue eyes, a bit like...' he decided not to finish the sentence.

'Snake, go and get your phone and pull out whoever's under there,' Hawk ordered, pointing the bottle towards the undercarriage of their home.

Snake wasn't best pleased but looked around for something to take as a weapon. He grabbed a broom and kicked off the head, leaving him with the handle and a chance to ward off at arm's length whatever was under there. He crawled underneath on his stomach.

'Shine some light under here, you lot,' he told his fellow riders. Three of them offered their phones and reached down to illuminate the darkness for him. He pushed the pole out in front of him and crawled forward. The light wasn't great, but it was enough to give him a warning if anything were to come for him.

The badger was waiting and attacked him with the same ferocity as it had Razor. The wooden pole did just enough to keep the badger at bay as it hissed and threatened the intruder.

'Pull me out, pull me out,' he shouted, poking it as hard as he could. His last lunge caught the badger full on the nose and stopped it dead in its tracks. It shook its head violently and then turned and ran off. As Snake was being pulled out, he heard shouting from the other side of the caravan as the animal ran for cover towards the hedgerow, avoiding the riders who swerved out of its way. They wanted nothing to do with the vicious creature.

'It was a bloody badger,' Snake shouted as he stood up, pushing Razor in the shoulder. 'Not a bloody dragon!'

'I'm going back to bed. Thanks for the entertainment, you morons,' Hawk said, turning around and heading back to his caravan.

'Go on, you lot, get back to bed. Nothing to see here,' Snake told the rest.

AMIR AND MARTIN tried desperately not to laugh as they made their way out of the campsite and away from the madness. They met up with Mo and Rory and burst out laughing as they explained what had happened.

'That was close, though, guys. Thank God for the badger, eh?' Mo said.

'Kendra was right to warn us. Some of them were still awake, so they were still feeling the effects,' Rory added.

'Man, are they in for a shock tomorrow when the double dose kicks in,' said Amir. They laughed and made their way back to the car and away, satisfied with another job well done.

18

MISCHIEF

The team was up and ready to go bright and early the following morning. After a light breakfast of cereal and coffee, the three teams and their backup left the still-sleeping laxative-delivering crew while they went off to their respective meetings.

Darren and Clive were at the community centre car park five minutes early and waited for Fellows to arrive. He was exactly on time, parking close next to their car and winding down his window. He reached out and handed Darren a yellow folder.

'Tell your boss that is everything I have. All the payments to myself and others that I've been involved in. I know it means nothing to you guys, but I'm resigning from the police today and handing myself in. Just thought you should know,' Fellows said.

He reversed out of the spot and drove off to meet his fate, leaving Darren to shake his head.

'That's a good thing, right?' Clive asked.

'Yeah, I suppose it is, but he's only doing it to save his arse. He deserves a lot worse than what he's likely to get,' Darren replied.

'Yep, nothing worse than a bent cop. He's got a lot to answer for, the horrible shit. I hope he rots in hell.'

KENDRA AND JIMMY arrived at the coroner's office and saw him waiting in his car. They both got out of their car and he did the same, meeting them under a tree by the side of the office, out of sight of the workers there.

'Here,' he said, handing over a brown envelope that felt very light to Kendra.

'There's not a lot in there,' Kirkbride said, 'just a couple of sheets of paper with some amounts, dates, those involved, and the body in question. I guess I'm ready to face the music now, eh?'

'That depends on how much you help the investigators who come to arrest you,' Kendra said coldly. 'Being corrupt is as bad a start as you can get, so you have a lot of explaining to do and many people to put forward. Only then will they decide whether you've done enough to avoid a lengthy sentence, but you'll never work as a coroner again.'

'I know that much. I had my reasons, but they were never enough to excuse what I did, so my life will change forever. It's like they say–if you don't want to do any time, then don't do the crime.'

'Yeah, well, you helped some very nasty people, so remember that tune when you're staring out of your cell window.'

With that, she turned and walked back to their car, followed by Jimmy. The soon-to-be ex-coroner stared, contemplating his miserable future yet accepting that it could be a lot worse.

Trevor, Izzy and Greg arrived at the deserted warehouse shortly before nine o'clock. They all now wore dark blue overalls and had the look of mechanics. Andy's convincing performance on the phone would make the delivery straightforward.

'I hope we've got enough room in the car,' he told the others as they waited.

The delivery van arrived just before ten, and Trevor approached the driver.

'Hello, mate, you got some tools for us?'

'Yeah, I'll just unload them now. Just give us a signature here, will ya,' he said, handing over a clipboard.

Trevor looked down and saw the list of goods that Andy had ordered on the bikers' account, likely paid for by Falconer, and smiled. He signed his name as J. Falconer II at the bottom, accepting the delivery and walking over to the back of the van.

'We're taking them to the new place that we found yesterday. This place is too far gone to repair now,' he told the driver. 'Reckon we can fit that all in the boot of the Mondeo?'

'Yeah, should be okay,' the driver said. 'It'll be a tight squeeze, but it's a big old boot.'

He started unloading boxes onto a trolley.

Trevor called the others over and said, 'Get this stuff in the boot, will ya,' before going to help the driver with more.

Their haul included a number of cordless drills, grinders, and other power tools, all the top professional brands. There were also several large toolkits, batteries, and more. It took a few minutes to load everything into the car.

'Thanks, mate, you have a nice day,' he said. The driver looked down at the clipboard to confirm it had been signed.

'Thanks, Mister Falconer. Good luck with the new place. Hopefully, it's not as remote as this one.'

They waved him off and were soon back on the road themselves, fully loaded with their goodies.

'Andy will be pleased,' Trevor said. 'Marge is getting an upgrade on her tools.'

BACK AT THE GYM, Andy picked out one toolkit, a new drill, and an angle grinder before the rest of the loot was loaded into the Land Rover.

'The delivery to Falconer's home should be today, too, so I'll keep an eye out and let you know how it goes,' Andy said.

'Thanks, Andy. Can you also let me know when Hawk is away from his two cronies? I need to contact them today and set up a meeting without him knowing all about it,' Trevor replied.

'Yeah, that won't be a problem. In fact, I don't think those two are at the camp at the moment. It looks like they went for something to eat in Cromer. Let me check.'

'Thanks, mate.'

Trevor went back to the gym to make a coffee. He pulled out the burner phone Andy had given him, containing the recording of Hawk. Andy had also added Snake and Razor's phone numbers, so once he knew it was safe to call, he would do so.

A few minutes later, he got a thumbs-up emoji from Andy on his regular phone, with the message, *'Call now.'*

'Okay, here we go,' Trevor said, puffing out his cheeks as he dialled.

'Hello?' came the quizzical response. 'Who's this?'

'That would be telling, wouldn't it, Kevin?' .

The pause was a long one as Snake digested the response. Very few people knew his real name, not even the Rejects.

'What the hell are you calling me for?' he asked.

'I have a proposition for you, Mister Talbot,' Trevor said, rubbing it in further with his surname.

'Just get on with it, mate. This conversation is getting boring. So you know my name, big deal.'

'I also know where your missing drugs are and who is responsible for their theft. Plus, I know something about your boss that you're gonna want to hear, both of you.'

'Why don't you go ahead and tell us what you wanna say and we can go from there,' Snake said.

'Well now, that would be too easy, wouldn't it? No, I like to do my business face to face, mano a mano, as our Spanish cousins like to say.'

There was another pause as Snake debated the offer. He covered the phone and told Razor.

'You up for it?' he whispered. Razor nodded eagerly.

'How do we know this isn't some sort of trick to take us out, too, like you did with Janice,' he asked Trevor.

'You don't, but I'll come alone and tell you everything you need to hear. You have my word that nothing will happen to you, unless you try anything stupid. You can name the place of your choosing and I'll meet you there. The only thing I ask is that you don't tell Hawk, because if he finds out we're meeting, then everything goes up in flames. I can tell you where the drugs are and you can do what you want with them. It's your choice.'

'Why are you doing this?' Snake asked.

'I want you off my turf. You're here under false pretences, serving someone who doesn't give a shit about you. I want you and your bikers out of this county. I'd rather do it quietly and without a fuss, but if you decline, I'll just do it the hard way and it won't be fun for you. Again, it's your choice. You can leave as rich men or in body bags. That's my offer,' Trevor said.

'Call me back in ten minutes and we'll tell you where to meet,' Snake replied, ending the call.

TREVOR LET the phone ring several times before answering.

'Meet us halfway down Cromer Pier in thirty minutes,' Snake said. 'And come alone.'

'I'll see you both there. Do me the same courtesy and we'll be just fine,' Trevor said, hanging up.

He walked back inside and found Mo and his nightprowlers all awake and drinking coffee.

'Amir, are you ready to take the beast back out? I'm meeting with the two scary dudes and need someone to cover my back in case they try anything stupid.'

'Yeah, no problem. When do you need me?' Amir asked.

'I'm leaving in about ten minutes, so if you leave now and get there before me, that may be prudent. I'm meeting them halfway down Cromer Pier, so park somewhere off the main drag and cover from a distance that won't cause any problems,' Trevor said. 'We'll know where their bikes are parked, so if anything happens, take the Land Rover and do some damage to them, got it?'

'Got it, leaving now. Fancy some ice cream, Martin?' Amir asked his new sidekick.

'Never trust a man who says no to ice cream,' Martin said, getting up. 'Count me in.'

'Right, get yourselves down there and I'll be ten minutes behind you. You know what they look like, but keep an eye out for anyone else doing what I've sent you to do, okay?'

'Yes, boss!' Amir saluted, before heading for the door with Martin.

'Mo, you may as well hang around here, in case anything comes up,' Trevor said.

Mo gave a nod as he slurped his tea.

Trevor headed for Marge to see Andy before leaving for the meet.

'Anything happening, Andy?' he asked.

'Nope, it's all quiet so far. I'm keeping a live feed open to Falconer's house so I can see the delivery turning up. I left them a message to just dump everything in front of the house,' Andy said, grinning.

'Yeah, that will be fun to watch. Got any ideas how else we can get this guy?'

'His banking security is very good. Even with his router password, I wouldn't be able to get into his accounts or transfer money like we did with the Albanians. He has two-step authentication set up on everything, along with other security measures. I can see his accounts, though, and almost all of them are almost empty. There is one left, though, that still has over forty million in it, which he has called the Investor Purchasing Account.'

Trevor whistled.

'Yeah, you can buy a lot of land and properties with that, but he'll need a lot more to carry out his plan. He's then got to develop it, which will be another massive amount that will probably come into the account when his plan has succeeded.'

'And there's nothing we can do with that?' Trevor asked.

'I'm good, Trevor, but I'm not the best. It'll take the best of them to find a way into that account. Fortunately, I know just the people,' he said, and grinned.

'Go on then, tell me!'

'I'm going to create an invitation-only auction on the dark web in one of the private areas that I have. I'll invite five or six of the top hackers in the world who'll have an excellent shot at getting in. I'll then basically ask for bids and see what happens. Someone may be up to paying seven figures for it if they are confident of getting in, who knows? Either way, we'll shaft Falconer good and proper and make some money doing it.'

'Do you think they can do it?' Trevor asked.

'I do, especially with the info I'll be showing them. I'll send screenshots of all the account info except for the account number and anything else that identifies the person or the account. They'll get the rest when I've been paid in crypto currency, which we can then use for many other things later,' Andy explained. 'Once I have that in my crypto wallet, then nobody can touch it.'

'Man, you have a very devious mind, you know?' Trevor said, shaking his head.

'I'm blessed with skills that only a few people have, yes,' Andy replied.

'Can you use some of those skills to let us know where the two bikes will be parked in Cromer for the meet? I want the boys to be close by in case anything bad happens.'

'Of course. I told you, I have super skills,' Andy said, grinning.

'Well, aren't you the lucky one? I'd better leave your sainted presence and go to my meeting with the devil's spawn,' Trevor said, heading out of the camper van.

'Let's get ready to shaft you, Mister Falconer,' Andy said out loud as he flexed his fingers and started typing away with a fury.

TREVOR PARKED in the public car park on Runton Road, close to the pier. He scanned the area, looking for more bikers, and saw nothing of concern. He spotted Amir lurking nearby and saw that he was sitting close to the bikes that Andy had just messaged him about. They had parked between a pair of cars on the same road.

He continued walking and was soon at the ornate approach to the Victorian pier. After climbing the unusual, scalloped steps, he entered the pier walkway towards the Pavilion Theatre and Cromer Lifeboat Station. He could see the attraction was busy and a good place to meet if you wanted to avoid any incidents. There were too many witnesses and only one way in and out.

As he made his way along the walkway, he saw the two Rejects waiting in the middle, leaning against the railings and looking menacing. People who saw them avoided eye contact and skirted around them to avoid confrontation. He reached them and looked from one to the other, gauging their reactions to meeting him.

'I thought you'd be bigger,' Trevor said, 'but you're definitely uglier.'

Razor's anger was quick to surface. It took a hand from Snake to hold him back.

'Listen, pal, just tell us what you know and we'll go our separate ways. But make no mistake, if you piss us off, we'll throw you over the fucking railings. Got me?'

Trevor laughed and nodded.

'Calm down, mate. I was just trying to lighten the mood. I told you I had something good to share and I'm a man of my word.'

'Well, spit it out then,' snapped Razor.

Trevor smiled, reaching into his jacket to pull out the phone.

'First off, I know where your drugs are, plus I know who screwed you over. It might surprise you to know that it was your boss, the one and only George Stellenberg,' he said, watching for Razor's reaction.

'What the hell are you talking about?' Snake exclaimed.

'Wait, his name is George?' said Razor.

'It's what I said, guys. Hawk screwed you over. He paid for some of the local muscle to break in and steal the drugs. There are two holdalls hidden at the campsite, right under your noses. He's not planning to share any of the proceeds, by the way.'

'You're lying,' Snake said, his face the picture of doubt. Trevor knew that the bait was well and truly hooked.

'There's more, I'm afraid,' he continued. 'You aren't gonna like this, either.' He pressed play on the recording and watched their expressions as Hawk's statements hit home.

'That's right, they do everything I say because they know I'm the boss. Without me, they're nothing, none of them.

'You're clever, old man, but in this world you're the shepherd or the sheep–a leader or a follower. I'm the biggest, maddest shepherd you'll ever meet. Razor and Snake will do anything I say because they're the sheep, expendable. They all are. Once I'm done here, they'll all be inside or dead. I don't give a shit.'

Snake's face darkened as Trevor switched off the recording. Razor's anger was clear to see. They both seethed, unable to decide what to do next.

Snake turned to Trevor.

'Where are the drugs?'

'They're underneath his caravan. He doesn't expect anyone to suspect him or to even consider that the drugs are at the site. He's telling everyone that I have them, but my source is the best, the guy who stole them from the warehouse.'

'How the hell do you know they're underneath the caravan?' asked Razor.

'Because what you guys don't know is that CCTV covers the site. Hawk crawled under there with two bags, so what else could it be?' Trevor had to think quickly on his feet with that question, one that he hadn't thought through properly.

'What happens now?' Snake asked, glaring at Trevor.

'First, remember that I haven't asked for anything, so stop looking at me like you want to gut me, okay? I'm not the one you want to get angry with, mate,' Trevor replied, standing his ground.

'Why are you doing this, then?' Snake asked.

'I told you: I want you bastards off my turf. Your boss is

helping someone take over the area and I don't want that. It's bad for my business. What I want is for you to sort your boss out and get the hell out of my town,' Trevor said. 'Nothing more, nothing less. I told you, this can happen peacefully, where you believe what I say and and piss off. Or we can do it the nasty, vicious way, where I take you out one by one and get my town back that way. It'll take a lot longer, but I will get it back.'

Snake and Razor exchanged a look and nodded.

'I'll call you tonight when you've realised that I'm on your side and we can talk again,' Trevor said.

The pair walked away, back towards their bikes, without even looking at Trevor again. As he walked back towards the car park, he saw the two bikes leaving toward Sheringham. Toward Hawk.

TREVOR WAS BACK at the gym fifteen minutes later, just in time to watch the hilarious scenes of Falconer berating his security staff and the driver of the lorry that had just dumped two pallets of goods onto his drive.

The driver pointed to his clipboard and then threw his arms up in the air and walked back to his lorry. Seconds later he was on his way, leaving Falconer to ponder what he was going to do with a pallet of motorcycle oil, hundreds of oil filters, and as many brake disks.

'He probably thinks it was Hawk ordering for his bikers, which is why he let the lorry leave – the doubt is there, isn't it?' Andy said.

'Should be a lot of fun watching them figure out where to put that stuff and who's going to do it,' Trevor replied.

'Nine thousand quid wasted,' said Andy, 'and it's about to get a lot worse for him. This is a tiny inconvenience compared to the loss he's going to experience after the auction.'

'When is that, by the way?'

'Tonight.'

19

AUCTION

Snake and Razor waited until Hawk had left the site, allegedly to meet with the benefactor about some supplies that had been delivered to his estate by mistake. As soon as he was clear of the site, they headed over to Hawk's caravan to find out for themselves whether he had betrayed them all.

'Keep an eye out. I'm going to get underneath and take a look,' said Snake.

Razor nodded and sat on Hawk's top step.

Snake turned on the torch on his phone and crawled underneath, wary of the vicious blue-eyed badger that had attacked the previous night. He checked the places where it was feasible to hide the two large holdalls, such as behind the wheel mountings and where the plumbing came out, but he saw nothing there. It didn't take long, however, before he saw something that he knew could be the holdalls – a strap that was hanging down from the chassis. He crawled over and pulled the handle. The holdall dropped beside him, confirming his fears. He saw the other one wedged in and pulled that one down, too.

'Is anyone around?' he asked Razor.

'No, it's dead quiet out here, except for lots of flushing toilets. It's weird.'

'Here, grab this,' Snake said, 'and put it somewhere that nobody can see it.'

He pushed the first holdall out to Razor, who grabbed it and quickly placed it behind their caravan, out of sight.

'Same again,' Snake said.

The second holdall quickly followed and was also hidden. Snake had one last look around to see whether he could find more, but soon decided that there wasn't anything and crawled back out.

'It's true,' Razor said, stern-faced. 'Hawk has been screwing us over.'

Snake was livid. He had trusted Hawk with his life, and this was how he was being repaid?

'Do you remember what he said on the recording? He doesn't give a shit whether we're inside or dead. Do you know what that means?' he said.

'What?'

'It means that if he's willing to screw us over with the drugs, then he's willing to sacrifice us to the cops. He's probably planning to grass us all up and keep the drugs money all to himself.'

'What the hell are we gonna do about it?' asked Razor.

'Well, first off, we're gonna hide these drugs where he can't get to them. We'll sort that out when we're done with Hawk, just me and you. Got it?'

'What have you got in mind?'

'I think we should give him a taste of his own medicine,

don't you? We wait until that other bastard calls us tonight and we'll deal with them both – our way.'

'Here's the plan,' Trevor told the rest of the team. 'I'm going to call the two bikers later tonight to see if they found the drugs. When they say they have, then I'll tell them I want to meet Hawk at Beeston Bump, where he killed Jacob. I'll tell Hawk to bring his two men if he's worried, and that I'll come alone.'

'What will the meeting be for?' Charmaine asked.

'To negotiate for the return of the drugs and to leave the area,' Trevor said. 'By now he may have heard from Falconer, so he's gonna need all the drugs and money he can muster.'

'What's he heard, Trev?' asked Darren.

'Andy, wanna tell 'em?' Trevor said, turning to him.

'Yeah, I can do that. Basically, we now know that Falconer is in trouble financially and is resorting to desperate measures for his development, including drug dealing on a grand scale, along with hiring the Rejects to cause havoc and scare the locals away,' Andy said. 'The drugs that were picked up by a buyer from Ipswich yesterday were intercepted by the police on the A14 near Claydon, on the way to their patch. There was a short chase, but the police were ready. Apparently, the buyers were well-known to them. Anyway, they ended up using a rolling stop and arresting them at gunpoint. The drugs were seized, and the buyers are currently in custody.'

There were cheers from the team.

'That's excellent,' Darren said. 'Nobody likes a scumbag drug dealer.'

'The best part is, they'll be blaming Falconer and going back for more drugs or their money back. His situation just got a lot worse,' Kendra added.

'Anyway, we're not done yet,' said Trevor. 'I'm calling for the meet, but I won't be going. I want to add some doubt and confusion to the situation. When they call to ask where I am, I'll just tell them I've changed my mind.'

'Ooh, they won't like that,' Amir said. 'Nobody likes to be ghosted, Trevor.'

'Things are falling apart for them, which is exactly what we set out to do. I won't stop until Hawk has paid for killing Jacob. The rest of them will pay for the carnage they've caused in this area. None of them will get away with anything, I promise you,' he added.

'What do we do next, then?' Mo asked.

'We want to see how the next phone call goes and the reaction to me not turning up to the meet. I'm guessing we'll have to get the police involved soon, so we can start getting the evidence ready. Can anyone think of anything else that needs doing or anything we should consider?' Trevor asked.

'Has anything happened yet with the bent cop and the coroner?' asked Jimmy.

'No, but that's not unexpected. The police will need time to conduct their own checks and investigations before putting a plan together,' Kendra said. 'It takes time.'

'But won't that give them time to destroy evidence?' Mo asked.

'Not really. Remember, we have some records already. They'll check bank accounts and phone records, along with computer records and anything else that can be used against them in court, stuff that can't be deleted from systems. If they are stupid enough to destroy anything, then it just makes them look that much more guilty – plus they'll leave themselves open to other serious offences.'

'Good, those bastards need sorting out,' Mo said.

'They will be, don't worry,' said Kendra.

'Alright then, just chill out here for a while and we'll update you when we know more,' Trevor said.

'I'm going to check and see how many have registered an interest in the auction,' Andy said as he left the gathering.

'I'll go with you,' Kendra said, following. 'I want to see the recording of the campsite again. I think we should put it on YouTube for the world to enjoy.'

'Kendra, nobody wants to see a bunch of hairy-arsed bikers running for the toilet,' Trevor said.

'You wanna bet? Our generation loves that sort of thing, right, Andy?'

'Hell, yes,' Andy said, 'it's gold.'

WHEN THEY WERE BACK inside the camper van, Andy switched on all the monitors covering the campsite and Falconer's house. Amir had retrieved the cameras from the warehouse as their work was done there, so only the two feeds were left for them to check.

'Right, let's see who's been in touch,' Andy said, logging on to his dark web account.

'While you're doing that, I'll just find that recording,' Kendra said, smiling.

'Holy crap on a stick!' Andy exclaimed.

'What is it?' Kendra turned to him, concerned.

'Sixteen people have registered an interest in Falconer's

financials. Two of them have put bids in of more than a million-and-a-half dollars.'

'Blimey, that's amazing,' she said. 'That means they're confident, right?'

'Absolutely, it does. Some of these guys specialise in banking fraud at the highest level, so they can do much more than I ever could. I can get into accounts that have nominal security, but these guys can get into far more secure accounts. They have people in banks that work for them: tellers, managers, owners, the lot. They use clone phones and technology to divert messages. You wouldn't believe the tech they have at their disposal. I know a couple that do work on the quiet for governments. That's how good they are!'

'What are you going to do?' Kendra asked.

'I'm going to ask them to send me sealed bids. They'll have one hour to comply and then we'll have a winner.'

'That's great, Andy. They do all the hard work and we get a nice little pay out,' she said.

'Having this persona on the dark web is perfect for our scheme. It's basically untraceable. Once I receive the payment in my crypto wallet, I can transfer it into our overseas account and nobody will have a clue where it's from.'

'It's helping a lot, isn't it? Having the money to buy what we need to bring scumbags to justice is so satisfying, especially as it's the scumbags who are funding it.'

'Yeah, that is the best part,' Andy said. 'Now, where is that recording? We have an hour to play with before I discover what the high bid is.'

'How much?' Trevor said. He couldn't believe his ears.

'Two-and-a-half million dollars!' Kendra said.

'Seriously? Someone has paid that just for some banking information?'

'Not just any banking information, Trevor, banking information for an account with forty million pounds in it. Also his router info and password; that's included and will help them greatly. By the way, almost all of that is investor money, so there'll be plenty more people going after Falconer when this comes out.'

'Wow, Andy, just wow. Two and a half million dollars? Man, you live in a very different world to mine. I'm just glad you're on our side!'

'I wouldn't have it any other way, Trev. Now, isn't it time you made that call?'

'I'll do it now,' Trevor said, taking out the burner phone from his pocket. 'Where is Hawk now?'

Andy checked the GPS tracker and said, 'He's at the Falconer estate.'

'WHAT DO YOU MEAN? Are you saying you didn't order this shit?' Falconer asked.

'That's exactly what I'm saying,' Hawk replied. 'Why would I order something and have it shipped here?'

'I don't bloody know, do I? I saw it was a bunch of biker stuff and assumed it was for you. What the hell is going on here?'

'What does the delivery note say?' Hawk took the slip from Falconer. He scrutinised it carefully before responding.

'Shit.'

'What?'

'According to this,' said Hawk, 'the order was placed and paid for from the business account that I set up for the Rejects. Only a couple of other people know enough about the account to do this. I bet it was that bitch Janice, as a parting gift.'

'Well, that's just dandy. Best you start moving this crap off my drive,' Falconer said.

'Dammit, why would she do this?'

'I don't give a crap, just get rid of it, okay?'

Hawk's phone rang. It showed as an unknown number, which he usually ignored, but in light of what had been going on, he answered.

'I'm in the market for some cheap oil and motorcycle spares. I heard you might have some,' Trevor said, laughing.

'What the hell do you want? I told you that our business is done and I don't care what you do,' Hawk replied.

'I think you do care, George. You care that you've got no drugs left. You care that your girlfriend has done a runner. But most of all, you really should care about what's still to come. Does Daddy know about the drugs being seized from the Ipswich mob yet?'

Hawk's blood ran cold. 'W... what are you talking about?'

He turned to look at Falconer, who was now also on his phone, and who looked equally agitated.

'You know what I'm talking about, boy. I know more about you than you think, all of you, and I won't stop until you have all been ground into the dirt.'

Hawk was lost for words. He covered the phone and turned to Falconer, who stood there in shock, white as a sheet.

'They know about the Ipswich buyer and about you. I

have a bad feeling about this. What does he mean the drugs were seized?'

'That was them on the phone, threatening to cut my head off if I don't give their money back because the drugs were seized by the police yesterday on the way from here. How the hell do they know any of that? What do they want?' Falconer asked, trying not to shout. Panic was seeping into their situation and, for the first time, he wasn't in control.

Hawk brought the phone back to his ear. 'What do you want?' he asked, trying to keep down the bile that was now threatening to erupt from his mouth.

'First off, I need to know you'll be leaving the area, make that the county–permanently. Second, I want you to tell me, face to face, exactly what happened with Jacob, at the same spot that you pushed him over the cliff.'

'Why the hell do you need to know that?' Hawk spat.

'I want to know exactly why he had to die. Why there? I need to know so I can tell his family.'

'Why can't I tell you over the phone?'

'Because I want to look into your eyes, those scary-ass, nasty eyes of yours, to see if you're telling the truth.'

'You won't be able to see Jack,' Hawk said.

'Well, that's the deal. If you want your drugs back, then that's what I want in return.'

'How do I know you're not gonna screw me over again?' Hawk said, touching the cheek that Trevor had hit the last time.

Trevor laughed. 'I did enjoy that. Thank you for the memory. Tell you what, bring your two henchmen with you and I'll come alone. I told you what I want, nothing more. You have my word that I won't lay another finger on you.'

'When?' Hawk asked after a momentary pause.

'Tonight's as good a time as any. Meet me at the top of Beeston Bump at ten o'clock and I'll bring the drugs. Simple,' Trevor said.

'I'll be there with my men,' Hawk replied.

'Just one thing, George.'

'What's that?'

'You try to double-cross me and I'll make sure that you all vanish from this planet. Every one of you, including Daddy,' Trevor said, ending the call.

'Well? What was that all about?' Falconer asked.

'We may be able to salvage something tonight. If he's true to his word, we'll get the drugs back they took from the warehouse. That, with what little you have left, may be enough,' Hawk said.

'Let's hope he's true to his word because we are pretty skint and I do not want to be using the investors' money– they'll skin me alive.'

'I'll sort it out,' Hawk said. 'If it means starting a war with this lot then it'll be worth it.'

20

BEESTON BUMP

The team gathered at the gym to find out what they needed to do next. They were nearing the end game and keen to see it through to its conclusion.

'We're close now, ladies and gents. Violence and drug issues have come to a standstill now. The bikers are still cowering down at the site feeling sorry for themselves, having gone through a record amount of toilet paper,' Trevor said, getting a few laughs. 'The bent cop has resigned but will still go to prison for being a corrupt shit. Same for the coroner. Neither will be able to even get a whiff of a decent job again after they're released.'

'Good riddance to bad rubbish,' Charmaine shouted out, to applause.

'Exactly,' said Trevor. 'Our friend Hawk has lost his girlfriend and almost all his bikes, so as a motorbike gang, they're pretty useless now. They also lost their drugs and a bunch of money. His daddy, Falconer, who started all this by hiring the bikers to do his dirty work, has just been told that the police have seized the drugs he's been selling–and that his buyers are after their money. It's not been a good couple of days for them, has it?'

'It's gonna get a lot worse,' Kendra added. 'He's now being investigated by the National Trust and also by English Heritage, who will stop him from carrying out any developments in the area by issuing protection orders. Everything he's doing will have been for nothing; he will lose everything by the time we're finished with him.'

'Wow, they won't be inviting us to any parties any time soon, will they?' Amir added.

'They will not. The only parties they'll be having are the ones where they're served porridge and a slice of bread and butter in prison, with an extra cherry at Christmas if they're well behaved,' Trevor said. 'I should also add that we may assist in the theft of his entire development fund, courtesy of some specialists. No, things are not looking good for them at all.

'What now then, Trev? What's left to do?' asked Mo.

'Now we wait and hope that we can avenge Jacob's death, the main reason we came here. I've arranged for a meeting with the man responsible tonight, but I'll not be going. I want him to stew a little longer. Then I'll set him up for the police to swoop in, hand over the evidence, and leave them to it. He'll go to prison for a very long time.

'There is one other thing we want to do,' said Kendra, 'which may be a little tricky. Before it gets dark, I need a couple of you to go up to Beeston Bump and place some cameras around the area of the meet. I'm hoping it will help us get more evidence of them at the place where they killed Jacob. It will be hard for them to explain it away as a coincidence.' 'Also, Dad has planted the seeds of discontent with his deputies, so they won't be too happy with their leader.

When the police show them the evidence, we think they'll turn on him. That's the plan, anyway.'

'Mo and Amir, are you okay with the cameras?' Trevor asked.

'Yeah, no problem,' said Mo.

'Andy will give you the kit. The earlier you go, the better. Keep an eye out just in case.'

'The rest of you hang fire for now,' said Kendra. 'There's not a lot we can do until the meeting is over and Dad calls back to stir the pot a little more.'

ANDY GAVE the twins four cameras each and showed them on the map where they should be placed. They were cameras with night-vision capabilities, so the detail would be more than adequate for their purposes. It wouldn't be easy, so they'd need to get creative.

'Take some wooden stakes, string, tape, whatever you think will help you put them somewhere they won't be seen by walkers while there is daylight. It won't matter at night, as nobody will see them,' Andy said.

'That won't be a problem, there's plenty of long grass and bushes to use, as well as the odd bench, lots of hiding places,' Amir said.

'As long as you get a good spread over the area, then they should give us some good footage of them at the site,' Andy confirmed. 'Let me know when they're in place and switched on so I can start the feeds.'

'Easy peasy. We can do this in our sleep.'

'Yeah, I know,' Andy said, 'but can you do it with all the dogs running around and peeing on everything?'

'What dogs? Pee?'

'Just make sure you don't put them anywhere a dog can cock its leg,' Andy added, laughing.

THE TWINS PARKED by the pitch-and-putt course and walked up the winding, narrow path to the place they knew, from Trevor's description, that Jacob had been thrown from. There were plenty of places to hide the cameras that covered a relatively wide area. The long grass helped, along with a park bench fifty metres away that they could use not only for the wide-angle view, but in particular that gouge in the cliff itself.

Amir made a beeline for the gouge first, knowing that it would be a great vantage point and the closest they'd be able to place a camera. He walked almost to the edge of the two-hundred-foot drop and dug a shallow hole at one side of the gouge, facing inwards. Placing the camera in the hole, he then covered it with the sandy soil, leaving just the lens showing.

'That should do it,' he thought.

He repeated the process on the other side, which would give a great wide angle for Andy to view on his monitors, giving a clear, unobstructed view of the path and both ways leading to the dreadful drop. If anything were to happen here, then these cameras would be of great benefit.

Mo walked to the bench in the distance and stuck a small camera on one of the rear wooden legs, facing the gouge and the approaches. He then walked back towards Amir and placed two more cameras, one on either side of the path, again facing the gouge. Amir had walked back towards the way they had walked and placed his remaining cameras similarly. The seven cameras gave a wide view of the area and were well hidden from passers-by.

As they walked back towards their car, Mo called Andy and told him that the cameras were in place.

'Can you check they're working?' he asked.

'Standby, old chap, let me just log on to the system. Ah, here we go. Seven cameras are online, in good shape and with lovely clear images. Good work, guys,' Andy said.

'Thanks, Andy. I figured I'd leave one camera for the parking area in case it was useful. Give me ten minutes and that will be online too.'

'Great, see you when you get back.'

The twins retraced their steps down the narrow path and exited by the putting course. The gravel and sand area leading to the road was often used by walkers for parking their cars. There was room for half a dozen if they squeezed them in. Mo figured the bikers would leave their bikes as close to the path as possible and so attached the final camera to the dog poo bin, figuring–rightly–that nobody would want to go near it unless they were making a deposit.

'He was wrong about the dogs, though,' Amir said as they walked the short distance to their car, 'but if that bin is anything to go by, then we had an escape, brother.'

'Maybe you did, but that smell is in my nose and won't leave, so lucky you. Now let's get back to the lovely warm gym. It was bloody cold up there, bro.'

SNAKE AND RAZOR were the first to arrive, thirty minutes early. The deputies wanted to make sure the area was clear and that they weren't being set up. They parked their bikes next to the low wall opposite the putting course and started their climb up the dark path. They were both familiar with the place from the time they had brought the victim to Hawk , so they walked slowly towards it, checking every bush for anyone who might be hiding, and using their phone torches to look for tell-tale signs. Fortunately, the place they were aiming for wasn't too far from the start of the path, so it didn't take too long to reach it.

There was plenty of moonlight for them to have the meeting without concerns; they'd be able to see people approaching – and anyone approaching at this time of the night was bound to be unfriendly. They could hear the waves below, ironically a peaceful, relaxing sound that people came from far and wide to experience. They checked the path past the gouge, moving away in the opposite direction, as far as the steep steps leading up to the highest part of the bump. Happy that there was no danger, they went back to wait for Hawk.

Hawk himself also turned up a few minutes early. He had prepared for the meeting with a couple of stiff drinks before the ride over. It helped his confidence and–in his eyes–gave him an edge. He was prepared for the worst but hoping for a swift conclusion to the disasters of the past few days. All he had to do was wait for the man responsible and deal with him as he saw fit.

'Nice to see you reprobates here nice and early,' he said as he approached his two deputies.

'Always prepared, boss,' Razor said, coldly.

'Happy to hear it, Razor,' Hawk replied, 'let's hope this bastard is true to his word, eh?'

'Yes, let's hope that, indeed,' Snake said, equally cold.

'What's up with you two wankers?' Hawk asked, suddenly

realising that his men weren't their usual aggressive selves, angry weapons that he had used so effectively in the past.

Before either could reply, Snake's phone rang. He knew immediately that it would be Trevor, or *the enemy*, as he liked to think of him.

'What?' he asked.

'Is Hawk with you? Put me on speaker.'

'What's going on?' Hawk asked.

'Hey, Hawk! What's up, bro? Sorry, man, but I decided not to take you up on your generous offer. I just can't trust you, man. You are more devious than anyone I've ever met.'

'What the hell are you talking about?' Hawk shouted. 'Are you taking the piss again? You brought us up here to have a laugh, did you?'

Trevor laughed out loud, enraging Hawk, who spun around angrily.

'That's right, Hawk, it's funny, isn't it? I'll tell you what I'm gonna do instead. I'm gonna send the police everything I have about you, including your confession to killing my mate. How's that sound?'

'What the hell are you talking about? What confession?'

'Wow, you forget so quickly. Tell you what, I'll play it for you,' Trevor said.

The first recording played through Snake's phone: *'Let's call it quits, eh? I killed Jacob, you smashed my face in. Or I tell you what, you can kill my brother. How's that?'*

The second was a bonus: *'You're clever, old man, but in this world you're the shepherd or the sheep—a leader or a follower. I'm the biggest, maddest shepherd you'll ever meet. Razor and Snake will do anything I say because they're the sheep, expendable. They all are. Once I'm done here, they'll all be inside or dead. I don't give a shit.'*

'Oops! You weren't supposed to hear that one,' Trevor said. 'Sorry about that. But you get the gist, right?'

'You... you... piece of...' was all Hawk could get out before Trevor interrupted.

'Anyway, gotta love ya and leave ya. I have places to visit, people to see, that sort of thing. Catch you later... George,' Trevor said, ending the call abruptly.

'Shit! Shit! That bastard!' Hawk screamed, stomping the ground like a teenager having a tantrum. He paid no attention to his deputies, who were staring angrily at him.

He didn't see them approach, both holding their favourite wrenches.

By the time he realised what was happening, it was too late.

'IF THAT DOESN'T DRIVE him nuts,' said Trevor, 'then I don't know what will. Hopefully, he'll do something stupid. His overconfidence will be his downfall, especially when his mates turn on him and give evidence against him.'

'Yep, looks like he's having a bit of a rage,' Kendra said, watching the feed.

'Oh, that doesn't look good,' Andy said, pointing to one of the monitors.

The view was from one of the two cameras that Amir had placed near the gouge, pointing inwards. It showed Snake and Razor approaching Hawk, both holding large wrenches.

'He hasn't seen them. Bloody hell,' Trevor said.

It took only two blows, one from each, to send Hawk to the floor. He put one hand on the ground to steady himself and one on his head where he was hurt. He was clearly dazed.

'Leave it, lads, leave it,' Trevor whispered, hoping it was payback for what Hawk had said and nothing more.

They did not leave it.

Grabbing one arm each, they lifted Hawk to his feet. He was unsteady and disoriented, so it took little effort to guide him towards the edge of the cliff. As they got there, the team lost the camera feed because of the acute angle. What came next was picked up from the camera that was attached to the bench, fifty metres away.

'Oh my God,' Kendra said, as they watched Snake and Razor push Hawk off the cliff.

21

ARRESTS

They found Hawk at the bottom of the cliff early the next morning, in the same place Jacob had been found. The dog walker who had found him was still shaking hours after he had discovered the body.

'Those eyes, I've never seen anything like it,' the man said, shaking his head as if to clear it of the memory. 'Staring at me, like something out of a horror film.'

'Don't worry, sir, they were probably just some of those fancy contact lenses that are so fashionable with youngsters nowadays,' said the police officer who handed him a cup of tea back at the station.

'Yes, I suppose you're right,' the man said, taking a sip.

'I'll be speaking to the council about that cliff. That's the second person who's fallen to their death there in the last few weeks,' added the police officer.

'Not sure how to process that,' Kendra said as they drank coffee back at the gym.

It had been a tough night, all of them unsure how to deal with seeing someone being thrown to their death.

'Poor Jacob,' Trevor mused. 'Watching that reminded me of him. It breaks my heart to think of what he must have gone through in the moments leading up to ... you know.'

'It isn't worth dwelling on it, Dad,' Kendra said. 'He would have died instantly and there's nothing anyone could have done about it. The man responsible has met the same fate, so I suppose justice has been served, in a way.'

'Not quite,' Trevor said. 'Hawk might have been the one who threw him off the cliff, but it wouldn't have happened if it wasn't for Falconer. He's just as much to blame.'

'Well, he will not be free for much longer, from my reckoning,' Andy said. 'Pretty much every agency in the country is going to want to talk to him.'

'It doesn't feel like it's enough,' said Trevor.

'You say that, but it will ruin his life on a massive scale,' said Andy. 'He'll be completely skint by tonight, probably. However you spin it, that was his son that was thrown off the cliff. Plus, his dream, everything he worked towards, is in complete ruins and will never happen. And if that isn't enough, he'll almost certainly be arrested and imprisoned for his part in this, if they can find the evidence.'

'Yeah, he's screwed,' said Kendra.

'What about those two?' Trevor asked, pointing to the screen showing Snake and Razor frozen in the act of throwing Hawk.

'Well, they're in a world of pain, too,' Kendra said. 'That is murder in anyone's book. We just need to send this anonymously and hope the police can use it to get a confession out of them. Additionally, they still have two holdalls of class-A drugs hidden back at the camp. They'll be away for most of the rest of their lives.'

'That's a point,' Andy said. 'What about the other two holdalls? What are you doing with those, destroying them?'

'I figure we give them back to the bikers. You know, give them a little hope for the future–just before the police raid them and arrest them all for dealing with those same drugs,' Trevor said. 'The area has been blighted recently, and the blame has been entirely placed on the biker gang, who went to great pains to be overt about it. It's backfired on them hugely, hasn't it? They thought they'd be rich from Falconer's plan, but they have now lost everything, too.'

'That could work,' Kendra said. 'How are you going to return them?'

'I'll send Amir and Mo back tonight and they can hide them somewhere the police will find them,' he replied.

'I'm okay with that. I mean, they're a nasty bunch, but they didn't kill anyone,' Kendra said.

'We did torch their bikes and give them the worst case of diarrhoea they've ever had,' Andy added, 'so a little time in the clink for drugs won't do them any harm.'

'Okay, I'll sort that out,' said Trevor.

'Can you have them retrieve the cameras from Beeston Bump, too, please?' Andy asked.

'Sure,' Trevor said as he left them.

'Can you put the footage on a flash drive that I can send to the police, please, Andy?' Kendra asked. 'It'll be anonymous, so hopefully they'll have some good shots of them doing the deed.'

'Yeah, don't worry. I'll sort it out.'

'It's all a bit surreal,' she said. 'It seems like it's all over, but it doesn't feel great, d'you know what I mean?'

'Yep, I do,' Andy replied. 'It turned into something much bigger and nastier than we thought it would, so it's natural to think that we've either done an awful job or we could've done it differently. Your dad must be thinking it's his fault that Hawk died. Whatever he thought of him, however much he hated him, I can tell you he didn't want him dead.'

'No, he didn't, because he's a good man, a decent man. I'll speak to him,' she said.

They sat in silence for a few minutes, thinking back on the events of the past week.

'Some road trip, eh?' Andy finally said.

IT WAS EARLY AFTERNOON, and the bikers were still struggling with the effects of the laxative. Snake and Razor had returned in the early hours of the morning and planned their next moves. They had left it until the following afternoon to let the rest of them know of Hawk's fate.

'Hawk is dead,' Snake told the rest of the gang. 'That bastard that has been messing with us threw him off the damned cliff in revenge for killing his mate.'

There was shock in the ranks as they struggled to process what they'd been told.

'What are we gonna do about it?' asked one.

'What's gonna happen to us now? We have no bikes and no leader,' asked another.

The grumbling started, much as Snake had anticipated. The gang had been through a lot. There had been the highs at the beginning, the promises, the new bikes, the money. Then there'd been the lows of losing the bikes, losing the drugs, the diarrhoea episodes, and now losing their charismatic leader, the man who had promised them the world. The man they'd believed in.

'There's bugger all we can do now; the police are all over it and the bloke responsible is nowhere to be found. We can't do a thing, and he knows it,' said Snake.

'What now then, Snake?' asked another. 'There's sod all left for us here, isn't there?'

'I don't know about you,' he replied, 'but I don't really wanna stick around much longer. Now that Hawk has left us, I'm gonna head back to London and see if I can figure out what to do next. I'll be leaving tomorrow morning.'

'Me too,' Razor added.

'What about us?' asked several bikers at once.

'What the hell do you want me to do?' replied Snake angrily. 'I'm in the same boat as you lot, aren't I?'

'Not really, mate, you still have your bikes. We haven't got diddly squat.'

'Listen, that's fair enough. I'm just upset about this whole thing, okay? Tell you what, I'll leave you with some money so you can all get home. Here,' he said, pulling out a large wad of cash that he'd taken from Hawk before throwing him to his death..

'Here's five hundred quid. You can hire a minibus or two and get yourselves back home. I wish I could do more, but I need some money for myself for when I get to London.'

'This won't help much, Snake, but we appreciate it. You didn't have to give us anything,' the man said, nodding his thanks.

'Spend some of that money on a good drink before you go, may as well, eh?' Razor added.

The bikers dispersed slowly, still grumbling, with very little hope for the future.

'That could've gone a lot worse,' Razor said.

'Yep,' said Snake. 'The sooner we get out of here, the better. We'll grab the two bags later when they're all asleep and transfer the drugs into our own bags, just in case. And we'll just go.

'I'll be glad to see the back of this place, Snake. Not a lot has gone right for us since we got here,' Razor said.

'Yeah, well, once we're back in London, we'll be able to clear up with the drugs,' Snake replied. 'It'll set us up for life, mate, don't you worry.' He grinned at his mate, who momentarily thought that he looked like a demon.

Better not keep my back to him, Razor thought as they made their way to their caravan.

Mo, Amir and Martin returned to the campsite that night. When they were happy that the coast was clear, they made their way to the static homes and hid the remaining two holdalls underneath two different caravans. With the tipoff to the police, they'd be found easily, and at least two lots of bikers would be in deep trouble. Fingers would be pointed, and the gang would likely all turn against each other.

While the trio were completing their job for the night, Andy was placing an anonymous call to Norfolk Constabulary Headquarters from an untraceable phone.

'I need to speak to the duty officer urgently,' he told the operator.

Eventually, after answering a bunch of questions and maintaining anonymity, Andy was put through to the night duty CID officer. It was the best they could do in the early hours of the morning.

'This is DC Allen; how can I help?'

'Listen carefully, DC Allen. One biker gang, the Rejects, has carried out the violence and the drug crimes in the Cromer and Sheringham areas these past weeks. They are about to leave town, having caused chaos, so you will have to hurry if you want to arrest them with a large quantity of class-A drugs.'

'I'm listening,' came the reply.

'Good, because you'll only get one shot at this. They are currently at the site in Overstrand, next to the farm in Craft Lane. It's the one with the pods and static caravans. They have hidden their drug supply underneath the caravans, so you'll have to search for them.'

'How do you know about this?' asked the DC.

'Because I saw them.'

'So you're one of them?'

'No, I am not, but I can promise you the drugs find of the century for North Norfolk, if you pull your finger out.'

'Okay, how many of them will there be?'

'There's over twenty there, and they're nasty as hell, so take lots of backup and a search team.'

'You sound like you know your stuff,' said the DC.

'I do. There's more,' Andy replied.

'Still listening.'

'There was a body found this morning at the bottom of the cliffs in Sheringham, where someone was thrown off Beeston Bump,' Andy teased.

'How do you know it was murder?' the detective constable asked.

'Because I have footage of the man being thrown off the cliff, that's why,' Andy replied, 'and they're also at the site.'

There was silence as the police officer mulled over the information.

'I know it sounds crazy, but if you give me your email address, I will send you the footage now,' Andy said.

'Oh, you're serious!' Allen exclaimed. 'You have video evidence of the murder?'

'That I have. Email address?'

Allen spelled out his email address twice to make sure.

'I'll send it via a file transfer site as it is too big a file for email,' Andy said, 'so it'll take a minute or two.'

'It's three o'clock in the morning and I was almost asleep when you called, so I'm good, thanks.'

'Like I said, you get one shot at this because they'll be gone to the wind tomorrow. If you're a good detective, then you'll know what to do. Are the files there yet?'

'They just turned up now. Let me just check. Okay, there's several videos. I'm just opening one up now.'

Andy waited on the line as the detective viewed the recordings.

'Bloody hell,' DC Allen exclaimed.

'Remember, you have little time. It's your chance to nick a couple of murderers and a stack of drugs like you've never seen. This could be your moment, Detective Allen. I suggest you grab it with both hands and hold on tightly,' Andy said, ending the call.

'Hello?'

Allen sat back in his chair. He'd been a detective for several years and was proactive and diligent, considered highly amongst his peers. He hated night duty because nothing ever happened–until now.

'Bloody hell,' he repeated. 'I'll not complain about night duty again,' he added, picking up the phone to his boss.

'Hello, Guv? Yeah, sorry for waking you, but this is urgent. Yeah, you can stick me on tomorrow, but listen up before you get too angry...'

It took just a few minutes to explain to his boss. DCI Montrose then called his boss and was also threatened and sworn at. Within thirty minutes, they had mobilised a reactive team of fifty officers from all over the county, including dog handlers and specialist firearms officers, along with a search team.

They did not want to let this lot get away.

AT SIX O'CLOCK IN the morning, the wooden gate to the site was quietly opened by one of the entry team. The forty-odd officers fanned out and surrounded the caravans, which were each then approached by teams of two or three officers with dogs, and firearms officers in attendance as back-up. At four-minutes-past six, the whistle was blown by the senior officer on site and the caravans were stormed. Strangely, few of them had locked doors, so it was a rapid entry and almost all occupants were arrested with minimum resistance. Several instinctively lashed out in their half-asleep state, but they were not at their best and were subdued without having injured any officers.

The result of the rapid raid was a tremendous success for the police, who had their targets in custody and two holdalls containing class-A drugs seized, along with smaller amounts for personal use, and some offensive weapons. All the targets were arrested except for two, who had left the site on their motorbikes well before midnight on the pretext of getting something to eat. The two that were wanted for murder. Snake and Razor had made good their escape from the rest of the bikers, with their rucksacks and panniers stuffed with drugs that would change their lives forever. They both laughed as they left the town and rode towards the A148 and freedom.

What Snake and Razor were unaware of was that Andy still had the tracker units on their bikes and knew exactly where they were. And so did the following police units, with whom Andy had liaised – anonymously, but in great detail. At the time of the raid on the campsite, Snake and Razor were both fast asleep at the Days Inn, at Birchanger Green Services on the M11 where they had stopped for a bite to eat and had stayed the night so they would face the challenges of London fresh the next day.

Shortly after five in the morning, the police team that had been hurriedly put together to arrest them was in position outside the two hotel rooms, ready to gain entry. The night duty manager had pleaded for them to avoid smashing the doors in and had provided key cards for them to use..

The doors bleeped when the cards were used, but the entry team rushed into the rooms to make the arrests before their targets had time to react. Snake had been lying on the bed fully clothed, with a bottle of beer in his hand, almost empty from the previous night's celebrations. When he heard the noise, he instinctively threw the bottle at the closest onrushing officer, striking him on the riot helmet that he was fortunately wearing. The bottle glanced off the side and struck another officer behind in the chest, where the bottle bounced harmlessly off the body armour. A second later, Snake was pinned to the bed by three officers, one on each arm and one on his feet, while two others came to restrain him in handcuffs.

'Is that all you got? Bastards, fight me like a man!' he screamed.

'We don't need to,' replied a woman PC, who sprayed him in the face with CS gas.

The screaming continued incoherently, but his struggling stopped immediately.

'That's better, isn't it?' the officer added, 'now be a good boy and sit down while we search your room.'

Two rucksacks and a pannier were quickly searched and found to contain exactly what their anonymous caller had described.

'The drugs are here, Sarge,' one officer told his superior.

'Wonderful, thank you.' She turned to Snake and said, 'Kevin Talbot, I am arresting you for the murder of George Stellenberg in Sheringham yesterday evening. You do not have to say anything, but it may harm your defence if you do not mention when questioned something which you later rely on in court. Anything you do say may be given in evidence; do you understand?'

Snake glared at the officer, but said nothing.

'No reply, please make a note,' she told her colleague, who had been recording the proceedings.

'I'm also arresting you for the possession of a controlled drug with the intent to supply it to another. The caution still applies. Do you wish to reply?'

Snake's face hardened as he finally responded.

'That ain't mine, missus,' he said, 'and I have no idea what you're talking about. I haven't murdered anyone.' He grinned. The confidence returned in his demeanour as he probed for a response from the officer. She turned to her colleague.

'Please make a note of Mister Talbot's denial,' she said. 'If we're finished in here, we can leave.'

As Snake was escorted from the room, with an officer on each arm, they saw Razor being similarly led away.

'That ain't mine!' he shouted.

'Ah, looks like your mate Fabian is unhappy, Kevin,' the sergeant said. 'Apparently, neither of you have any idea that they caught you on film throwing your colleague off the cliff. It's pretty impressive evidence.'

Snake's confidence evaporated and his heart sank as realisation dawned upon him.

'Yep, you'll be going away for many, many years, Kevin,' she continued. 'By the time you're released–if ever, your nasty tattoos will look pretty silly on your shrivelled old face.'

They led away the bikers, their fates sealed and their futures very dim.

22

SOGGY BOTTOM

Jeremy Falconer was nursing another epic hangover when his phone rang.

'Who is it?' he asked, his voice gravelly and his feet slightly unsteady.

'Mister Falconer? Jeremy Falconer?'

'Yes, yes, who is this?'

'This is Jennifer De Ville from the National Trust. I'm calling to arrange a meeting so that we can discuss some matters that have been brought to our attention relating to land and properties that you now hold. When will it be convenient for you to come and see us?'

'What on earth are you talking about?' he said. 'What does the National Trust have to do with my property?'

'Well, sir, we've been made aware of some recent purchases in the Overstrand, Sheringham, East Runton and West Runton areas that have been earmarked for development. Is that correct?'

'Yes, what of it?'

'As I said, we'd like you to come and see us so that we can discuss your plans moving forward, as they may adversely impact the local area, which has been deemed an area of national importance. Our lawyers will explain how the process of compulsory purchase will work,' De Ville continued.

'W... what? Compulsory purchase? What the hell are you talking about?' he spluttered, his gut tightening in fear.

'It's as I said, Mister Falconer. Our lawyers need to discuss the issue in person. When are you able to attend?'

Falconer ended the call. He sat down heavily on the sofa and held his head in his hands, trying to make sense of what had just been revealed.

As his head cleared and the fog left, his brain went into overdrive as he pondered potential solutions.

I need to divert some of the money now before the investors find out, otherwise I'll have nothing, he thought.

He hurried to his desk and sat at the computer. He typed in his bank login details and clicked enter.

Sorry, we don't recognise those details. To log in, both your customer number and date of birth need to match our records. Please check them both and try again.

Falconer tried again, making sure to double-check the details before clicking Enter.

Sorry, we don't recognise those details. To log in, both your customer number and date of birth need to match our records. Please check them both and try again. Still having trouble?

The feeling in his gut worsened as panic set in. Logging in to his bank was never anything he'd had problems with. He had activated all the recommended security protocols such as two-step authentication via text message or email and had always logged in without incident. He tried a third time with the same result. He grabbed his phone and called his account manager.

'This is Peter Waldron; how can I help?' came the reply.

'Waldron, this is Jeremy Falconer calling. For some reason, I can't get into one of my accounts, so I'm calling to see if you can check and let me know why?'

'Of course, sir. Before I do that, can you please confirm the first line of your address and postcode?'

Impatient, Falconer gave the details.

'Can you tell me the second and fourth digits from the pass code you have registered for phone banking?'

Again, Falconer provided the information, biting his knuckles so as not to shout down the phone.

'Thank you, Mister Falconer. Which account is it you are calling about? I see that you have several with us,' Waldron continued.

'It's called the Investor Account, account number 00783347,' Falconer replied.

'What is the problem with it, Mister Falconer?'

'I already told you; I can't get into the account online and I do not know why.'

'Sir, you only changed the password a couple of days ago. Did you make a note of the new password?'

Falconer froze. He had no recollection of changing the password or anything to do with that account. Had he done it inadvertently when he was drunk? He tried to think back, but had no memory at all of doing so.

'Sir?' Waldron enquired.

'I did not change anything to do with that account, Waldron,' he replied coldly.

'Mister Falconer, it could only have been you. You are the only person with access. All the relevant security protocols were conducted correctly and you responded with the correct codes. Are you sure that you haven't noted the new login information?'

'Yes, I'm damned sure!' Falconer shouted.

'There's no reason to shout, sir. I suggest you go to the Norwich branch with your documentation and ID, and they can reset it for you so you can get back online.'

'Yes, yes, I'll do that. Are you able to transfer some funds from that account into my regular bank account, ending in 2990?'

'How much do you wish to transfer, sir?'

'Three million pounds,' Falconer replied.

'Under normal circumstances and with further security procedures, yes, I would, Mister Falconer. But in this case, that isn't possible,'

'Why on earth not?' Falconer asked.

'Mister Falconer, there's only one hundred pounds left in the account. You transferred the majority out when you last logged in, for the development projects that you set up the account for, don't you recall? Sir, are you sure you haven't just forgotten? Mister Falconer?'

The phone dropped from Falconer's hands as he slumped to his knees.

'Mister Falconer, are you there, sir? Is everything alright?' Waldron was barely audible, but Falconer didn't care. Nor could he do anything. The pain in his chest had intensified as the conversation had gone on and had culminated in a sharp stabbing when Waldron had revealed the balance. One hundred pounds. Not forty million pounds, one hundred pounds. How was it possible? Who was responsible?

It was the last question he asked himself before he toppled to one side, unconscious, before he hit the floor.

'How are you doing, Kendra?' Rick Watts asked. 'And more to the point, when are you coming back? We're short-handed here, so I was hoping you'd come back a little earlier.'

'Sorry, Rick, I need another couple of days. I have a funeral to go to tomorrow that I can't miss, then I'll drive back to London. Is that okay?'

'Yeah, that works. There's been a spate of armed robberies and it's one of those operations that will be very much intelligence-led, so I need your help as it's right up your street.'

'Sounds good. I'll see you in a couple of days.'

'Oh, before you go, I have some interesting news for you,' Rick continued.

'Oh? What's that, then?'

'Your mate Eddie Duckmore and his sidekick Dave Critchley were both suspended after their DPS interview. They screwed up and gave conflicting answers and basically lied to the investigators. Their honesty and integrity were questioned and so the investigating officer had no choice but to suspend them for gross misconduct,' said Watts.

'Wow, that happened fast,' Kendra said. So I take it that nothing more will happen to us?'

'Correct. I doubt that you'll see or hear from those two arseholes again.'

'Well, there you go. Christmas came early. That is good news indeed, thank you.'

'Okay, well, I'll let you go, and I'll see you in a couple of days,' Watts said.

'Thanks, Rick,' she said, ending the call. 'And good riddance to bad rubbish,' she said out loud, happy to have seen the back of Duckmore in particular.

'You'll like this,' Andy said, as Trevor and Kendra joined him in the camper van.

'Will we?' asked Kendra. 'I mean, you say that a lot, Andy, and it mostly isn't something we like, is it?'

'What she said,' Trevor added.

'Fine, gang up on me all you want, but this time it's true, you'll like this a lot,' Andy continued.

'Spit it out, man,' Trevor insisted.

'I was contacted by the buyer who paid for Falconer's information. He told me he'd cleared the entire account, except for a hundred quid or so.'

'That's brilliant news! That means he's properly skint now, right?' Kendra asked.

'Yes, it does, Detective,' Andy said, 'but there's more.' He paused as he looked from father to daughter with an impish grin on his face.

'Honestly, you keep doing that and you know I don't like it,' Trevor said.

'Okay, okay, I just love milking things. So the guy was so grateful that we basically gave him access to forty million pounds in exchange for only two-and-a-half that he sent us a little bonus to keep us sweet,' Andy said.

'Bonus? What, like more money?' asked Kendra.

'Even better. He's giving us Soggy Bottom!' Andy exclaimed, flinging his arms wide in excitement.

'Seriously, Andy, I get why my dad feels like thumping you so much. You can be a right royal pain in the arse. What the hell are you talking about?'

Andy leaned over and tapped the keyboard.

'This is Soggy Bottom!' he exclaimed again, pointing to a

picture of a motorboat on the monitor.

'He gave us a boat?' Trevor asked, confused.

'He gave us *his* boat,' Andy said. 'A 2003 Hardy Commodore 42, all forty-six feet of her, with two powerful diesel engines. Isn't she a beauty?'

Trevor and Kendra were speechless, staring at the blue-and-white boat, more confused than ever.

'Oh, come on, you two. This is a gift from a grateful client. What's not to love? This lovely piece of engineering can sleep five and is fully operational and recently serviced. It's currently berthed in Hackney, but we can easily move it to Tilbury and moor it there. It's a proper bonus, this. We're bound to need a boat sometime soon, right?'

'Can you sail her?' Trevor asked, 'because we can't. I don't know anyone who can, do you, Kendra?'

'Nope, I don't. Can you sail her, Andy?'

'Erm, how hard can it be?' he replied. 'I'm sure it won't take long to learn, right?'

Trevor and Kendra stood up and left without a word.

'Come on, how hard can it be?' he asked as they walked away.

23

FUNERAL

The ornate antique carriage was towed by a polished and restored vintage tractor as it made its way slowly towards the cemetery. Jacob's coffin had been picked up from the undertakers and taken to his home early in the morning, where it would begin its last journey.

Dozens of people had lined the route, parents and students alike who had benefited from Jacob's kindness, from his faith in the youngsters and from his dedication to making their lives better. Many wept openly as the colourful carriage went by, followed by his family, his people, and his friends. The route took him past the places that had meant so much to him during the years he had lived in the town, giving him a chance to connect with them one last time before being laid to rest.

After leaving the marital home, the colourful convoy went to the restaurant where Jacob had proposed to Maureen, where it paused for a few minutes before moving on. It stopped at their favourite pub, and eventually reached the gym, where many people waited to show their respects.

Some threw flowers into the carriage. Others bowed their heads.

The cemetery was close to the gym and the hearse arrived there just a few minutes later. Eight young men that Jacob had trained carried his coffin, several with tears streaming down their faces as they thought of the man who had changed their lives. Eventually, the coffin was lowered slowly onto a pair of wooden staves that suspended it above the hole in the ground. As people approached it, the coffin was quickly strewn with roses.

Manfri was one of the last to leave. He approached the coffin and placed an old pair of boxing gloves on the lid, the leather worn and cracked in places. The gloves that Jacob had used for so many years when he had boxed. The gloves that Manfri had kept as a treasured memento of his son's success, hanging them in pride of place in his caravan.

'I thought you might need these, son. Maybe you can teach a few more youngsters while you're up there.' He blew a kiss at the coffin and stepped back.

The sound of the coffin being lowered was drowned out by the weeping, as Jacob finally came to rest.

Trevor could not hold back the tears as he saw his great friend lowered into the ground. Kendra held him tightly as she wept, mainly for the pain that her father was enduring but also for Jacob's family, now that she had gotten to know them.

'He will be sorely missed, Dad,' she whispered.

Andy and the rest of the team stood behind, bowing their heads in respect. They could see the pain that Trevor and Jacob's family were going through. It was small comfort that they had avenged his death when such a decent human being had been lost to them forever.

They watched as Maureen was led away in tears by family members, followed by her children. Trevor would wait until later to speak with her privately.

Before leaving the cemetery, Manfri came to Trevor and shook hands.

'I can never thank you enough for what you have done. If it wasn't for you all, his death would have gone unavenged, which would have made our lives painful and miserable forever.'

'It was the least we could do, Manfri. He was like a brother to me,' Trevor said, weeping.

'God bless you, son. If we can ever be of help to you, just call and we'll come running. I hope to see you at the wake?'

'We'll be there,' said Trevor.

Manfri nodded and walked away. He was more stooped and slower than Trevor remembered. Although he put on a brave face as the Rom Baro, he was now showing his age. Grief seemed to be taking its toll.

Many other family members came and thanked them, some shaking their hands, others hugging, all grateful.

Finally, Rufus Donald approached.

'Thank you, Trevor. Please, thank your team for everything. I dread to think what would have happened if you hadn't had been here. The area would have been decimated,' he said, shaking Trevor's hand enthusiastically. 'It's opened my eyes to a few things which I'll mention later. We're having the wake at my house, so I'll see you there shortly.'

Trevor stood for a few more moments, his head bowed, keeping his thoughts to himself, as he paid his final respects. Eventually, it was their turn to leave.

'Let's go,' he said, leading his daughter and the team away.

THE WAKE at Rufus's house was a traditional affair, rather than a typically lively Romany one. Manfri and his family had celebrated Jacob the previous night, as was their tradition, so it was a more sombre event at the farmhouse. There was a violinist to merge the two traditions, but drinking was moderated out of respect for Rufus and Jacob's wife Maureen, who was struggling deeply.

The team mingled with the guests, enjoying the company and listening to Jacob stories, giving everyone positive memories to hold on to.

Midway through, Rufus Donald asked for everyone's attention and stood facing them all.

'My friends, it is a sad day for us where we must mourn the loss of a husband, in your case, Maureen, and especially for a child, as it is with you, Manfri. Such a day is today. I know it is of small comfort to you, Manfri, but I hope that a small gesture from me and my wife will help ease the pain and make all your memories of Jacob good ones. We have decided to create a special lease for the campsite to your family for one month per year for the next one hundred years, so that you may all continue your tradition of coming here once a year. I have also ensured that the site will remain in trust after we're gone and cannot be sold unless full approval is given by your family, whereby you will benefit to the tune of one twelfth of the sale price – if you approve the sale. I hope that this gesture further cements our relationship and gives us all hope for the future. Jacob, may you rest in peace knowing that your family will continue to celebrate here every year. Thank you.' He raised his glass, as did everyone else. As soon as the glasses were lowered, there was a round of applause as Manfri approached Rufus and gave him a hug.

'Thank you, my friend,' he told Rufus, tears in his eyes. 'Thank you.'

Rufus nodded and wiped his own tears away.

'Let's have another drink, shall we?' he said.

Trevor saw that Maureen had sat alone by the fireplace and went to join her.

'How are you doing?' he said, holding her hand. She squeezed his hand and nodded.

'It's been tough, Trevor, but I think I'll be okay. Manfri and the rest of Jacob's family will always be around, so I won't lose touch with them,' she said.

'That's good. You know the same applies to us, right? Anything you need, all you have to do is call me, okay?'

'That's so kind, thank you. I need some time to think about the future. The security company will have to close, as will the gym, so I suppose I must think about retiring,' she said, with a disappointed look on her face. 'It's such a shame. We had great plans,' she reflected.

'Would you be open to an alternative?' Trevor asked. He had thought about it and discussed it with Kendra and Andy. Both had agreed that his plan was a good one.

'Alternative? What do you mean?'

'About the gym and your business,' Trevor said.

'I don't understand.'

'What I mean, Maureen, is that you don't have to retire if you don't want to. You don't have to close your company if you don't want to. And you certainly shouldn't have to close the gym if you don't want to.'

'I'm confused, Trevor. What are you saying?'

'I'm offering to buy the business and the gym from you, if

it's acceptable to you,' he continued. 'I'd pay you a salary to keep them both going. I can't think of anything better than keeping the gym open in Jacob's memory.'

'Are you serious?' she said, her eyes widening as the legitimate offer dawned on her.

'Absolutely,' he said. 'Those youngsters need the gym and you are too young to even consider retiring.'

Maureen cried. Trevor hugged her tightly.

'He was my brother, Maureen, which makes you my sister. I'll do everything I can to see that you are okay. Please let me do this. I'm not doing it for charity, I'm doing it because it is viable and needed in the area.'

He released her and sat back down. Maureen dried the tears with a tissue and nodded.

'Then I accept, with my heartfelt thanks,' she said, smiling for the first time in many weeks.

'I have just one condition,' Trevor said, smiling back.

'What's that?'

'You change the name of the gym,' he said.

'To what?'

'Jacob's.'

EPILOGUE

Specialist Rehabilitation Centre, Norwich, Norfolk.

The nurse pushed the wheelchair through the double doors and into the lounge area where many other patients were resting. Some watched TV and others played games. One favourite game that always had four players was Monopoly, which the same four patients played in almost complete silence every day. Many others sat alone, sleeping, or watching the rest of the room. The room was diligently kept clinically clean, as all specialist care homes had to be, and there was a hint of chemical smells in the air. Other than the sound of the TV, there was very little to hear.

The patient in the wheelchair had been with them for a few months now. He'd had no visitors and no callers. As the nurse reached the TV area, she stopped and applied the brake, lining the wheelchair up at a nice angle.

The patient did not move, except for his eyes. His eyes darted around in all directions, at speed, as if watching out for approaching danger. This continued even when the nurse stopped him and said, 'Here you go, love. Just in time for the local news.'

As she walked away, his darting eyes slowed down slightly, the room and the surroundings becoming more familiar. Another nurse watched and approached her colleague.

'Such a shame, isn't it, Maria? He isn't that old, either, is he?'

'No, I think he's in his early fifties, Gary. It's very unusual for someone of his age to suffer such a nasty brain injury. They don't have a clue how long it will take to recover from it; it could take years from the sounds of it, poor thing.'

'Isn't this the rich guy who gave everything away to charity, or something like that?' asked Gary.

'I'm not sure. I know the National Trust was involved, maybe English Heritage? It's weird, though,' she said.

'Why's that, then?'

'About a week ago, we did this very thing, much like we do every day at this time. I brought him here, put him in front of the TV, just as the local news came on. His eyes were doing the same weird high-speed dance that they always do–until the news started. As soon as the reporter started talking, his eyes stopped and stared at the TV. It's not happened since,' Maria said.

'That is strange. What was the reporter talking about?'

'Well, that's the thing. The story was about a large area in North Norfolk where the National Trust had just gained land and properties to preserve. Something about it being an area of national importance.'

'You think it was his?' Gary asked, intrigued.

'I can't say, but he reacted to it, for sure. I mean, his eyes were glued to the TV.'

'Yeah, that's weird alright.'

'The other thing was the tears. Not sure it was because he stared for so long without blinking, but it sure looked like he was crying.'

The patient sat in the wheelchair facing the television, his eyes darting all over. One thing that the nurses hadn't spotted was the tiny item he was holding in his left hand. When nobody was looking, his eyes would dart back and forth to the little red plastic hotel that he had picked up from the games table one day when nobody had been watching.

THE END

'London's Burning'

Book 4 of the *'Summary Justice'* series with DC Kendra March.

https://mybook.to/Londons-Burning

Or read on...

BOOK 4 PREVIEW

The room was buzzing with its usual excitement as the auctions continued to garner larger than usual bids. It was one of those rare occasions when there were two or more interested parties in many of the rarer items. Christies was a world-renowned auction house, having auctioned billions of pounds worth of goods in recent years. One of the largest in the world, they scrutinised carefully the items before making them available to their prestigious clientele.

It was time for one of the rarer and more unusual items on offer today. The auction house had ensured that it was placed strategically between some of the more expensive items so that it would raise awareness and hopefully increase bidding.

'Ladies and Gentlemen, we now come to lot five three six, a most unusual item that we hope will attract much bidding. The proceeds of the sale will be going towards improvements and equipment for a charity that helps single women, including a gym and club that helps with their physical and mental wellbeing. The item has been generously donated for these causes by a London company that wishes to remain anonymous,' the auctioneer said.

He indicated towards a colleague that approached the dais holding a crimson velvet cushion that displayed a unique bejewelled eye patch. It was made of gold and encrusted with diamonds and other gems of many colours. The leather strap had also been worked so that it held several smaller diamonds along its length, with the exception of the last five inches of each side that was fabric used for the knot.

'This very unusual, one-off jewel-encrusted eyepatch was made by Tiffany and Company in Paris and is made with twenty-four carat gold. It is magnificently encrusted with eighty high-colour Carre-cut diamonds totalling forty-four carats, four Zambian emeralds totalling six carats, eight Mozambique rubies totalling ten carats and finally four black opals totalling two carats. I have online bids and will start the bidding at three hundred and twenty thousand pounds.

There was a buzz in the room as the starting bid was announced, with many intrigued by such a curious item.

'Do I have three fifty?' the auctioneer asked. He glanced to the side where the assistants were dealing with online bidders.

One of them raised their arms.

'We have three fifty from an online bidder. Do we have three seventy-five?'

An elderly woman in the audience raised her paddle, showing the number five seven nine, indicating a bid.

'We have three seventy-five on the floor, thank you madam. Do we have four hundred thousand?'

One of the assistants stood up, raised her arm in the air and called out.

'Five hundred thousand!'

There was a collective gasp from the audience as the bid was announced.

'We have a bid of five hundred thousand pounds from overseas, ladies and gentlemen. Does anyone care to raise the bid to five hundred and fifty thousand?'

He looked at the audience ahead of him, some shaking their heads, others wide mouthed at the development. Looking at the assistants, he saw more shaking heads. The bidding seemed to be over.

'Ladies and Gentlemen, this beautiful, one-off item is unlikely to be seen again so don't let it get away.'

He looked again and there was no movement.

'Going once, going twice ... and sold, sold, sold to our overseas bidder for five hundred thousand pounds, ladies and gentlemen! That will be a tremendous boost to the charities that it was intended to help, thank you all for your bids.'

There was a round of applause as the auction ended and the eyepatch removed from the dais by the assistant. The buzz of excitement continued for several minutes until it was no longer in the room.

'Moving on to the next item, never seen before, a small twentieth century self-portrait by the master artist David Hockney, oils on canvas circa nineteen seventy-four. The bidding starts at sixty-five thousand pounds.'

'GOODNIGHT, Winston, make sure to try those cookies on your break, Marion spent hours baking them yesterday,' the auctioneer told the security guard as he left the building.

'Thank you, mister Crawford, and please thank missus Crawford too, they look delicious,' the guard replied, saluting as the auctioneer waved one last time before exiting via the front entrance and onto King Street, walking towards St James's Street as he took his usual route towards Green Park tube station.

There was little daylight left and streetlights were now illuminating the now-quiet road. As he neared the junction the scaffolding that covered the entire building on the corner appeared to be the only place that the lighting hadn't penetrated, the pavement still in darkness under the wooden boards that surrounded the building. It wasn't helped much by the white transit van that was parked alongside it, which cast more shadow on that part of the pavement.

Crawford had used this route for more than seven years and had no fear about the unlit pavement. His mind was on the successful auction that he had conducted today, which had exceeded everyone's forecasts and estimates by several million pounds. His bonus would be a good one.

He did not see the sliding door of the van open slightly as he approached and then went under the scaffolding. He saw the sliding door open suddenly as he came alongside it and two large men jump out silently, one either side of him. They grabbed an arm each. A quiet well-spoken voice echoed from within the van.

'If you struggle, we will not be so gentle with Marion. Do you understand?'

Crawford's blood froze as he nodded and acquiesced to being led to the van. Within seconds he was inside the van, sat on a bench between the two hulking men, facing a well-dressed elegant woman who sat opposite him, fanning herself with a multi-coloured, intricately patterned lace fan.

'Now then, mister Crawford. I need you to answer some questions for me. Then we can let you be on your way to your charming wife. Does that sound okay to you?'

Crawford, who by now was shaking as the adrenaline took over, nodded quickly.

'That's a lovely art deco fan, that would fetch a pretty penny at the auction,' he thought to himself as his fear increased.

Chapter 1

'What do you mean, you want to be a Captain?' Kendra asked as she sipped her latte.

'If I want to use the boat it means I should train up and get a Boatmasters license,' Andy replied.

'So go get one,' she replied.

'I will. I'm looking forward to using *Soggy Bottoms*, but you won't believe how much paperwork is involved,' he continued.

'Well, as an ex-cop you should feel right at home, shouldn't you?'

Soggy Bottoms was the motor cruiser that Andy had been left as a bonus by a grateful dark web hacker that had acquired tens of millions of pounds because of his tip-off. The tip off, which had been sold on an online auction, had cost the hacker a couple of million pounds, but the forty million that had been gained as a result was such a huge mark-up that he had gladly given Andy the boat as a gift. The hacker was now sitting on a much larger, newer, motor cruiser that was moored at St. Katherines dock in Central London, waiting to be taken out for the first time.

'Well, I'm not a cop anymore, so I'm entitled to have the occasional whine, okay? I've always wanted a motor cruiser; it would have been perfect if all it took was to switch the engine on and drive the damned thing, not have to take exams, get a license, various certificates and all the other bullshit.'

'And it's taken you this long to figure that out?' Kendra asked.

'Yeah, well I needed some time to unwind since the last adventure. I've made sure we're fully stocked up again and we're ready for the next one. How's it going at work?'

'I can't complain. They've got me checking on some armed robberies that they think are connected. It's not as boring as I thought it would be,' Kendra replied.

'Is Rick still asking you to go back full time?'

'He asks every week, hoping that I'll either change my mind or cave. He's trying to wear me down, bless him.'

'He's a good boss, K, you can't blame him for wanting you around more. I wouldn't mind that myself,' Andy replied.

'Yeah, well we both agreed not to go there, remember? Or are you having another of those mid-life crises that you have every month?'

Andy laughed.

'Nothing wrong with that, K, it keeps me on my toes. Life would be boring as hell if everything was perfect, wouldn't it? It's the little things that you either can't control or don't want to control that make it interesting.'

'Well, that's a human trait, we have to keep learning new stuff or we wither and die,' Kendra replied.

'Yep, it surely is.'

'Getting back to the saggy trousers business...'

'It's *Soggy Bottoms*, and it's a cool name for a boat,' he corrected.

'Anyway, getting back to the boat, how long is it going to take to get your license?' she asked.

'Probably a few months. It's not difficult, more a formality and a paper exercise, I'll do it in my spare time.'

'You may as well start; I've been looking for something new for us to take on, but nothing seems to stick out at the moment. It's all quiet on the western front, as they say.'

'Okay, well that's settled then, I'll start tomorrow. Is your dad still coming over?' he asked.

'No, he's going to spend the day visiting one of the clubs. He's bought some new kit that he wants to surprise them with. Those clubs are starting to look very professional and slick now, thanks to our criminal donors.'

'Yeah, we've done well with that. Long may it continue. Our coffers are full, and we are fully stocked up and ready to go. God help the criminal fraternity and especially the ones that we pick on next,' he said, pumping his fist in the air with one of his typically exaggerated poses.

'Well, don't get too excited, like I said there's not much for us to do at the moment.'

'This is great, Trev,' Charlie said as he examined the new

kit that was being unloaded from a van. 'The kids will get a kick out of this stuff.'

'Yeah, I'm very pleased with it, Charlie. It wasn't cheap but well worth it if they engage with us more.'

Along with two very modern treadmills that featured a large screen for users to view as they ran, Trevor had brought a rowing machine and two new boxing target trees that featured strike pads at various angles and positions. There were also several boxes of new pads, gloves and even tape. He had thought of everything.

'One last thing,' Trevor said, opening the boot of his car. He pulled out a Bose Pro PA system that had built-in Bluetooth connectivity, a smart speaker that would allow for the club to have the very best quality sound quality.

Charlie laughed.

'You know they'll be fighting each other to see whose music they should be listening to, don't you?

'That's where you come in, Charlie. You play our music, not theirs. I want them to listen to something other than that foul mouthed violent crap that they seem to like. Get 'em used to something nicer, you know? It will help their mental health as well as sooth their souls. Boxing shouldn't be about violence, it's more about routine, mental strength and they should channel their energies into the bags and pads – not their heads.'

'Don't you worry about that, I'll make sure that they get plenty of soul and jazz,' Charlie replied, 'and maybe the odd rock anthem.'

'Nothing wrong with some good old-fashioned rock. Now, show me that kid you keep talking about, the middleweight. Danny, isn't it?'

'Danny Baptiste, yeah. He's only seventeen but he boxes

like he's a seasoned pro. He has a great boxing mind and is a future champ, for sure,' Charlie replied. 'He's just over there, come and say hello.'

They walked over to the young man that was helping to place one of the treadmills. He was tall and thin, his hair completely shorn, wearing a tracksuit. He was still very much a young man with plenty of growing ahead of him.

'Hey, Danny, come here, son,' Charlie said, waving him over. 'Come and say hello to Trevor, the owner.'

'How're you doing, boss?' Danny replied, shaking Trevor's hand firmly.

'That's a good, strong grip you have there, young man. How are you enjoying the club so far?'

'It's great. I'm between jobs at the moment so I'm spending more time here than normal. It's helping take my mind of the whole unemployed situation.'

'You looking for a job? Anything in particular?' asked Trevor.

'I don't mind. My last couple have been in fast food joints, so it would be nice to try something different,' Danny replied.

'Have you considered anything in security? Like learning a trade or two in the industry?'

'Not really, but I'd give anything a go.'

'That's good to know. I may have something that would be a good fit for you, if you're up for it?'

'Yes, sir, I'd be very interested, thank you!'

Trevor turned to Charlie and said, 'bring him to the factory tomorrow. I'm looking to take on more apprentices and interns, maybe he'll be a good fit.'

'I'll bring him over in the morning then, show him around until you speak to him,' Charlie said.

'Alright then, I'll see you both tomorrow' Trevor said. He

shook both their hands and went back outside. He stood there, looking around at the familiar surroundings, taking a deep breath.

'I love this place,' he said out loud, 'you just can't beat London town.'

ACKNOWLEDGMENTS

As I continue with this very satisfying journey as an author of the '**Summary Justice**' series I continually think myself as very lucky.

Lucky to have the support of those that have helped me through my journey, lucky for the support of the readers who take the time to contact me with their comments – good and bad – and lucky that I still have many friends and ex-colleagues that are still able to help me out with some of the newer processes that I am now unfamiliar with.

With '**Road Trip**' I had to call on several friends for this very thing. Alastair Allen graciously and patiently went through the current interviewing procedures, Dick Watts and Bob Dabbs helped me with motorcycle information that was alien to me.

My thanks again go to editor Linda Nagle, who continues to right my wrongs in the most supportive way.

I must also give huge thanks go to my partner, Alison, for her help with the cover for this book and for her ongoing support.

M. G. Cole and Jack Gatland, two successful authors – and good friends of mine – both continue to give their valuable time and assist me with the finer details like amazon advertising and reader magnets, with which this journey would come to a swift end. I highly recommend their crime novels.

I will be eternally grateful for all those that have assisted, regardless of the outcome of this journey.

Thank you, all of you.
    TH

You can reach me at: theo@theoharris.co.uk

ABOUT THE AUTHOR

Theo Harris is an emerging author of crime action novels. He was born in London, raised in London, and became a cop in London.

Having served as a police officer in the Metropolitan Police service for thirty years, he witnessed and experienced the underbelly of a capital city that you are never supposed to see.

Theo was a specialist officer for twenty-seven of the thirty years and went on to work in departments that dealt with serious crimes of all types. His experience, knowledge and connections within the organisation have helped him with his storytelling, with a style of writing that readers can associate with.

Theo has many stories to tell, starting with the 'Summary Justice' series featuring DC Kendra March, and will follow with many more innovative, interesting, and fast-paced stories for many years to come.

For more information about upcoming books please visit theoharris.co.uk

Printed in Great Britain
by Amazon